SINFUL PRINCESS

KNIGHT'S RIDGE EMPIRE
BOOK 17

TRACY LORRAINE

Editing by Pinpoint Editing

Proofreading by Sisters Get Lit.erary

Photography by Wander Aguiar

Models - Zakk Davis & Evan Keys

I watched one of my best friends get married.

Fucking *married.*

In Las Vegas.

I shake my head and then rest it against the tall leather bench behind me and close my eyes.

There's a whole myriad of feelings warring for dominance inside me. The sadness I've been battling since the moment I drove away from Evie on Monday evening only gets worse with every day that passes. The regrets grow as I think about finishing things like that after the time we spent together. It just solidifies what I already know. I'm not good enough for her.

Then, there's the loneliness...

I knew walking away from her was going to rip me to pieces, but I couldn't have imagined it would be this bad. That it would hurt so much.

I barely know her. It's crazy to be this attached already.

But it hasn't just been a few days. You've been pining for this girl for months. You fell the second you saw her.

"Hey," Calli shouts over the music, sliding into the

booth with me. The others are all on the dance floor having the time of their lives.

It's been the same since we got into that Hummer outside our building at the arse crack of dawn on Tuesday morning.

Everything since has been a blur of excitement, disbelief, and happiness—for everyone else. Well, I am happy. I'm so fucking happy for Nico and Brianna, that's not in question. It's my own misery I'm drowning in.

I'm doing my best to play my part, because I know I'll regret not making the most of this crazy trip. But I just can't shake myself out of it.

I don't even know what day it is right now with the time difference and everything.

Alcohol.

I reach forward and grab my drink, finding the level way lower than I was hoping for.

Alcohol is my friend. It helps to drown the sadness, and it blurs the concerned expressions on my friends' faces every time they look at me.

That exact look stares at me right now when I glance over at my companion.

Her eyes soften and she reaches for my hand.

"Getting a bit much for you?" I ask. We've barely stopped since we got here, and I'd be lying if I said I wasn't worried about her.

Yes, she slept most of the flight here, and when we'd eventually crashed into bed when the sun had been starting to rise the last few mornings, she's slept a solid ten hours, but I'm still worried.

She's growing our future queen, and that's a really fucking important—and exhausting—job.

"My feet are killing me," she confesses, kicking her shoes off under the table.

"How's blob?" I ask, dropping my eyes to the very slight bump she's sporting in her fitted dress.

Over the past few weeks, it's been easy to forget she's growing my niece or nephew, but that's all about to change.

Everything is about to change.

We've got a handful of exams left between us. Calli is going to start waddling around like she has a bowling ball stuffed up her shirt. Brianna is going to return as a teacher to Knight's Ridge College as Mrs. Cirillo. Seb and Stella, Theo and Emmie, Toby and Jodie... they're all making plans for their summers, for their futures. And here I am. Alone. Miserable as fuck.

I throw the rest of my drink back and groan to myself that it no longer burns. I need that pain, that punishment, anything to make the ache in my chest lessen for even a few seconds.

"Where's D?" I ask, turning to search for him in the crowded nightclub before me. He's never very far away from his angel.

"Bathroom," she says, leaning closer so we don't have to shout at each other too much.

"I wish you'd talk to me," she begs, squeezing my hand tighter.

I shake my head. "What's the point? It won't fix anything."

"No, but it'll get it off your chest. Maybe I'd have some killer advice for you."

"Maybe," I mutter.

Problem is, I already know what she'll say, and it won't help.

"I hate seeing you sad, Alex," she says, resting her head on my shoulder.

"I'll be fine," I say weakly.

"We're in Vegas. You should be up there with them, having the time of your life." Seb and Stella break through the crowd as she says that with wide smiles on their red, sweaty faces.

They take one look at us in the booth we snagged and dart toward the bar for more drinks. Something I can totally get on board with.

My phone burns a hole in my pocket. I've got a couple of messages from her sitting there, taunting me.

I should have deleted them. And her contact. I don't trust myself when I'm wasted, and the last thing I want to do is give her hope that something will happen when I return.

It can't. She deserves so much more than anything I can offer her.

Part of me hoped I'd get a notification that she's online. At least that way, I'd get to watch her, punish myself with what I could have had if I were someone else. But it's been eerily quiet.

Is she missing me as much as I am her?

A bitter laugh spills from my lips.

Why would she care when she could have her pick of every single guy in the city?

She's beautiful. Sexy. Kind yet sinful. Gentle yet wicked. Innocent yet wild.

She's... everything.

I'm so lost in my thoughts that I don't notice Daemon join us. Not until he steals his girl from my side, anyway.

Loneliness seeps through me at the loss, and it doesn't

get any better when I look up and watch him cup her cheeks in his hands and brush his lips against hers.

What starts innocently quickly turns heated. I should look away, but I'm powerless but to torture myself.

"Here you go, perv," Stella announces, putting a tray full of whisky and shots in front of me.

She plucks the one soft drink from the centre and slides it toward Calli—not that she notices—before throwing back two shots.

I do the same as the rest of our group descends on our table.

Brianna and Nico are still sporting the same wide smiles they have been since we got here. I never thought I'd say it, but marriage looks good on him.

Despite their wedding being two days ago, Brianna still insists on wearing a veil in her hair. She picked it up at a souvenir store the evening of their wedding and stated that their wedding day wasn't just the day of the ceremony but our entire trip. She hasn't taken it off since.

It's great. As I said, I'm stupidly happy for them. All I can hope is that somehow, I find a way to show them I really mean that.

"Excuse me," I say, sliding from the booth and skimming the dance floor in my need to escape.

I pass the insane line for the ladies' bathroom and duck into the men's.

Thankfully, there's a stall empty and I lock myself inside, lowering the toilet lid and sitting down.

It's quieter in here, and it only allows my regrets to get louder. Those, the sound of men pissing and the disgusting scent that fills my nose ensures I won't hide out here for very long.

Stuffing my hand into my pocket, I stare at my phone and all its notifications.

I haven't posted on Instagram for days. None of us have publicly said that we're here or what we're doing. For now, it's our little secret, and I'm happy with that. It gives me the perfect excuse to vanish for a while.

But that doesn't mean my account stops. The comments continue to stream in. And not nice ones.

Opening up the app, I scroll down the trolls' comments and let them feed the darkness that's already consuming me.

Pointless.

Waste of space.

Vain and arrogant.

Egotistical.

And those only scratch the surface.

It's the death threats that really help pull me under, and before I have a chance to question myself, I open the baggie that was hiding with my phone and throw back two little pills.

With the alcohol no longer drowning everything out, maybe these will let me forget about everything and actually enjoy myself.

Tapping my photos app, I scroll up a few days to find the handful of photos I took on Monday.

It's a mistake.

Staring at her happy, smiling face is like a knife through my heart.

She shouldn't matter so much after only a few days, that little voice pops up again.

But she does.

Brushing my fingertips over her face like a pussy, I lock

my phone and shove it back in my pocket, hoping my depressing thoughts can disappear with it.

I walk out, praying for those little pills to kick in. I could really do with letting go right about now.

There are two shots left when I get back to the table, I throw them back and force myself to get involved.

Grabbing both Stella and Emmie's hands, I drag them out onto the dance floor while Seb and Theo bark demands at me. Something about keeping my hands where they can see them or some shit.

I flip them off over my shoulder as the girls sandwich me between them, and we set about showing Las Vegas how it's really done.

Thankfully, it doesn't take long for my high to kick in and I'm flying.

Everything aside from this moment slips away, and I dance until my shirt is stuck to my back and my head is spinning.

The others join us at some point, and I receive more than a few warning slaps from both my boys and their girls when I get a bit too handsy. But fuck it. It's not like I'm going to bend them over and fuck them or anything. I'm just doing what they've been trying to convince me to do since we got into that Hummer. I'm fucking enjoying myself.

Long before I'm ready, they call it a night and I'm dragged out of the club, complaining that it's too early to leave. Something that's proved not to be the case when we step outside to blinding sunlight.

"Ow fuck, that hurts," I complain, shielding my eyes with my arm.

"Come on, party animal," Daemon says, throwing his arm around my shoulder and dragging me down the street—

I assume in the direction of our hotel, but I'm fucked if I know right now.

With my twin on one side and his girl on the other holding my hand so tightly I wonder if she's worried I'm going to vanish. I'm taken to the suite I'm sharing with them, stripped out of my clothes and thrown into bed.

And that's the last thing I remember before my brain decides to torment me with dreams of her. Her touch, her scent, the sinful curves of her body and the way her voice gets all raspy with need when she's about to fall for me.

Each image is so vivid it might as well be real.

So much for the drugs taking everything away. If anything, all this shit is heightened.

Everything I walked away from is more painful than ever.

And when I'm finally woken with a sharp shove to my shoulder, I'm actually grateful for the clarity real life brings.

But only for a few seconds, because everything rushes back, threatening to suck me under once more.

"Alex, for fuck's sake. You need to wake up," Theo barks, none too gently shoving me again.

"Fuck off," I grunt, my hangover making itself known the more my body wakes. And it is not pretty.

"No can do. I've found something you're going to want to see."

2
___

ALEX

I crash through to the bathroom, following our Boss's demanding orders.

With my legs barely able to hold me up, I'm forced to take a posh piss and sit down like a child.

Hanging my head, I breathe in deeply through my nose in the hope it'll help settle the riot that seems to be happening in my stomach.

I've no idea how long I sit there, and I'm not aware of falling back to sleep, but I startle when Theo barks my name in irritation.

"Will you fucking hurry up?"

"Sorry, sorry," I mutter, finally staggering to the basin to brush my teeth.

I feel marginally better once I have a fresh mouth, but it's going to take more than a squeeze of Colgate to fix me up this morning... this afternoon... this evening.

Fuck. What day even is it?

Still dressed in only my boxers, I head out to the living area.

Loser.

"Do you ever have a day off?" I mutter, finding Theo alone at the dining table with his laptop in front of him.

"Drink this and sober the fuck up," he grunts, sliding a takeout coffee toward me.

"Yes, Boss," I quip before tipping the cup and burning a layer of skin off my tongue. "Ow, fuck. It's boiling."

He glances up at me with this brow quirked and a 'well what the fuck did you expect?' look on his face.

"Fuck off," I snarl before pulling out the chair next to him and dropping my exhausted body into it. "Why the fuck are you working? We're on holiday."

"Because, dipshit, I've been looking into the trafficking ring we're meant to be bringing down, and they didn't get the memo that we're away and put all activity on hold."

"Well, aren't you in a sarcastic mood this morning? Didn't Emmie put out?"

"Didn't Emmie put out?" he mocks, rolling his eyes. "Thought you knew her better than that. You really want the details?" he asks.

"No," I blurt. "I don't need yet another reminder that everyone around me is getting laid regularly and I'm here with my right fucking hand."

"Ow, pup," he teases, making me want to punch him in his overused dick. "You've got a left hand too."

I push the chair back and take two steps to escape this bullshit, but his commanding voice stops me dead.

"Sit the fuck back down, Deimos."

His tone is deadly, but there's more in it that forces my body to move of its own accord. My arse hits the cushion again and I cross my arms over my chest, glaring at him.

"Go on then, oh great one."

He rolls his eyes again but chooses not to comment.

"I was hunting through the dark web—"

"Of course you were," I scoff.

"I'd start taking this seriously, if I were you," he warns as he clicks something and a new page fills the screen.

I blink once. Twice. Then, I shake my head, because what I'm seeing can't be real.

I swear to God, my stomach actually falls out of my arse.

"Theo," I growl, snatching his laptop with trembling hands and dragging it closer. "For the love of all that's holy, tell me this isn't what I think it is."

"It's exactly what you think it is."

"No," I bark, flipping his computer into the middle of the table as I jump to my feet. "NO," I bellow, refusing to believe what I just saw. "It can't be. No. No."

I retreat until my back hits the wall. Then, I bend over, sinking my fingers into my hair as images of my girl play out in my head like a movie.

No. This can't be happening.

She can't be for fucking sale on the dark web.

She can't.

This has to be a fucking joke.

"Alex?" I hear Theo repeating my name, trying to bring me back, but it's like he's at the other end of a tunnel. "For fuck's sake," he grunts before pain explodes through my gut.

"What the fuck?" I bark out, clutching my stomach. "You fucking hit me."

"You were freaking out. How the fuck is that going to help?"

I shake my head. "I-I don't—"

"Look, I know this isn't ideal—"

"Isn't ideal?" I bellow. "The girl I—" I suck in a breath

and swallow whatever was about to tumble from my lips. "She's for fucking sale."

Jesus. I'm too fucking hungover to deal with this.

Theo's concerned eyes burn into me as I slump back into the chair and push his laptop back toward him.

"Okay. How do we fix this? I just buy her, right?" I didn't pay all that much attention to the price tag, but even if I don't have it, we'll have enough between us.

We have to. There's no fucking way I'm going to allow some other motherfucker buy her.

"No," Theo says, forcing all the air from my lungs, and any hope I was feeling goes right along with it. "It's too late. She's sold."

Time stops fucking dead as I stare at him in disbelief.

"Who?" I whisper.

He shakes his head. "I don't know. They don't advertise that shit."

"No, but they put an eighteen-year-old virgin up for fucking sale quite happily."

I'm back on my feet, my hangover forgotten as I pace back and forth through the living area.

"What do I do, Theo? Tell me. I need to fucking fix this."

He studies me for a few seconds before turning back to his computer and tapping away at the keyboard.

"Go and get dressed and packed. She only sold this morning. We're going to figure out a way to intercept her."

I nod. "Yeah, okay. That makes sense, I guess."

"I'm gonna call Toby to come to help me dig deeper into this. Go," he says, nodding to the bedroom behind me. "And Alex," he calls, long before I get to my suitcase.

"Yeah?"

"Is she really still a virgin?"

I swallow, hating that I fucking allowed that to still be the case.

"Yeah," I call back reluctantly.

"Okay. When you get her, can I suggest you fix that?"

"Let's fucking hope I get a chance," I mutter to myself as I shove my boxers down my legs in favour of a clean pair. Here's hoping that by the time I change them again, I'll have her to help take them off me.

3

———

EVIE

The sound of deep, rumbling voices is the first thing I hear when I come back around.

For a few blissful seconds, I forget what happened before everything went dark and assume it's just Dad and Derek talking. But then, it all comes rushing back.

"Someone has paid a pretty penny for your innocent cunt, and your job is to do as you're fucking told."

My stomach revolts, and I push onto my hands and vomit all over the floor.

"Hey, she's awake," someone says.

Lifting my hand, I wipe my mouth and sit back, looking around.

I'm in a small room. There's a tiny window, but it's got bars in front of it, stopping anyone from breaking out. And the rest of the room is concrete. Cold, unforgiving concrete. With a single sink in the corner and a drain slightly off centre.

The only door in the space opens and a dark figure dressed head to toe in black steps into the room, quickly followed by another.

"Good afternoon," one of them says.

There's a slight accent. I wrack my brain for any kind of familiarity, but there's nothing. Not a flicker. And it doesn't help that I can only see their eyes, thanks to the skull-covered bandanas hiding the bottom half of their faces.

Lifting my hand, I rub the sore spot where I remember Derek plunging a needle into my neck before... well, before whatever he did that ended with me here.

My stomach turns again, bile burning up my throat as I think about what he and my dad have done.

Blakely is going to kill them...

"What do you want?" I ask, my voice rough and my throat dry.

"We don't want anything. Just got a job to do," a second man says, his voice much colder, harsher than the other, and it sends a shiver of fear racing down my spine.

As they walk deeper into the room, I scramble back, tucking into a corner and curling in on myself.

One of them eyes the puddle of vomit on the floor and quickly steps over it.

"We can do this the easy way or the hard way. It's really your choice," he continues, but I don't miss how his voice lightens when he offers the hard way.

Well, that sounds ominous.

"On your feet and strip," the softer one demands.

"W-what?"

"You heard," the evil one barks.

Finding some confidence from somewhere, I lift my head and hold his eyes. "Why?"

"Because we told you to," the evil one sneers.

A shriek rips from my throat when he reaches out and lifts me to my feet, his fingertips digging into my upper arm so hard that there's no doubt it'll leave bruises.

"Strip, or we'll do it for you."

"Tell me why?" I demand, refusing to look away.

"To make sure you don't have any kind of tracker on you," the other concedes.

"Can't you just scan me or something?"

The evil one chuckles. "And what would be the fun in that?"

Silence fills the small room as they wait for me to make a decision.

"Fine. Hard way it is," the evil one decides, taking a step toward me.

"N-no, wait," I cry.

I might not want to do as they say, but like hell are they laying another hand on me if I get a say.

Lifting my hands, I wrap my fingers around the hem of my tank.

"Is this really necessary?" I ask before doing something I could avoid. Not that they give the impression they're joking in any way.

"Yes," the evil one growls. "You're more than welcome to change your mind and allow us to help."

"Get fucked," I mutter under my breath, but it's not quietly enough, and the evil one's eyes flare with fire.

Sucking in some confidence, I pretend they're not really here.

Just two men on a screen. They're not right in front of me. They can't touch me.

But it doesn't matter how many times I tell myself that. I never believe it.

Their scents fill my nose. Their breaths echo in the room.

An involuntary whimper spills from my throat as I drag my tank up my body, leaving me exposed to them.

I close my eyes, refusing to watch their reactions to my body. Something tells me one of them will be more than interested.

Tucking my thumbs beneath the waistband of my sleep shorts, I shove them and my knickers to my ankles, kicking them from my bare feet.

"Happy?" I sneer, holding my arms out from my sides, trying to appear confident. "I'm not hiding anything."

Finally, I open my eyes and look at them. Just as I expected, the evil one's eyes are locked on my body, hunger filling the dark, cold depths of his orbs. But the other one has turned away.

No one says anything, but Evil's eyes make my skin prickle as he continues to eat me up.

My stomach twists, the tremors wracking my body getting worse by the second.

"Necklace?" he growls.

I gasp, my hand flying to the piece of priceless jewellery Blakely only gave me yesterday.

Thoughts of Blake and Zay threaten to break me. A massive lump climbs up my throat, cutting off my air as my heart fractures in my chest.

A sob rips from my lips as I clutch my necklace tighter.

"No, please. It's just a locket. There's nothing."

Before I know what's happening, my arm is in Evil's grasp again and I'm shoved against the wall.

His grip doesn't loosen as he growls at his mate to remove the necklace.

"Please, no. It was my mother's," I sob. It's pointless, I know it is. But I can't help it.

I half expect them to rip it from my body, but to my relief, fingers lightly brush the back of my neck to remove it properly.

"Can I get it back?" I ask, my voice weak and broken.

"I guess that depends on your new owner, doesn't it?" Evil snarls.

I'm dragged from the wall and pushed toward the sink.

The quieter guy stands back, his eyes downcast, as Evil grabs an extendable tap and points it at me.

His eyes are alight with excitement.

"Wait. No. Please," I cry.

"Sorry, I'm not the one who makes the rules, sweetheart. Your new owner is. And he wants you as pure as he can get you."

All the air rushes out of my lungs as the meaning behind his words hit me.

He wants me because I'm a virgin.

I did this. Me and my stupid intentions of waiting, of it meaning something, and this is what I get. Some sick fuck who's paid God knows how much for me.

Twisting around, I heave once more. But this time, nothing but bile comes up. Pain shoots from my stomach as my body continues to revolt, but there's nothing in there.

Nothing but desperation.

"Can we get on with it?" the other guy asks, barely looking at me. "I've got other shit to be doing."

"Don't pretend you're not enjoying this, man. I know you're as hard as I am right now, playing with this innocent little toy. If only we had permission to really play, huh?"

I heave again.

"You've seen her dance, right? Sinful." Lust and dark intentions drip from his voice, which turns my blood to ice.

I shoot a look at the nicer guy, silently begging for him to keep sticking up for me. But he doesn't get a chance to say a word before Evil turns the tap on, spraying me with ice-cold water.

My scream of shock echoes off the walls, but something tells me it can't be heard through the concrete.

My body freezes as he keeps the spray of water aimed at me, soaking me through.

It only takes seconds for my teeth to start chattering as the cold seeps through my skin to my bones.

"You feel that?" Evil sneers. "Rebirth. Baptism. Exorcism. All rolled into one. Everything about your past has been wiped away when you walk outside this building. Anyone you loved, anyone who impacted your life, anyone who touched you." A whimper spills free as I think about Alex.

He held back. For me. So many times when we were together, he could have claimed me, taken my innocence away. But he didn't.

Why did he have to be a gentleman? Why?

"When you walk out there, you're a new woman. An owned woman. You will do as you are told and obey your new man. No matter what."

Fear races through me, making the trembling that's taken over my body almost violent.

"Please," I whimper. "Stop."

But despite everything, I refuse to let any tears spill free. They might burn red hot at the back of my eyes, but I will not give this twisted fuck the satisfaction of knowing he broke me.

It is not happening.

Finally, the water cuts off. Not that it helps all that much. Every inch of me is covered and my hair is dripping, causing little rivers of ice to run down my skin.

Goosebumps cover my body as I wrap my arms around myself in a pathetic attempt to warm up.

"Here," the nice guy says, throwing a dry shirt at me.

Anger swells within me when I catch sight of my necklace still in his hand. How dare they take something so precious from me? Isn't the rest of this humiliating enough?

"What? No internal exam?" I sneer. "I could be hiding a tracker in my arse."

I regret the words the second the words roll off my tongue. Evil prowls toward me, his dark eyes pinned on mine.

"I'm more than happy to check," he offers.

"Get fucked," I hiss.

His arm lifts, and I brace myself for the hit, but thankfully, it never comes.

"Enough," the other man booms. "You heard the boss. He wants her perfect. Untouched."

Opening my eyes, I find him studying me over Evil's shoulder.

He nods at me before something that makes me relax glitters in his eyes.

Is he... is he on my side?

No. That's crazy. If he were, he wouldn't be standing there, allowing me to be degraded like this.

Remembering I'm clutching a shirt in my hands, I quickly tug it over my head and cover myself up. The loss of my necklace still sits heavy on my chest.

"Now what?" I ask as Evil bundles up my clothes and shoves them into a carrier bag.

"Now, we go find your owner."

I'm shoved toward the door.

"What kind of man buys a woman?" I ask in genuine disbelief. This is the kind of shit you see in movies. It's not real life. It's just not.

"The same kind of man who sells them. How is your daddy?"

My spine stiffens as a level of hatred that I've never felt before rolls through me.

I've always considered myself a gentle person, but in the past few days, I've wished Grant dead after the way he touched me on Sunday night, and now my father.

But then again, I've never been exposed to such evil before. Or at least, I wasn't aware of it.

"Hopefully, breathing his final few breaths. He won't get away with this," I warn.

"Oh yeah. And who do you think is going to do anything about it? You're no one. The only part of you anyone is interested in is what's between your thighs. And from what I've heard, it went for a pretty penny."

"You won't get away with this," I repeat, unable to come up with anything else.

"Thanks for the warning. I'll make sure I sleep with one eye open in case your whore of a sister comes after me at night." He laughs as if Blakely coming after him is nothing but a joke.

I mean, yeah. It probably is.

I just have to hope some other people out there might be willing to fight for me. Ones who are better trained, deadly...

I shake my head as I'm led down a deserted hallway.

It's pointless hoping.

Alex turned his back on me.

He's not coming.

He couldn't even return a message.

None of them are.

From here on out, I'm alone.

Me and my new owner.

My stomach rolls as I imagine the kind of man I'm about to be delivered to.

Nothing good is going to be waiting at the other end of this journey.

The two men move closer behind me as we approach a heavy door, and I startle when one of them grabs my hands and pins them behind my back.

"Seriously?" I hiss.

I might want to fight. To kick, scream and punch, anything to get myself out of this. But I'm not stupid. I stand no chance in overpowering either of them. And even if I did, there are more of them. I might not be able to see them, but my skin tingles with awareness. Whether they're standing in the shadows or sitting behind cameras, I'm being watched. I'd put my life on it.

"We can't have you running off now." I relax a little when the nicer one of the two leans in and speaks.

Evil grunts in irritation before stepping in front of us and pulling the door open.

The bright summer sun burns my eyes, making them water immediately.

"Fuck," I curse. I haven't fought this hard to remain strong to be undone by the fucking sunshine.

"Your destiny awaits," Evil says, gesturing to the blacked-out SUV ahead of us. "Real shame, if you ask me. We could have some real fun with you. But alas, you're already spoken for. I really hope your new owner treats you well." He sneers, making a shiver run down my spine. "I know I would."

My lip curls in disgust as I'm frogmarched closer to the awaiting vehicle.

Thankfully, the next time he speaks, he's farther away.

"What's happening?" I whisper, hoping the other guy will give me some kind of clue.

Leaning around me, his warmth presses against my

back. Despite the sun's heat on my still-chilled skin, I stupidly lean back into him, desperate for warmth and comfort.

"Now you get in this car and head off to your new life." He shifts behind me, his grip on my wrists tightening before something hard presses into my palm. "But I need you to do as you're told. I promise it'll make all this easier." His accent, American, is stronger with this warning.

My fingers wrap around what he just placed in my palm and hold it for dear life.

I nod in agreement.

I knew he was on my side.

Although, I second-guess that not a second later when something's placed over my head, cutting off my vision.

"We're not all evil, Evie," he whispers so quietly that no one else has a chance of hearing him.

My heart pounds and my heart races as he straps me in.

There are so many questions dancing on the tip of my tongue, but all of them are too dangerous to ask right now.

The door slams, leaving me alone in the back of the car. I blink against the darkness, but no matter how hard I try, I can't see anything.

His words ring in my ear, his warning to be good. And foolishly or not, I take them seriously.

I leave my hands behind my back, my fingers clutching what I hope is my necklace.

Deep voices rumble outside the car, and I pray to anyone who might listen that the nice one gets in the driver's seat and gets me the hell out of this situation.

4

———

EVIE

It takes so long for someone to join me that I startle when the door is ripped open and someone drops inside, making the car wobble.

"Remember what I said?" a familiar voice says.

I've no idea if he can see, but I nod in agreement. It's the only movement I make as the car rumbles to life.

"We've got a bit of a journey, so I suggest you relax," he says as we begin moving.

"Relax?" I hiss, unable to keep my mouth shut. "When I'm in a car with fuck knows who with a bag over my head?"

He chuckles, which does nothing for the fragile grip I've got on my emotions right now.

"Just do your best. I'll tell you when it's safe."

"Safe? I'm meant to believe I'm safe right now? You could be taking me toward a man who makes a hobby of skinning innocent virgins alive."

He laughs again.

"I can assure you, I'm not."

"Really? Know this man well, do you?"

"Something like that," he mutters.

"Wait? Is it you? Are you the sick fuck who's purchased me to do... well, whatever you want me to do?"

"No, princess. I couldn't afford you."

Finally, I pull my arms from behind my back. They're going dead, and quite frankly, this 'do as you're told' bullshit is already getting old.

Lifting the bottom of the hood that's covering my head, I stare down at the locket in my palm. A small piece of my heart slots back into place.

"Not sure if that's actually a good thing or not," I mutter, remembering his comment.

"I guess that all depends on how the rest of this plays out, huh?"

"So you might be delivering me to a skin-peeling psychopath."

"There really is nothing like a mystery," he says absently as we take a corner.

"Where are we going?"

"What about the hood makes you think we want you to know?"

"Are you always this funny?" I quip.

"I try."

Silence falls between us as I try and figure this out.

"Who are you?"

"Nice try."

"You could be sending me to my death. I should at least get to know who the man is who rescued my necklace."

"I'm no one."

"A ghost, right. Where are you from? Surely you can tell me that."

"Here and there."

"A ghost with no home. Don't tell me, you've been

trafficked too? Did some rich, lonely woman buy you to do her worst with?"

"No, princess. No one would want me. I just do my job."

"Ah, a good boy who follows orders. So do you sleep well at night, knowing you're ripping poor, innocent girls from their lives and depositing them in hell?"

"Watch your accusations there, princess. I'm not the worst man you've experienced today by a long shot. You should be thanking me."

"Oh, sure. Thank you for locking me in a cell while I was unconscious, forcing me to strip naked in front of two strangers, and then dousing me in freezing cold water. How could I be so ungrateful?"

He laughs. "You're welcome. You're not what I was expecting," he confesses.

"Why? Because I'm not crying for my daddy?"

"No. I'd never expect that after learning what he did. I thought you'd be... I dunno, scared."

"You think I'm not scared?" I ask in disbelief.

The fact I'm rambling like an idiot and asking a million and one questions would be enough to tell anyone who knows me that I'm a world away from my comfort zone right now.

"You don't sound it," he admits.

"Just think, if this were another life, I could have been an actress."

"It could still happen," he murmurs.

"You think my new owner will allow it?"

"I think he'd give you the world if you asked."

My brows pinch, but I don't get a chance to say anything, because he takes such a hard right that I go flying across the back seats despite the seat belt he wrapped around me.

"A little warning would be nice," I snap, righting myself.

"Sorry. We've got to make a little pit stop."

"I hope it involves snacks. I'm starving."

The car pulls to an abrupt stop, the engine dies, and he climbs out.

The slam from his car door still echoes in my ears when mine is opened and the bag is ripped off my head.

"Gotta say, princess. I'm impressed you kept that on so long."

Amused eyes stare down at me, but still, it's all I can see of him. His hood and the bandana still cover his features, hiding his identity from me.

"Are you trying to tell me that I could have taken it off?"

He doesn't respond. He doesn't need to. I can see the answer shining in his eyes.

"Wanker."

"Now, now. Remember, you should be thanking me.'

"Really?" I sneer.

"Oh, come off it. You offered that cunt the chance to strip search you for trackers. You know he'd have taken you up on it if it weren't for me."

"I don't—what the hell?" I bark as he lifts me from the car as if I weigh nothing.

"Time to move, princess."

A dark van parked two spaces away catches my eye.

"Oh no," I start, my heart dropping into my stomach when the side door opens.

A body gets thrown out, landing right at our feet before two other guys jump out.

"All yours," the oldest one says before picking up the

dead weight they threw on the floor and putting him, none too gently, into the back of the car I was just in.

"What the hell is going on?" I ask as I'm led toward the van.

"Probably best you don't ask, princess."

"B-but," I stutter as he lifts me and places me in the back of the van. "Where are you taking me?"

"If I told you to trust me, would you?"

"Not a chance."

"That's a shame, because you really should. Make yourself at home. Sleep off whatever is running around your system you're trying so hard to fight."

"I don't know what you're talking about."

"Okay, sure." He shoves me back a few steps, then swings the door closed.

"Hey," I scream, slamming my curled fists on the door. "You can't just lock me in here."

The only response I get is rumbled laughter.

There are voices, and then someone climbs in the front of the van and the engine starts. Then, we're off.

I stumble as we move, cursing myself for not sitting down or even looking at my surroundings.

"Oh," I breathe, taking in the massive pile of cushions and blankets tucked into one corner.

The exhaustion I was trying to ignore suddenly hits me, and with no way of seeing out or having anyone to talk to, I make myself a little bed and curl up under a blanket.

Despite the riot in my head, the confusion, the fear, all the questions that are spinning around, with the gentle rocking of the van as we drive wherever we're going, I fall asleep faster than I thought possible.

And when I come to again and stretch my legs out, it

becomes apparent very fast that I'm no longer curled up in a back of a van but... in a bed?

My eyes spring open and I gasp as I stare at the vast room around me.

The blinds are closed, but there's a soft glow coming from the bedside lamp next to me, allowing me to see the luxury I'm surrounded by.

My first thought is that I'm in a hotel again.

Memories from my short stay in The Empire last weekend flicker through my mind.

But there's something about this room that feels different. Less... hotel-y and more personal.

Hesitantly, I drag my body until I'm sitting with the covers pooled at my waist.

As well as the massive bed I'm in, there's a sofa that faces what I can only assume are floor-to-ceiling windows when the blinds are open. There are two heavy oak doors on the other side of the room, one for an en suite and another for a dressing room, maybe. This place gives me the vibes that whoever owns it has a dressing room. Maybe it's what is obviously a very expensive piece of art staring at me on the opposite wall. It's even got a little light above it like it's sitting in a gallery. You don't go to that much effort if it's a bargain from Ikea.

Twisting around, I hang my legs off the side of the bed. Something tickles my chest as I move, and when I lift my hand, I find my locket hanging around my neck.

Pulling it from beneath the shirt I'm still wearing, I wrap my fingers around it.

Everything else in my life might be beyond fucked right now, but I still have this. Hope.

Blakely will know I'm gone by now, and she won't rest until I'm safe. She'll find me. Somehow.

But how?

Dropping my head into my hands, I let myself wallow for two minutes.

I have no idea where I am. No clue who the man was who drove me here, and then what? Carried me to bed and tucked me in.

I'm grateful. I am. If it was Mr. Evil, then God only knows where I'd have ended up.

But without any answers, I'm struggling to see anything good here other than the fact I'm unharmed and alone.

But how long for?

If what I've heard is to be believed, then someone has paid a lot of money for me.

That has to mean they want me for something, and I assume not to lock up like a damsel in distress.

Pushing my feet into the thick carpet, I wiggle my toes.

Whoever owns this place clearly has money.

Fancy house, priceless art, expensive carpet, eighteen-year-old virgin.

It's what every man has on their bucket list, right?

Padding across the room, I poke my head into the first door and find I was right. A dressing room. Only, it's empty.

Not what I was expecting.

Maybe I'm wrong and this is a hotel.

The second door reveals a very flashy en suite. The tub is the biggest I've ever seen in my life, and it sits in front of a huge window that showcases outside—or I assume it would, if it weren't the middle of the night.

Twinkling in the darkness has my feet moving closer to the window.

I might have lost the plush carpet, but the tiles beneath my feet are warm.

Unable to stop myself, I step right up to the window and press my palms to the cool glass as I stare up at the inky black night sky.

A gasp slips past my lips when the twinkling of stars far above me holds my attention.

"Where am I?" I whisper, already knowing that the city is far behind. I don't think I have ever seen this many stars.

My heart pounds steadily in my chest as I continue to stand there and stare.

It's so peaceful, so serene. All the while, there's a riot going on inside me.

Bringing my trembling hand to my locket once more, I lift it to my lips, a silent promise to Blake and Zay that I'm going to find a way out of this. That I'm going to get back to them and do whatever it takes to get them as far away from Dad and Derek as possible.

"I hoped to be able to give Blakely a better life, but she screwed that up for herself long before I even realised. But you, my sweet girl... I can give you everything."

Dad's words come back to me in a rush. They didn't mean anything to me at the time, but now...

My bare feet slap against the tiled floor as I run for the toilet, throw the lid up and drop to my knees.

But just like the last time my body tried to expel all of this, there's nothing to bring up.

My stomach muscles scream as the heaving continues. My knuckles turn white as I clutch the seat, desperately trying to get my body back under control. Tears flood my cheeks, then drop, splashing onto the backs of my hands, and my head spins.

It's night, that much is obvious, but I've no idea what day, or how long has passed since Derek turned up at the flat, deciding it was time to start my life over.

I heave once more, nothing but pain wracking my body.

Slumping back on the warm tiles, I wrap my arm around my legs and lower my head to my knees.

My entire body trembles, my limbs exhausted despite the sleep, my veins filled with fear and apprehension.

Wherever I am, it might be all kinds of opulent, but that doesn't mean anything. Ugly people often have what look like the most beautiful lives. This might not be a house set for a princess, but a beast.

A beast who paid God knows what for a young, innocent girl.

My stomach clenches violently again, but thankfully, there's nothing more as I consider the reasons why anyone would want to buy me.

None of them are good. Not one.

I've no idea how long I sit there silently freaking out, begging anyone who might be up there listening for this nightmare to be over. For me to wake up and discover that it's all been a sick and twisted dream.

But I never do.

I'm already awake. This is my new reality.

A place where I've no idea what's happening, where I am, or who I'm expected to be.

Ice rushes through my veins, making the journey back to my feet harder than it should be.

I stagger toward the basin, my eyes darting around the counter, looking for any signs of life here.

It's the first time I notice that this bathroom is as desolate as the dressing room.

The only sign that it's ever been used is the fact that there's a roll of toilet paper on the stand.

There is nothing else.

I'm lost. Totally out in the middle of the ocean without a paddle.

My eyes gloss over the white marble counter, following the wiggly grey lines cutting through it as I try and come up with a plan.

If this place is totally empty then...

I look up and stumble back when I find my reflection.

I barely even recognise myself.

My skin is pale, my eyes dark as if they're bruised. My hair dangles limply around my shoulders. The man's t-shirt I'm wearing hangs from my body as if I'm nothing more than a skeleton beneath it.

Looking at me, it would be easy to think this ordeal has been going on for a long time, not only... hours. Days, maybe.

I look weak and pathetic. The exact opposite of how I want to look.

What would Blakely do?

I stare into my eyes, trying to channel her fire, her grit, and determination. She hasn't got where she has after everything by being weak.

She's strong. So fucking strong.

After Mum died, she picked herself up and became the mother that Zay and I had just lost without questioning it, or at least without ever letting us see that she had.

I need that strength right now, if I'm going to find a way out of this. A way back to my family.

A small mark on the corner of the mirror before me catches my eye and I reach out, tucking my finger beneath it.

I tug gently, just in case I'm wrong. But I'm not.

"Thank God," I mutter when I pull the hidden cabinet open and find a whole stash of new toothbrushes.

A lot of things might be wrong right now, but the state of my mouth is right up there.

I rip open the packet and reach for a new tube of toothpaste and set about fixing at least one of my issues.

Ignoring everything else in the cabinet that points toward this place not being abandoned like I first thought, I make my way out of the bathroom.

I pause the second my feet hit the carpet, my eyes locked on the only other door I've yet to open.

What the hell am I going to find on the other side of that?

A man?

A monster?

Hell?

5

———

ALEX

"It's delayed. Again," I bark down the phone the second the call connects.

Theo sighs, unable to come up with a response that will calm me down.

"Trust us. Just focus on keeping your head together."

"How the fuck am I mean to do that exactly? I'm stuck in Harry Reid International waiting for a plane that doesn't apparently want to come, and Evie is—" I cut myself off, unable to force those words out. "Tell me something, please, Theo. Lie to me. Tell me we've got her and that she's waiting for me."

"Alex," he growls.

"Fuck's sake, man," I bark, earning myself more than a few irritated stares from the bored passengers sitting around me.

"Mommy, he said a bad word," a little girl says, scowling at me like I'm the devil incarnate.

Her mother pierces me with a death stare and I turn my back on them, striding toward the windows that look out over the planes that I am not getting on.

The second I was dressed and packed, Theo stole my phone and handed me a burner and basically shoved me out of the suite, telling me that I had a seat heading home later that afternoon.

Well, that flight was meant to take off hours ago, and I'm still fucking here.

"I know you're freaking, but we're doing everything we can," Theo assures me.

"Give me a job. Give me anything," I beg. I need to do something, I need to feel useful.

Silence fills the line for a few seconds and I imagine them looking at each other, at a loss for how to respond. Well, other than to tell me to sit tight and wait it out.

"Go shopping," a familiar soft voice says.

"Baby C," I sigh.

"I'm serious. Go and find something you can give her when you get back to her. She's going to need a pick-me-up."

"Won't I be enough?" I ask, but I refuse to feel any hope that I'm going to see her again, let alone that she'll be happy about it.

Logically, I know this isn't my fault. But I can't help but feel the guilt that I left destroying me from the inside out. I walked away and left her to this.

If I hadn't...

Fuck. I don't know. But surely it wouldn't have been this fucking devastating.

The Riveras, and the Hawks, are both after this corrupt human trafficking ring, and I unknowingly stumbled right in the middle of it. Or more so, I found a girl who was about to be at the centre.

I'm sure Reid and Luciana are foaming at the mouth at this chance to infiltrate them and take out the leaders. But all I feel is dread. All-consuming dread that we're going to be too late.

The people who have been trafficked... Many men, women, and children have never been seen again, either forced to start new lives somewhere else, or killed by the psychos who pay for ownership of other people.

Of course, I want it eradicated. I want it for all the people whose lives have been touched by it to get closure, to know that the people at the top have suffered in a way their loved ones might have. But mostly, I just want my girl in my arms where she belongs. Not with some corrupt cunt who's going to do God knows what with her.

My stomach rolls.

That's not true. I know exactly what they're going to do with her. She was advertised as an eighteen-year-old virgin, for fuck's sake.

My grip on the burner in my hand tightens to the point I'm sure it's about to crack.

"Alex, you'll be everything," Calli says softly, reminding me that she's there. "Just... please. For me, go and find something."

"Fine," I sigh, unable to deny her of anything.

The last thing I want to do is go fucking shopping, but sitting here waiting for the inevitable isn't a better option.

"They'll get her," she assures me. "Trust them. Trust us."

"But—"

"No buts. It doesn't matter how many thousands of miles away we are, we can fix this."

"Calli." My voice cracks as I whisper her name and lean forward, pressing my brow to the cold glass before me.

I probably look like a right headcase to the rest of the passengers, but I don't care.

All I care about is her, and I've no idea where she is or how to get to her. Theo didn't allow me to hang around long enough to even hear his plan. Assuming he had one.

He had to, right?

Pressing my hand to the window, I look out to the horizon and send up a silent prayer.

I'm not religious in the fucking slightest, but there's no harm in trying, right?

"Daemon came back, Alex. Evie will too."

My palm slides down the glass as I remember my twin's state when he returned.

If anyone has so much as laid a finger on Evie...

"Go find her something pretty. Something that will show her how much she means to you."

"Tell them to call me if they find anything."

"Of course. They're doing everything they can. Have faith."

I end the call with my heart in my throat and dread knotting my stomach.

But what if that's not enough?

Intrigued stares of the bored people around me burn into my skin as I continue standing there, drowning in my misery. I let it fuel me for a few seconds before I drop the burner phone into my pocket and take off, keeping my eyes ahead, refusing to meet anyone's stare.

I focus on Calli's suggestion and search the rails and shelves in the array of shops that surround me. I don't see most of it. My head is too full of fear and desperation to focus on buying a meaningful present.

But then, I walk past a jewellery counter, and something calls to me.

I pause, studying it, my finger trailing across the glass cabinet that protects it.

There's no price, but that doesn't matter. It could clear out every penny I have; if it means I get a chance to see her again, to give it to her, it'll be worth it.

"Can I help, sir?" a chirpy shop assistant asks.

"Y-yes," I stutter, clearing my throat before I can continue. "That bracelet. I want it."

I continued wandering around the airport with the bag and Evie's gift swinging from my fingers for hours after purchasing it.

Every time I looked at the departures board, our time had been moved back.

I got to the point when the anger had faded and nothing but desperation set in.

But there was nothing I could do. I was over five thousand miles from London. If she was even still in London.

My burner had been ominously quiet. I could only hope that no news was good news and things were in place. That Theo and Toby had located her and found a way to intercept her before she ended up with her owner.

Owner...

Every time that word floats around my brain, my stomach threatens to revolt.

Evie isn't an object to be owned. She's a young, beautiful, sassy woman who deserves the chance to live her life as she sees fit. Not be shackled to whoever might have purchased her like she's nothing more than a new pair of shoes.

I sent Theo a message when we took off as I promised, but since then, I've forced myself to sit here and just hope they're making progress while I'm flying halfway around the world.

I wanted them to come with me. It made sense in my head for them to return as fast as possible. But also, their need for a decent connection to hack into whatever the hell they were hacking sounded sensible. Plus, we had no idea if whoever is running that shitshow knows that any of us are after them. And if they are and they're watching us... well, us all returning unexpectedly might raise some alarm bells.

I got it. Although it sounded far-fetched to me. But what the hell do I know? I'm just the easy-going pretty one who seduces information out of people.

As I watch the little aeroplane move across the screen before me with our progress, I try to devise a plan of my own. My need to go and spill enough blood to drown in consumes me. But without knowing who did this, I've little to go on.

There's only one face that keeps coming back to me.

Vincent.

"He's in charge of the girls. If you want to know anything about them, he's your man. Might even be able to secure you an hour or two with your mystery dancer, for the right price."

Every word Matteo said to me that night in Paradise rings alarm bells.

He could have done this if he's her pimp, or whatever.

Matteo made it very clear that he was selling his girl's time for the right price. But was he selling more than the promise of a good time in one of the back rooms?

I should have spoken to him for longer. I should have shown more interest in her. Maybe he'd have offered her to me.

I'd have paid it. I'd have paid anything to stop this from happening.

Why her? She's got family who loves her.

Her sister... she freaked out when she suspected I'd drugged her. She must be going crazy right now.

But Blakley lives the same life.

What if they've been sold together? What if Blakely has gone too, and their little brother is alone? What about their father?

Too many questions to compute race around my head.

I've had nowhere near enough sleep and way too much alcohol and pills for this shit.

I've no idea how it happens, but when the captain's voice comes through the speakers to let us know that we'll be beginning our descent into Heathrow Airport, it wakes me up.

I blink, staring at that little plane in front of me again, my groggy brain not believing that we're nearly there.

My heart jumps into my throat when I see that the captain is right.

Thirty minutes until I'm back on English soil and I can begin my own search for my girl.

Powering up the burner, I connect to the aeroplane's Wi-Fi that I've refused to use this far. I knew I'd only be torturing myself while waiting for news from the guys.

The second it syncs, I get a message from a number I recognise as the burner Theo's been using.

My hand trembles as I open it.

> Theo: Your driver will meet you in Arrivals.
> Look for a familiar face.

"That's it?" I bark, making the woman beside me shriek. "Sorry," I mutter, although I'm not really.

My grip on the phone once again tightens and my thumb angrily taps at the screen.

> Alex: Landing in twenty-five. Is that all you've got for me?

> Theo: Right now, yes. We'll catch up when you're on a secure line and not surrounded by people.

"The fuck?" I hiss, shaking my head in frustration.

I swear the next forty-five minutes are longer than the entire flight back.

We might have landed on time, but I'm sure we've done five laps around the fucking airport since.

"Thank fuck for that," I mutter, barging my way past the woman beside me to drag my bag from the overhead locker and force my way down to the front of the aeroplane to escape.

The second the door's open, I run, leaving all the pissed-off passengers I shoved out of my way behind.

Thankfully, the queue for passport control isn't too long, and an hour after being told someone would be waiting for me, I spill through the huge doors welcoming arrivals and my eyes land on a pair I more than recognise.

"For the love of God, you had better have some information for me," I bark at Ant, not stopping for any pleasantries. Instead, I wait for him to fall into step beside me as I march toward the exit.

6

———

EVIE

My heart pounds in every inch of my body as I twist the handle and pull the door open.

But unlike I feared, there isn't a man on the other side waiting to scare the bejesus out of me.

It's empty.

Silent.

I want to shout out, but I swallow it down.

If there is someone here, then I figure it's better not to warn them that I'm coming.

My eyes widen when I step out of the bedroom and find a long hallway with multiple doors on each side. There's more artwork hanging on the walls between each doorway. Although with the only light coming from the room I just left, it's hard to see what's on them.

But none of the doors have locks on like I'd expect from a hotel, confirming my thoughts.

Hesitantly and silently, I make my way toward the stairs at the very end of the hallway.

The need to open every single door and check out every

inch of this floor burns through me, but I lock it down. There will be time for that later... maybe.

My heart is racing when I get to the stairs, my entire body trembling.

While up here is in darkness, there's a light on downstairs. The thought of being here with some unknown person makes me want to vomit.

Be brave, Evie.

For Blake. For Zay.

You need to figure a way out of this.

Sucking in some confidence, I make my way down the polished wooden stairs on unsteady legs.

The stairwell opens up when I get about a third of the way down, allowing me to see the lower floor. And what I find makes my eyes go so wide they hurt.

The space is huge, and, even in mostly darkness, breathtaking.

My legs move faster, my need to discover more is too much to ignore.

"Wow," I breathe when I finally get to the bottom and get a chance to see the huge fireplace and massive living room that was beneath me.

One of the walls is entirely glass, I assume giving perfect, uninterrupted views of whatever lies beyond.

The sofas are huge, covered in soft, comfortable-looking cushions. There's a massive TV hanging on one wall and every game console that exists on a shelf beneath it.

Spinning toward the light that illuminates the space, I find an incredible kitchen. That alone is bigger than our entire flat. The island in the middle is bigger than most people's dining tables.

But the most noticeable thing is that there's no one here.

Convinced I must have missed something, I spin around once more, searching the walls until I find a light switch.

If it's possible, the place gets even more breathtaking as I flick more and more lights on.

Spotting a short hallway behind one of the sofas, I take off in that direction in my search.

I find an office, a smaller den, a laundry room, and a locked door at the end.

"Hello?" I eventually shout, my voice echoing around the vast space. "Is anyone here?"

Silence.

Walking through the house, I find more evidence that someone might live here. Ornaments, DVDs under the TV, a bookcase full of paperbacks. Although, there is nothing personal to give me any kind of clue as to whose house this might be.

I pad back to the kitchen and find something on one of the counters I had missed.

Rushing over, I take in the pile of clothes and, more importantly, the note on the top.

Evie,

Make yourself at home. Anything here is yours to make use of.

Relax.

Company will be arriving soon.

Your ghost.

A smile twitches at the corner of my lips at the sign off, but mostly, any amusement is swallowed by the previous sentence.

Company will be arriving soon... if that doesn't sound ominous, then I don't know what does.

Moving the note to the counter, I find a new set of underwear, sleep shorts, and a tank similar to what I was wearing when I was taken, whenever that was. A pair of leggings, a t-shirt and a hoodie. And right at the bottom, a pair of sliders.

A frown pulls at my brows when I discover that it's all my size.

But while ditching the shirt I was forced to wear and pulling on some underwear is high up my list, it's not as high as dealing with the growling in my stomach.

Spotting a huge American-style fridge freezer, I pull the door open and gasp when I find it full.

Ignoring the food for now, I reach for a bottle of water and twist the top.

The cool liquid slides down my raw throat, and I sigh in relief before making my way through the cupboard to see what I can find to eat. The fresh food in the fridge isn't going to cut it right now.

"Yes," I hiss when my eyes land on a packet of chocolate-covered Hobnobs.

Snatching up the packet, I rip it open and take a bite.

"OhmyGod," I mumble as the sweetness coats my tongue.

I eat the first one fast, quickly followed by another.

I'm five down by the time I turn around, my eyes landing on the clock on the wall-mounted microwave.

Midnight. Guess that explains the stars.

With the biscuits still in my clutches, I take off around the ground floor again. But this time, I focus on the doors that lead outside.

Locked. Every single one of them.

Another light switch catches my attention as I stand before the wall of windows. Reaching over, I flip it, revealing just a little bit of what hides behind the veil of darkness outside.

"Wow," I breathe as a large deck is revealed, complete with a huge hot tub. I can't see beyond the railing, but something tells me there's nothing. The good kind of nothing.

I think of the recurring daydream I have of sunbathing naked in complete solitude with only the birds to see, and I can't help but wonder if somehow, I've found myself in the middle of it.

Surely not. I can't have gone from a concrete cell with Mr. Evil to paradise.

That isn't how this kind of thing works.

I haven't been bought by some nice, lonely, wealthy man who's just looking for some company of a young woman.

I might be innocent in some ways, but I'm not that naïve.

Shaking my head, I turn away from the deck. All of this is a dream, it has to be. It can't be real.

I grab another bottle of water when I get back to the kitchen, followed by the pile of clothes, and I make my way back to the stairs.

As I climb up, I think that I should probably be trying to escape. The doors might be locked, but surely there's a way out? But I refuse to do that while wearing a man's shirt and no knickers. And despite having no clue where I am or who my company will be, I feel weirdly comfortable here.

My grip on the pile of clothes in my arms tightens as I pass each door upstairs. My need to throw each one open and look inside almost gets the better of me. But I manage to refrain in favour of making use of that bathroom.

Placing the clothes on the counter, I open the mirrored cabinet again and find a bottle of shampoo, conditioner and shower gel before placing them all into the cubicle and turning the shower on.

Water sprays from every direction, and my thoughts immediately take me back to Alex's shower.

A pained sigh falls from my lips as I remember how it felt to stand under that torrent of water while his body was pinned against mine, his hands roaming over my body.

God... that night was all kinds of ugly yet beautiful.

The perfect kind of contrast. Just like him.

Light and dark.

Perfect and dangerous.

Gentle and rough.

The ultimate contradiction.

Peeling the shirt up my body, I let it drop to the tiles behind me before I step under the water.

A low moan rumbles deep in my throat, and my muscles instantly relax with the powerful jets.

I've no idea how long I stand there in the hope that everything that's happened in the last however long will just wash down the drain and I can return to his shower that night and have a do-over.

But what would I do different?

What made him pull away like he did when he dropped me off on Monday?

It's something I've thought about non-stop since he drove away, leaving me shattering on the pavement in front of our building. But no matter how much I repeat our time together in my head, I never come up with anything that will have flipped that switch in him.

One moment, he seemed to be all in, and then, it was over.

It's why it hurt so much. At least if something

happened, if we had a disagreement or something, I'd have understood.

The only thing I can come up with was that the reality of who I really was and where I lived was too much for him.

I was a poor Lovell girl, and he was a Knight's Ridge prince. Not exactly compatible.

We were fighting to live from one day to the next, and he was living in his fancy building and driving around town in his custom Audi which probably cost more than our flat is worth.

I roll my neck, wincing as my muscles crack and pull.

With pruned skin, I finish up before stepping out and discovering I don't have a towel.

Maybe this isn't paradise, after all.

I didn't bother going back downstairs after I finally found a thick, fluffy towel stacked on the dresser in the bedroom waiting for me. Stupid place to put them, if you ask me. Instead of plotting my middle-of-the-night escape plan, I opened the blinds and dropped my exhausted body onto the sofa in front of the windows.

With the lights illuminating the deck below, I was able to make out the trees just beyond the building as they swayed in the wind.

By the time I'd munched my way through the entire packet of Hobnobs, I could barely keep my eyes open, and I pulled the blanket from the back of the sofa and curled up into the corner, giving in to the exhaustion.

I awake with a start, my eyes flying open as my heart races.

The house is still in silence, but I'm sure something woke me up.

Shoving the blanket from my body, I swing my legs off the sofa and slide to the edge, on full alert.

Long seconds pass with nothing. But then, there's a bang.

My heart jumps into my throat.

Company will be arriving soon.

I squeeze my eyes closed, but they spring open once more when there's another noise.

Someone is downstairs.

My breathing increases until I can barely catch my breath. The trembling in my hands becomes so violent, I can feel it in my toes.

Footsteps land on the stairs and a squeak of terror rips from my lips.

I look around the room in a panic.

I've no idea what to do.

Sit here and wait for my fate to be revealed or...

My legs move before I've made a decision, and I pull the dressing room door open and slip into the darkness.

The pounding of my heart and the blood racing past my ears drowns out the sound of the person approaching.

But that doesn't mean I miss the bedroom door being thrown open. I gasp, my eyes wide as my hand flies up to cover my mouth and muffle any sounds I might be making.

I look around, but there's nothing but darkness.

This was a really stupid idea.

My legs tremble, my knees about to give out, when the person on the other side of the door shouts, and my world tips on its axis.

"Evie? Where are you?"

7

———

ALEX

"The fuck is that?" I bark as Ant leads me to a basic and inconspicuous light blue Ford Focus.

"Careful, Deimos. Your wealth is showing," he quips.

"Fuck that. Tell me that this isn't your car."

He snorts, telling me what I already knew as we both pull the doors open and drop inside.

The second we slam them behind us, I turn to him, the tone of my voice turning serious.

"Tell me what the fuck is going on right no—"

"She's safe," Ant interrupts, making all the air rush out of my lungs.

"We've got her?" I ask, needing to hear the words straight from his lips.

"You've got her," he confirms.

"Fuck," I sigh, sinking back into the hard seat.

Some of the tension that's been locking up my muscles since the moment Theo told me what had been happening while we were living it large in Vegas loosens.

"Why the hell are we still sitting here? Take me to her,"

I demand. Okay, so I might not be all that relaxed. I won't be until I've got her wrapped in my arms where I can keep her safe.

He glances over at me but wisely keeps his mouth shut as he navigates us out of the drop-off car park and finally gets us moving.

"Long flight?" he asks when we're finally flying down the fast lane of the motorway, the speedo almost hitting one hundred—something I wouldn't have said this car was capable of when I first clapped eyes on it.

"Longer than you can even imagine," I mutter, combing my fingers through my messy hair. After a night in Las Vegas, a long-arse delay in Harry Reid, and then an international flight, it really needs fucking washing, but that's hardly my priority right now. Neither is how I smell, which even I can admit is less than pleasant. "What do you know?"

"You haven't spoken to Theo?" he asks, sounding shocked.

"No."

"Okay. Well, he's the one with the details. I was just sent to chauffeur your arse to your girl."

"How did they get her? Did they manage to track her phone? Intercept her?" That's what Theo was talking about before I left, but a lot of fucking hours have passed since then.

"Pretty much, yeah. And thanks to your girl, now you have their location for Luciana," he says, letting me know he's up to date with what we're up to, even if it's not a Mariano job.

"I would say they're welcome, but I'm fucking not. Is she okay? Did they touch her or—"

"I don't know. This is your party, not ours. I'm just doing a friend a favour."

"Thank you," I say, clenching and unclenching my fists on my lap.

It's dark out, the middle of the fucking night, and I hate the idea of her being alone somewhere, scared of what's happening, missing her family.

"Can't you go any faster?" I bark, getting more and more impatient.

"Dude, the wheel is shaking like a motherfucker. Any faster and it's likely to fall off. There are snacks in the back if you're—"

Long before he's finished talking, I've unclicked my seat belt and heaved my exhausted body through the gap in the front seats.

"Jesus Christ," he growls.

"See something you like?" I tease, wiggling my arse in the air. "Oh shit," I grunt as I slip lower, getting wedged as I rummage through the bag of goodies he brought.

"With you smelling like that?" he barks behind me. "Come off it."

"You would, and you know you would," I tease.

I throw a couple of packets of crisps, chocolate bars and sweets onto my seat before grabbing energy drinks.

"Ow, you fucking prick. That hit my head."

"Just focus on driving instead of checking out my arse."

"You fucking wish."

"Nah, I've got my sights on a redhead. Jealous?" I ask, planting my palms on the back seats and trying to free myself.

It takes longer, and hurts more, than it should, but eventually, I drop my arse back into the passenger seat without crushing the food I threw into it.

"Welcome back," Ant laughs.

"You didn't answer my question," I point out while ripping open a packet of salt and vinegar McCoys.

Ant glances over, irritation in his dark eyes.

"I thought we were forgetting about it?"

"It's totally forgotten. I'm just curious."

"Well, don't be. Just focus on her."

A pathetic-sounding sigh falls from my lips as I do as he suggests, seeing her dark red hair sprawled over my pillow, her gorgeous body laid out for me to take. But it's more than that. I've been with more beautiful people than I'd care to admit, but none of them have spoken to me on a deeper level like she has. My attraction to her, my obsession... it runs so much deeper than her looks. It's in her eyes, in her soul, her heart.

Lifting my hand, I rub at my breastbone as if that'll help banish the ache that's only been growing there since I left her on the pavement outside her house on Monday.

Fuck. That feels like a lifetime ago.

"Tell me about her? She's the girl I saw you with coming out of the lift, yeah?"

"Yeah," I agree. "I can't get enough of her."

"I'm pretty sure the feeling was mutual from the way she had her hand in your pants."

My dick jerks just thinking about her touch.

"She's too good for me," I mutter, absently staring out the window at the lights in the distance.

"Bullshit. You're one of the best people I know. I'm not sure I've met anyone who loves as hard as you do."

"And there lies the issue," I whisper. It's more for myself than it is him, but that doesn't stop him from answering.

"I'm talking about your family, Alex. Your friends. Fuck

anyone else who's been a part of your life, no matter how briefly."

I scrub my hand down my face, images of all the faceless, nameless people I've 'worked' with over the past couple of years flickering through my mind.

"She deserves better. Not some glorified—"

"Stop. Just stop," he demands, slamming his palm against the wheel in frustration. "You don't get to decide what she does and doesn't deserve, Alex. It is her choice."

"Not if she isn't aware."

"So tell her. She's just been sold in a human trafficking ring, for fuck's sake. She can handle this. Handle you. Just give her the opportunity. Trust her with your truth, Alex. She might just surprise you,"

"Or run the other way screaming," I murmur.

"You really think that?" I shrug. "So it wasn't you who ran away, leaving her on the pavement outside her apartment with no promises of tomorrow like a pussy?"

I glare at him. "How do you know that?"

He smirks. "I know everything."

"Prick."

He chuckles darkly before taking the exit, finally taking us off the motorway.

"Where are we going?" I ask, suddenly realising that I have no idea what's going on.

"Call Theo," Ant suggests. "I'm merely the driver."

Sliding my phone from my pocket, I find his contact, not bothering to figure out the time difference or worrying about him being asleep. Honestly, I barely know what day it is right now. Attempting to work out something that complicated might make my head explode.

Hitting call, I place it to my ear.

"Voicemail."

"Helpful," Ant deadpans.

I try Toby but get the same response.

"When are they flying back?" Ant asks.

"Umm..."

"Let's just get you to your girl. The rest can wait. She's safe, and you guys have intel. That's all we need right now."

"So where are we going?"

M y need to jump out of a moving car has never been as strong as the moment Ant turned off the main road and started taking the track that leads to a secluded place I haven't been in in too long a time.

Soft lights from the cabin ahead of us glow through the trees, and my stomach twists and tumbles with a mixture of nerves and excitement.

I've no idea if she's sitting in there waiting for me or has no idea what's happening.

The only people who know and I trust to explain aren't answering their fucking phones.

I have my belt off and my fingers curled around the door handle long before Ant pulls up out the front next to a black van.

My heart jumps into my throat, my exhaustion instantly forgotten as my body revs up to fight whoever might be here for the girl inside that cabin. No sooner have I got the door open—the car still moving—does a familiar face step out with his hands raised.

I stumble as I launch myself from the car before Ant has pulled to a stop, and I run at full speed toward the door.

My hand trembles as I press it to the scanner that will

allow me entry into the building. Sucking in a breath, I force myself to calm down as an owl hoots in the trees somewhere around me.

"Get it together, dickhead," I mutter to myself before shaking my hand and doing it again.

This time, it works, and the little red light turns green and the lock disengages.

"Yes," I hiss, crashing through the door and letting it slam behind me without thinking. "Shit."

The cabin is in darkness. I can only see anything because of the glow from the outside lights.

My heart pounds so hard as I move toward the stairs that I can feel it in every inch of my body.

The cabin spins around me as I begin to ascend the stairs. Everything that's happened in the past fuck knows how many hours—all my panic, desperation, and need to wrap her in my arms and promise her that everything is going to be okay—becoming too much, and I trip up the next stair.

"Motherfuckers," I curse my legs.

Scrambling up, I manage to get to the first floor unharmed, my legs carrying me past all the closed doors faster than the rest of my body can keep up with.

With my eyes locked on the slightly open master bedroom door, I picture her curled up in bed, safe and sound despite everything that's happened.

But when I finally get to the door and shove it open...

My stomach bottoms out at the sight of the empty bed.

Panic like I've never known floods through my veins as the thought of someone else beating me here slams into me.

Surely not.

No one knows she's here.

She's safe.

She's—

"Evie? Where are you?" I bellow, refusing to believe my worst fears.

Silence greets my question as I rush into the room, looking around for evidence of where she might be.

I flick on a lamp right as the sound of someone moving fills the room.

Spinning around, I search for where it came from.

But then the door on the other side of the room opens and the most beautiful sight appears.

Her eyes are wide, her hair is a mess, and she's dressed in just a tank and tiny shorts.

"Alex?" she gasps, blinking at me as if she might be seeing things.

"Vixen," I whisper, taking a step forward.

"Oh my God, you came," she cries before taking off across the room.

In a heartbeat, her body collides with mine, her arms wrapping around my shoulders, her legs around my waist.

"You came," she repeats against my neck.

My grip on her tightens as she trembles against me.

"Yeah, Vixen. I came for you."

Threading my fingers into her hair, the other on her arse, I keep her pinned to me as I walk toward the bed, lowering down on the edge.

The wetness of her tears soaks through my shirt, making a lump the size of a basketball climb up my throat.

"It's okay, baby. It's okay," I soothe, hoping like hell I might help.

Pressing my lips against her scalp, I breathe her in, forcing myself to believe my words.

"I've got you. Everything is going to be okay."

8

EVIE

I don't think I've ever felt relief like I did when I heard his voice.

Everything that has been wrong since the moment Derek pulled the rug from beneath me back in our flat started to right itself. If he's here, then I'm safe.

Everything will be okay.

I truly believe that.

As my sobs subside, I pull my face from the crook of his neck and take his rough cheeks in my hands.

He looks wrecked. His eyes are bloodshot with dark circles beneath them. His skin is pale and clammy, and if I breathe in… yep, he smells pretty rank, too.

"I'd advise you don't do that," he whispers, an amused lilt to his voice. "It's been a long…" He shakes his head. "I don't know. Fuck, Evie."

He doesn't say anything else. He doesn't need to. I can read it all in his eyes.

Shifting a little, I lean forward, capturing his lips with mine.

He hesitates for a beat, but the second I tease the seam of his lips with my tongue, he opens up for me.

A deep groan rumbles in his chest as our kiss deepens, quickly turning wild and desperate.

He grows hard beneath me and I roll my hips, teasing us both.

"Fuck, Evie," he groans, his fingers digging into my arse to halt my movements as he pulls away from my lips so we can both drag in some much needed air.

"Y-you..." My words trail off as I stare into his tired eyes. My thoughts are racing at a mile a minute. But none of them matter right now.

He's here.

Why he's here or how got here isn't important.

"There's a massive tub in the bathroom. You look like you could make use of it," I say softly.

"You've no idea," he groans. "But I'm only getting in if you come with me."

His eyes glitter with excitement, and I can't help but sigh in relief. That cheeky boy is still there under the exhaustion.

"I'm sure that's something I can do," I tease.

"Fuck. I missed you," he confesses.

I suck in a sharp breath, both shocked and delighted by his words.

"You never needed to leave, you know."

A sad laugh rips from his lips.

"There's so much you don't know, little thief," he says softly, brushing his fingertip over my swollen lips.

"So tell me."

Resting his brow against mine, he stares deep into my eyes.

"I will," he promises. "Just... not tonight. Tonight, I want you in my arms, and I want to sleep."

I refrain from telling him that he looks like he needs it. Instead, I unwrap myself from his body and place my feet back on the carpet. Taking his hand in mine, I pull him until he's at full height and then drag him into the bathroom.

"I came here to take care of you," he tells me.

"Right now, I think you need it more. I'm okay. I think," I tack on when I realise that I might be lying. And after everything, that's the last thing I want to do.

I could be anywhere, with anyone, but I'm not.

I'm with him.

I've no idea how, but I'm too relieved and too concerned about him right now to put too much thought into it.

I tug him into the vast bathroom and force him to sit on a bench that lines the wall while I put the plug in and run the taps.

Returning to the hidden cupboard, I find some bubble bath and tip way more than is actually required into the running water, watching with delight as the white foam explodes.

While it fills up, the vanilla scent filling the room around us, I turn back to Alex.

"Time to get naked," I say, letting my eyes drop to his body as my teeth sink into my bottom lip.

He groans.

"I'm a fucking moron." He chastises himself as he pushes to his feet and drags his shirt from his body.

My mouth runs dry as he exposes his toned abs and chest to me.

"Looks like you missed me, too."

I swallow, trying to summon up some words as he undoes his fly, kicks his trainers off and then shoves his jeans and boxers down his thighs, letting his dick spring free.

Without instruction from my brain, my tongue sneaks out and licks my bottom lip as I vividly remember how he tastes.

"I should be angry at you," I tell him.

"Not as angry as I am at myself."

Stepping up to me, he wraps his fingers around the bottom of my tank and peels it up my body.

My shorts and knickers hit the floor seconds later, and a shriek of surprise rips from my lips as he sweeps me off my feet.

"Do your ribs still hurt?" I ask, unable to miss how his bruises have started healing from the fight last weekend.

"Not enough to stop me having you in my arms."

He steps into the tub, hissing a breath when the water burns his feet.

"You like it hot, huh?"

"Guilty."

"I can deal," he says, lowering us down.

"Jesus, Alex. It's scorching," I gasp, reaching for the tap to turn the cold up a bit.

"You're scorching," he says, refusing to release me.

He settles me between his thighs and pulls me back until I'm lying on his chest.

A contented sigh falls from his lips as he rests his head back.

As we lie there clutching on to each other, all I can hear is the steady beat of his heart beneath me while the bubbles pop around us.

There are so many things that go unsaid between us, but there's nothing that could force me to break those few perfect minutes as we lie there, unapologetically us.

His erection continues to poke me in the back, but neither of us makes a move to do anything about it.

My skin erupts in goosebumps as he trails his fingers up and down my arm that's running along the side of the tub, his other hand splayed possessively over my stomach.

Twisting around, I snuggle deeper into his chest, craving his touch, his warmth, the sense of safety I get whenever I'm around him.

I don't know why he's here. There could be many reasons. But there's one I settle on.

He found the listing, and he bought me.

It's why I'm here. Why I was waiting for him. Why no one told me anything about it. He wanted to be the one to confess. And while that whole scenario is beyond fucked up. I think I like it. No. I know I like it.

If I have to belong to anyone, then I'd want it to be Alex a million times over.

It doesn't answer my questions about why he left me last week. But I'm sure there's an explanation.

His world. His life. I'm not sure I'll ever understand it. Honestly, I'm not sure I want to. But I do know that he's capable of all of this and more. And I know in my heart that, for whatever reason, he'd do whatever it took to protect me.

His large hand cups my scalp as I nuzzle my cheek into his chest.

"I've got you, Evie," he whispers against my hair. "Mine."

I didn't realise it was possible for your heart to ache and sing at the same time, but that's what happens as he whispers that final word.

"Yours," I promise back.

Silence falls once more as we lie with the warmth of the

water surrounding us, the stars twinkling in the inky sky outside the huge window.

More questions teeter on the tip of my tongue, but I swallow them all down, too content to get into any of it.

Eventually, the water begins to cool around us, so unless we want to end up lying in cold water, we really need to get moving.

He groans when I sit up, dragging my body from his.

When I twist around and look at him, I find his eyes hooded as if he was actually just asleep.

I squeeze a generous amount of shower gel onto the puff I grabbed from the cupboard and set about cleaning him up.

He moans as I brush over his skin, drawing circles down his arm, studying the ink on his bicep and the lingering bruises across his chest.

"We need to repeat this when I'm not dead on my feet."

"You're not on your feet," I tease.

A smile pulls at his lips, his eyes closed once again as he enjoys my attention.

Plunging the puff under the water, I scrub his abs and work my way down his legs and to his feet.

When I get back to his waist, his cock knocks the back of my hand.

"Thought you were tired?" I joke.

"Hmmm, but you're naked, Vixen. My body wants you, no matter what."

And what about your heart?

I've no idea how I manage to keep those words to myself, but I do.

My hand skims up his chest, resting right over the organ I was just thinking about. It thuds steadily behind his ribs, and for a few seconds, we stay just like that.

But then, he opens his eyes and finds mine instantly.

A small gasp falls from my lips at the burning intensity in them.

"I fucked up," he admits quietly. "I'll do it again. Probably often. But..." He swallows nervously. "Will you forgive me?"

A burst of air rushes past my lips.

"You're here, Alex. When I needed you most. There's no question."

Something dark passes through his eyes, but it vanishes so quickly I wonder if I imagined it.

"Let's get to bed. I want to fall asleep with you in my arms."

I swoon. Hard. "See, how could I not forgive you when you say things like that?"

"Many, many reasons," he counters.

"We'll talk tomorrow. Or even the next day. Just... relax now."

He nods, too exhausted to do anything else.

We climb out of the tub, and I wrap myself in a towel for the second time in only a few hours.

"There are toothbrushes in the cupboard," I say, but then I immediately feel stupid. "But of course, you already knew that."

He studies me as he tucks a towel around his waist, but he doesn't say anything about my comment.

"You made yourself at home, huh?"

I'm frozen to the spot as he stalks across the room, grabbing a new toothbrush and loading it with blue and white striped toothpaste. His muscles pull and ripple in the most delicious way as he moves.

I eat up every flex until my eyes find the dimples just above his arse.

"See something you like?" he asks around his brush.

My eyes jump to his in the mirror, and he chuckles at my reaction to being caught.

"Look all you like, Vixen," he mumbles before tugging at the towel, letting it pool at his feet. "I'm all yours."

I can't help but laugh when he clenches his butt before giving it a tempting little wiggle.

"You're an idiot," I laugh, making my way to the bedroom.

"I've been called worse."

Abandoning my towel over the arm of the sofa, I saunter toward the bed, putting a bit of extra sass into my step the second my skin tingles with awareness.

I glance back over my shoulder before I crawl under the covers and find exactly what I was expecting, Alex standing in the doorway with his eyes locked on my body.

How is it possible that one person's presence alone can make you forget the dire situation your life is in? Or is it dire?

If I'm right and I'm his, everything could have just become so much easier.

I think back to Blakley's suggestion of using him to help get us out of our shitty life all those weeks ago and sigh. Is it possible that I ended up here anyway? Not that I'm here to use him or take his money, of course. I just...

"Stop overthinking, Vixen, and get into bed."

Alex pushes from the doorframe and stalks toward me. His long legs eat up the space quickly. He pulls the covers back on his side, and together we slide into the cold bed.

"I'm sorry if I scared you," he says softly, pulling my body into his.

I want to tell him he didn't, but I think the fact I was hiding in the walk-in wardrobe probably says it all.

"I freaked out when I couldn't find you and—"

Pressing my fingers to his lips, I silence him.

"Not tonight." Moving them aside, I lean forward and brush my lips against his in the sweetest of kisses.

Hooking his hand around the back of my thigh, he wraps my leg around his waist, getting us as close as possible.

Our kiss is slow and gentle but full of silent promises and apologies that make my eyes burn with tears.

"You undo me," he murmurs, his eyes closed, his voice sleepy.

"The feeling is mutual," I confess, but I'm too slow. His breathing has already evened out and he's succumbed to his exhaustion.

I lie there for the longest time watching him sleep. His eyes move behind his lids as he dreams. I can't help wanting to know what's going through his head. Is he dreaming about me? And when his lips pull up into a smile, I find myself copying the move.

Despite how we first met and the intensity of our proper first interaction, everything seems so easy when we're together. As I lie here studying each of his features, the thickness of his brows, the length of his lashes, the small scar on his cheek and another in his lip, it's easy to push aside how we ended up here, the truth of what I've dealt with recently.

I have so many questions, and I can only hope that he has all the answers, because if he doesn't then—No. I'm not going there. He has to know. He has to fix all of this, because I need to get back to my family. To Blake and Zay. They'll be going out of their minds.

9
_____

EVIE

I wake the next morning feeling lighter. After seeing Alex, being wrapped in his arms, I'm a little more hopeful.

I want to believe that everything I went through, being forced to strip in front of Mr. Evil and his friendlier mate, was some twisted joke to test my strength, my ability to be a part of Alex's life. Either that or a nightmare that never really happened. Sadly, I know that neither of those is the case.

Stretching my arm out, I search for him on the other side of the bed, but I come up empty.

"What the—" I sit up in a rush.

Please, no. Please tell me I didn't dream it.

I look around the room, finding no evidence of his presence, although, with the blinds down, it's almost impossible to see anything.

Scrambling out of bed, my heart is in my throat at the thought of him here last night being nothing more than a figment of my imagination.

It can't have been. It felt so real. His voice, his touch, his kiss.

I race into the bathroom and come to a grinding halt when I find the pile of clothes he discarded last night.

All the air rushes from my lungs.

He's here. He's really here.

I make quick work of freshening up. Then, I pull on my tank and shorts and go in search.

The house is silent as I make my way toward the stairs, although the scent of something sweet cooking rises up to me, making my stomach growl hungrily.

As I descend the stairs, the deep rumble of his voice flows through my ears. But as my feet hit the wooden floor and I look around, I can't find him.

A warm breeze washes through the living room, and when I turn the corner, I come to an abrupt stop.

He's lounging in a chair out on the deck, wearing just a pair of black boxer briefs. The angle of the sun makes the definition of his stomach even more mouthwatering than it usually is, and the V-lines that disappear into his boxers look deeper than ever. His hair is mussed from sleep and the scruff on his face is beginning to turn into a beard.

I stand in the shadows of the living room, watching him as he listens to whatever the person on the other end is saying. He doesn't like it much, whatever it is, because a deep frown appears on his brow.

"Are you seriously telling me that we've got this far and now you've hit a wall?"

He shakes his head.

"I thought you and Toby were shit hot at this," he complains. I know from what Emmie and Stella told me about their group that Toby is one of their friends.

"Yeah," he sighs, pushing his hand through his hair. "I

know I get it. I just... I don't fucking want this for her, man. She deserves better."

My breath catches. Is he talking about me?

"Yeah, I know. Everything I could dream of, but that's not the point."

He falls silent again, slumping lower in the chair and resting his head back. Closing his eyes, he grits his teeth making his jaw tic with frustration.

"Yeah. You got it." He laughs, but it's not his usual carefree one; it's full of tension and unknowns. I hate it. "I'm sure I can cope. Please just... make sure they're safe, yeah? It's important." Pause. "I know." Sigh. "Get his motherfucking name, Theo. And don't let anyone else fucking touch him. I don't care how badly Daemon might want to watch him bleed. That cunt is mine."

Shock at the viciousness in his voice rocks through me to the point I have to reach out and steady myself on a piece of furniture.

"Limb from fucking limb. No one touches what's mine. No one."

The roughness of his voice, the possessiveness in each word sears through me, making my legs weak.

He's talking about me, right? Please, let him be talking about me.

It's fucked up. Irrational. I don't belong to anyone, no matter how much anyone might have been willing to pay for me. But I want to be his. When he said it last night before falling asleep, it meant everything to me.

It's insane. I've known him for what? A handful of days. But this connection, this live wire that crackles between us whenever we're close? It's addictive. He's addictive. And despite everything, he's the one I want by my side right now to get through whatever the hell is going on.

He lets out another heavy sigh, his legs falling wider and his other arm dropping in defeat.

"Yeah, okay. We'll be here. Enjoy that fancy jet. Can't say I'm sad to be missing all the action, even if I did have to fly commercial and sit next to some randomer who looked more than a little freaked out by me." He laughs, and this time it's more genuine, more him. "Yeah, I guess so. Sure. See you soon," he promises before hanging up. He drops his other arm, letting it hang over the armrest, his phone still in his clutches before he lets out a frustrated groan.

Unable to watch from a distance any longer, and happy that I'm not going to interrupt, I make my way toward the sliding doors.

I pause when I've stepped over the threshold and he lifts his hands, dropping his phone onto his lap and clenching his fists.

His shoulders tense as he lets out a pained sigh, not opening his eyes once.

Birds tweet in the trees as a soft breeze blows across my skin.

It's paradise, or it would be if my life hadn't been thrown into a blender and Alex wasn't suffering from whatever he just heard on the phone.

Unable to keep the distance between us, I move closer, my footsteps light on the decking, but it's enough to announce my arrival.

He opens his eyes and immediately finds mine where I'm standing right in front of him.

"Evie," he breathes, almost as if I'll vanish if he speaks any louder.

"Hey," I say, suddenly feeling shy under his intense stare. Wrapping my arms around myself, goosebumps erupt across my skin.

"What's wrong?" Alex asks in a rush, pushing to his feet and taking my face in his hands.

A laugh bubbles up my throat.

"What's wrong?" I ask in disbelief. "It would be faster to tell you what's right."

"Shit, yeah," he agrees solemnly, dipping lower at the same time he tilts my head up so he can rest his brow against mine. "Stupid question, huh?"

"Blakely and Zayden," I blurt. "Where are they? Are they safe?"

Out of everything I've been through in the—

"What day is it?" I ask before he gets a chance to respond to my first question.

His eyes hold mine, searching for God knows what while he prepares his words.

"Sunday," he whispers.

"Right. And—"

"They're safe, I promise you."

"But my d-dad, Derek, they—"

"I know, Vixen," he breathes, stepping closer, letting the heat of his body warm mine. "I know what they did, and I need you to know that they won't get away with it."

I blink up at him, struggling to comprehend that it's true. I mean, I knew it was. I've lived through the last few days and experienced everything first hand. But to hear the words spoken aloud...

"He sold me." The words sound foreign, my voice not like my own as they roll off my tongue.

"Baby," Alex whispers. It's so quiet I'd have missed it if he weren't so close. "I'm so sorry."

Then, his arms are around me, his warmth heating me from the outside in, and I break.

Loud, ugly sobs rip from me as I finally get the chance to unload everything I've been through.

I was fighting the inevitable, but the relief of hearing that Blake and Zay are okay, having it confirmed that I'm not just experiencing the world's worst nightmare right now has pushed me over the edge.

One second, I'm standing, pinned against his hard, naked chest, and the next, my feet are off the floor and we're moving across the deck.

I don't look up to see where we're going. I blindly trust him to know what I need as he holds me up, literally.

I'm still sobbing into his neck when he lowers us. My feet hit something soft as he cradles me on his lap and then we start... swinging.

I'm so confused, I pull my head from the crook of his neck and blink away my tears.

Warm fingers wipe my cheeks as I stare out at the beautiful view as we gently rock back and forth on a swing chair hidden under a wooden gazebo.

With a shaky breath, I rest my head against his shoulder and stare absently through the trees, watching the shadows twist and dance as the wind blows the branches, making the leaves flutter.

Alex's hand slowly moves up and down my back, soothing me and giving me little choice but to relax.

"Are you sure they're safe?" I eventually ask again, needing the reassurance.

"I promise."

"My dad?" I ask, unsure I actually want the answer.

"Where he deserves to be."

"Derek?"

Alex stills, his answer not as immediate as the previous ones. It tells me everything I need to know.

"When you're ready, I need you to tell me everything."

I shake my head. "I don't know anything. I was just at home. Dad said some really weird stuff about me making someone a good wife, and then Derek turned up, explained that someone had paid for me, and then... everything went black."

If I thought he'd tensed up before, then it's nothing compared to his reaction to the final part of my statement. He's basically a statue beneath me.

"They hurt you?" he growls, his voice low, barely audible.

"N-no. They drugged me," I confess. "When I woke up, I was somewhere. I don't know." I shake my head. The memory of that room makes me want to vomit all over again. The dark stare of Mr. Evil shakes me to my core despite him not being here. "There were two guys. One was..." I noticeably shudder. "Evil. His eyes were dead. The way he looked at me..."

"I'll kill him," Alex growls. "When we find him, and we will, I'll kill him for ever laying those eyes on you."

"Alex," I breathe, unsure if I'm terrified or turned on by this threat of violence.

I know which I should feel, but I'm not sure that's the reality.

"Didn't you get the memo last night?" he asks, his voice soft once more, his fingers dancing over my cheek. "You're mine. And no one else is ever going to get the chance to have you."

My heart practically explodes in my chest.

It's possessive, arrogant, and borderline psychotic that he can claim me quite so fiercely after knowing me for so little time.

But it feels right. It has done since he forced me to my knees in his bedroom at Christmas.

And I can't help but think he feels the same way.

"There was a moment there when I didn't think I'd have you in my arms again," he confesses, tucking my head under his chin and holding me tighter.

"I'm going to need you to tell me everything," I warn him.

"I don't know everything," he counters.

"Don't be a smart-arse," I tease.

Silence falls between us again, but it's loaded with all the things he's not saying.

I want to trust him, but has he earned that? There's so much I don't know about this enigma of a man.

And pushing everything I do know about him aside, he's in the freaking mafia. He's a soldier. And that threat he just made to kill Mr. Evil wasn't a joke. He meant it, and I truly believe he has the means to follow through.

"Where were you?" I ask, needing an answer but also not ready to dive into the heavy stuff.

He says I'm his, and right now, I'll grab onto that with both hands, because it makes me feel safe. But really, it only scratches the surface of all this. It fixes nothing.

Whether I am his or not, my family is still broken. My father is... I don't even know what he is. But the men who are doing this need to be brought to justice one way or another, and whether Alex wants me to help or not, I'm willing to do whatever it takes to make that happen.

Any of the girls I've been dancing with could be at risk.

"Las Vegas," he says, breaking through my dark thoughts.

"Vegas?"

A laugh spills from his lips. "Yeah. Nico, one of my

friends, decided it would be fun to surprise his fiancée and the rest of us on a trip to get married."

"Your friends got married?" I ask in surprise. "Aren't they all eighteen?

"Nico's nineteen, and Bri is... I dunno actually, like twenty-two, twenty-three maybe."

"Oh, almost ancient," I deadpan.

"Well, she's older than us. She's already done uni. She's training to be a teacher at Knight's Ridge."

"Nico's left though, right?" I ask, frowning.

"Uh... well, he's doing his exams. So I doubt he'll be taught by his wife."

"And they say Lovell Academy is bad," I mutter as my stomach begins growling embarrassingly loudly.

ALEX

"I need to feed you," I say, my face tucked into her neck so I can breathe her scent in, remind myself that she's right here in my arms.

She looked terrified when I opened my eyes and found her standing on the deck with me earlier. I hated it. All I want to do is make all this better, make her life better. But right now, I don't even know where to start with that.

Actually, that's a lie. I know exactly where to start. With her grumbling belly.

Way to a girl's heart, right? Or is that diamonds? Either way, I've got it covered.

"You want to stay here?" I ask as I shuffle my arse to the edge of the swing seat. "I'll bring the food to you."

"That depends," she says, making me pause.

"On?"

"If you're cooking or just throwing some cereal into a bowl."

Shifting her on my knee, I find her eyes, searching them in an attempt to figure out what she means. I raise my brow in question, and she answers my silent question.

"Well, if you're cooking, I want to watch."

"Okay. Well then, I guess I'm cooking. Kind of," I add. I'm not sure putting the oven on and placing a baking tray inside counts, but hey.

"Then I want to watch you work. I bet you'll look hot in an apron."

"Oh yeah?"

She bites down on her bottom lip, her eyes lighting up with desire.

It makes me want to do anything I possibly can to help her forget this situation.

I know shit is fucked up, but I didn't lie to her earlier.

Blake and Zay are safe. More than safe. She doesn't need to worry about them. She just needs to relax and pray that Theo and Toby figure this shit out sooner rather than later.

They're all up in the air right now, but he assured me that he's filled the boss and the others in on everything that's happening. Damien has met with Luciana, and the whole city is working on finding Derek, Vincent, and everyone involved in their little operation. I mean, assuming they're the ringleaders. Until this happened with Evie, everyone was scrambling around clutching at straws, as far as I could see. And I still have no idea how Tessa and Jude fit into it all. If they even do. It's not my job to figure it out. I played my part, got the intel we needed. I should be able to put it behind me and move on. I usually do. But everything is different now, because it involves her.

Standing with her still in my arms, I effortlessly carry her back into the cabin and lower her to a stool at the breakfast bar, dropping a kiss on the end of her nose.

Her attention makes my hairs stand on end as I move

across the kitchen and drag forward the board of croissant dough I left out earlier.

Unable to ignore temptation, I rolled one and baked it long before she woke up.

It was worth it. Just thinking about the crisp layers and fluffy inside makes my stomach growl almost as loudly as hers did.

"What's that?" she asks, eyeing the pale dough now in my hand.

"Wanna see me work some magic?" I ask with a wink.

"With your hands?" she asks coyly. "Here I was thinking I'd already seen your tricks."

A wide smile pulls at my lips as she teases me.

How does this feel so right? So natural?

Everything about her just fits. She fits.

Pushing reality, and everything outside of this cabin and our little bubble aside, I smile. "Oh, baby. You haven't seen anything yet."

I knead, roll and shape the croissants just like our maternal grandmother taught us, while Evie watches my every move.

I didn't spend all that much time in the kitchen with her—that was Daemon's thing, really. But I had my moments, and almost everything I do know about cooking is thanks to her.

"Well, a bad boy and a pastry chef. It's like I don't know you at all."

I swallow nervously. "You don't," I say, unable to keep the words inside.

Her entire body tenses at my words as the air sweetens around us despite the obvious tension.

"Tell me something. Something not many others know."

Resting back against the counter, my fingers curl around the edge as I think.

Her eyes hold mine, but something tells me she's desperate to drop them. Having her study my body with such unabashed interest is the main reason I'm still standing here in my boxers.

That and I'm afraid that if I cover up then she will too, and I fucking love being able to see the outline of her nipples through her tank.

There are so many truths that want to make their way out. Confessions about my life, about the things I do. Hell, even about the things she does.

That cam call fills my mind, and guilt knots up my stomach.

"I'm scared of my own blood," I finally settle on.

Her lips twitch. "Bullshit. Last weekend you were covered in it, and you didn't so much as blink."

I return her smile, pushing from the counter and moving closer. Her magnetism draws me in, my need to be in touching distance too much to deny.

"I mean real blood. Like when I got this," I point to the scar marring my upper arm. "Or this one." I drag up the leg of my boxers, letting her see where I got stabbed when out on a job with the guys one time.

"How'd you get them?" she asks, her attention on my upper thigh making my blood heat.

"Story for another time." I don't want to scare her off with the dangers of my life yet. "What about you?"

She lowers her head for a beat. "There isn't much to know. I'm the shy girl with no life who loves to draw."

"Bullshit," I state just like she did me. "You're one of the most interesting people I've ever met."

"One of?" Her brows lift.

"I've met some crazy-arse people, Vixen. The worst of them I sadly consider family."

"I can't wait to meet them all. Stella and Emmie are—"

"Insane?"

She chuckles. "Yeah, something like that. I've known of Emmie all my life. She's always been one of the untouchable ones. Hanging out with Archer Wolfe and co in Lovell gives you that protection. But despite being younger than me, she was always so..."

"So..." I prompt.

"Confident. Sure of herself. Beautiful."

"Not as beautiful as you," I counter. She's right about Emmie's confidence, though. She has it in spades, and it does give her this untouchable aura. "But you're just as confident. I don't know many girls who would have the balls to do what you do."

Her cheeks brighten and she keeps her eyes on the counter.

"Now that's bullshit," I say softly, reaching out to cup her cheek and lift her eyes.

Her light blue orbs find mine.

With her slightly swollen post-crying eyes, no make-up and messy sleep hair, she looks younger than her eighteen years.

Like this, it's hard to believe that she does have the confidence to don her sexy corset and high heels and dance in front of hundreds of people. Men.

The wave of possessiveness that rocks through me thinking of all those sets of eyes on her makes me wobble on my feet.

"The way you wear your confidence... it's fucking mesmerising. Breathtaking."

She tries to look away again, but I refuse to let her.

"I know you think that Blake is the sexy one of the two of you, but that's just not true. I've only ever seen your sister across the room, and sure, she's beautiful, you'd have to be blind not to see that. But she's got nothing on you, Evie. You captivate me like no one I've ever met before. No one I've ever seen before."

She licks her lips and swallows nervously.

"Somehow, I'm going to find a way to make you believe me," I breathe, leaning forward to brush my lips against hers. "I remember the first time you walked in the room. Out of all those girls at Dad's Christmas poker night, you were the only one I saw," I confess, gently kissing her again. "I couldn't take my eyes off you."

"I know," she whispers. "I felt it."

"Yeah?" I ask, tingles erupting as her confession wraps around me. "I was so angry when I found you in my room. I know what those girls can be like, and I thought you were different. But there you were—"

"I wasn't stealing, Alex. I promise, I—"

"I know that now, little thief," I tease.

"Do you?" she asks, holding my eyes firm.

"Yes." The tweeting birds from outside fills the space around us as my heart continues to try and beat out of my chest. Having her here, all too myself... it's the thing dreams are made of. "I knew I fucked up the second you ran, but I was flying too high from that mind-blowing blow job to think straight, and by the time I chased after you, you'd gone."

My hand drops from her cheek, slipping around the side of her throat, allowing me to feel her racing pulse.

"I looked for you. But all I had were your red shoes and the memory of your lips wrapped around my cock. Not all that much to go on, in the grand scheme of things."

"Like Cinderella," she says, making my brows pinch.

"Huh?"

"She left Prince Charming with a glass slipper. He went all around town trying to find the girl it fit."

"Trust me, Evie. If I didn't think I'd have ended up with a million girls with size five feet, I'd have done the same thing."

Her head tilts to the side as she studies me.

"Do all the dangerous men you work with know how romantic you are?"

"Can't say I've ever confessed my feelings for them quite so honestly, so no, I kinda hope they don't."

She laughs. The soft sound floats around me, making my hairs lift and my balls tighten.

Fuck. This woman.

I'm addicted.

"I wouldn't have stopped looking for you," I tell her honestly.

She shakes her head in disbelief.

"You'd have got bored eventually, found someone else to chase."

I pull back a little, raising a brow at her. "You trying to suggest I didn't have options or offers?"

She snorts. "I would never suggest such a thing. I'm not sure your ego could take it."

Leaning closer, I brush my nose against hers.

"The only girl I need stroking my ego is you."

She stills, her eyes filled with amusement as they bounce between mine.

"Your ego. Sure."

Moving around the counter, I spin her stool and spread her legs wide enough so I can step between them.

Grabbing her hand, I place it on my cock.

She gasps when she discovers just how hard it is.

"Other options and offers meant nothing to me," I say, hoping she can hear the sincerity in my voice. "There was only you from the moment I saw you."

"Alex," she moans before I step closer and claim her lips.

Her hand moves against me slowly as we kiss, the simple touch building me higher and higher in only minutes.

"Can't get enough of you," I confess, kissing down her jaw before sucking on a sensitive patch of skin beneath her ear.

"More," she begs, making my dick jerk in her grasp.

I almost cry out in frustration when she moves her hand, but the second her warm fingertips brush the skin just above my waistband, I almost sob in relief.

Pushing her hand into my boxers, I find her lips once more, letting her know how badly I need her.

Her delicate fingers wrap around my shaft and she strokes me once before the timer goes off on the oven.

"Saved by the bell," she teases before tugging her hand free.

"Fuck. Evie," I groan, dropping my head to her shoulder. Sucking in ragged breaths, I will my heart rate to slow down and desire to stop pulsing through my body like lava.

"I thought you were feeding me," she says innocently, blinking up at me like butter wouldn't melt.

Dropping my lips to her ear, I nip her skin before growling, "I'll give you something to suck on."

"Alex," she half moans, half laughs.

"You know you want it." My voice is deep and rough with need, but also amusement.

Her cheeks heat and her tongue sneaks out to lick her lips.

Backing away from her, I reach for the oven and turn the incessant ringing off before pulling the door open.

A rush of warmth hits my bare skin before the scent of freshly baked pastry fills the air.

"Oh my God," Evie barks when I turn back to her with oven gloves covering my hands and a steaming tray of croissants in my grasp.

"I just got even hotter, right?" I tease, walking over and placing them on the side.

"They look insane. I'm starving."

"Trust me when I tell you that I know how to look after my girl."

"Oh yeah?" she asks when I lower a plate in front of her and then drop a croissant onto it.

"Yep," I state confidently. "Fresh pastry, my outstanding personality, and my cock to boot. What more does a woman need?"

She snorts, trying to keep her laughter in. But one look at my serious face and she loses it.

"You're not even joking, are you?" she manages to get out between her laughter.

"Why would I joke when it's true?"

"Bloody hell, you really are something."

"Yeah," I agree, walking behind her and trailing my fingers up her arms, making goosebumps erupt in their wake. "And I think you like that something." She shudders as my breath races down her neck.

"Maybe. Or maybe I'm planning my next big escape."

I freeze, my heated blood turning to ice in a split second.

"You really, really don't want to do that, Evie," I warn, my voice suddenly dark and haunting.

She stills, hearing the seriousness in my tone.

Releasing her, I pull the stool out beside her and lower my arse to it.

"Please," I say softer. "Don't leave here unless I'm with you."

Her eyes narrow, searching mine.

"Please," I add again, desperate to hear her say the words.

It's unrealistic of me to think that we're going to be able to lock ourselves up here and wait until the guys have everything fixed.

There's every chance it's not all going to happen that fast, and as much as I'd love to lock myself down with only Evie for company, we both have lives. I still have a couple of exams to take and she... Well, I have no idea. She's not going back to work, that's a given. But she's going to want to see her brother and sister, maybe others. I don't know.

Just like she said only minutes ago, we don't really know each other.

We might have a good idea about each other's bodies and how to make them sing. But we've barely scratched the surface of what makes us tick, who we really are under the bravado and confidence we both wear like armour.

"Am I in danger?" she asks timidly.

I don't want to lie to her, but I also really don't want to tell her the fucking truth.

"I don't know the details of what's happening outside of this cabin. I was on a long-haul flight, and now my friends are. Theo and Toby, they're in contact with the boss and other players who are involved in this. We have to just do as we're told and trust they can handle it."

"You knew about… about all of this?" she asks, nibbling at the edge of her croissant.

"The trafficking ring, yeah. Had no idea you were involved until I saw your face on the screen."

My stomach turns over as I think back to that moment, and when I turn to Evie, she looks equally as green.

"I was for sale on the internet?" She blanches.

"Not the normal internet, no. Your everyday person wouldn't have stumbled across you." She frowns. "The dark web, Vixen."

"Oh."

"It's where all the—"

"I-I know what the dark web is. I've seen enough Netflix crime series." Lifting her breakfast to her mouth once more, she takes a bigger bite. I don't think she actually tastes it, which is a fucking travesty, because these fresh croissants are the bomb. "I just can't believe that—" She swallows her words. "How did you find me?"

Her half-eaten croissant hits the plate again as she holds my eyes, begging me for the truth.

"We've been tasked to look into this trafficking ring. Well, not me specifically, but you know," I ramble. "Anyway, Theo is a bit of a nerd and he was doing some digging and came across your listing. Brought it to show me and, well, here we are. He booked me on the first flight out of Vegas so I could get to you."

Her eyes go all soft, as if I did anything worthy of such a look.

My lips part to continue when a thought slams into me.

Does she think I bought her?

My heart rate increases as I reach for her hand, my thumb brushing each knuckle.

Would it be such a bad thing if she believed that? It's

got to be better than knowing that some sick cunt out there paid for an eighteen-year-old virgin.

Bile sloshes in my stomach, threatening to rush up my throat just thinking about whoever he is having his hands on her.

"Thank you," she says, breaking me from my turmoil. "For coming for me. For... yeah."

Shit.

She does think...

"Anything, Vixen."

"But..." She rips her eyes from mine, and my heart sinks, because I know what's coming next. "Why did you leave me on Monday? If you'd go to all this, why go MIA on me?"

Lifting my free hand, I rub the back of my neck nervously.

Dipping my head, I look up at her through my lashes. "Because I was a fucking idiot. I'm... I'm not a good person, Evie. I've done things. I *do* things. Things that you don't need anywhere near your life."

"Seems like I might just have got myself right in the middle of it," she says, lacing our fingers together.

"Yeah. And there I was, trying to protect you."

"You still are." She smiles shyly. "This place, it's crazy," she says, gesturing to the cabin with her free hand. "I've never been anywhere like it."

"It's pretty flash."

"Everything in your life is pretty flash, Alex," she says.

"Get used to it. You're not going anywhere."

"I'm just a Lovell kid. This isn't what my life is like, it's—"

"It is now." Tightening my grip on her fingers, I pull her from her stool. Twisting her around, I drag her between my legs and wrap my arm around her waist. "Eat up," I demand, lifting her croissant to her lips.

"These are really good."

"I know."

"So arrogant," she mumbles around a mouthful.

"I know good pastry when I try it."

We eat the entire tray of croissants between us. Okay, fine. She has one and a half and I have the other three and a half while I keep her pinned to my body.

"What do you want to do today?" I ask, trailing my lips up her shoulder.

"I didn't think I was allowed to go anywhere," she breathes, tilting her head to the side to allow me better access.

"I can think of more than a few things we can do without stepping foot out of this place, Vixen."

"I'm sure I could be convinced to spend the day with you. You do seem to have a way of making a woman bend to your desires."

"You've no idea," I mutter, her words hitting a little too close to home.

As she shudders in my hold, her nails lightly digging into my forearm that's around her middle, all I can hear is Theo's warning to fix the fact that she's a virgin.

I know it needs to happen. I can't risk her still being one and keeping that high price on her head.

But also, I don't want that to be the reason why we finally take that step together.

11

EVIE

Even though my skin is prickling with desire and my blood is almost at boiling point, I manage to lock down the suggestion that we head up to the bedroom and spend the rest of the day shutting the rest of the world out and drown in each other.

That would have been the easy option.

What I really need is more answers. And even more than that, I need my family.

"Can I talk to Blake?" I ask after a few seconds of silence.

Alex stills behind me, a move that has me on full alert.

He promised me that she and Zay are safe, and I believed him without a second thought. Was that naïve of me?

"Yeah, I'll set it up. Why don't you go and relax while I clean up this mess, then I'll come and join you?"

Twisting around in his arms, I study his eyes, searching for a lie.

"I promised you that they're safe, Evie. I wouldn't lie about that."

I nod, desperately wanting to believe him, but now the seed of doubt has been planted, I need to see it with my own two eyes.

"Video call so I can see Zay too?" I ask.

"Anything you want. Go and get this sexy body out in the sun," he says, sliding his hands down to cup my bottom, dragging me tighter into him. "You know, there is no one else for miles," he whispers, brushing his lips down the column of my neck. "You could lie out there naked and no one would ever know. Other than me, of course."

"I think you might just like the idea of that a little too much," I counter when I feel him growing hard against me again.

"I like the idea of you in any form I can get you." He licks across my collarbone, and a needy whimper escapes my lips. "And don't deny that you want to watch me in the sun naked too. I saw the way you were checking me out earlier."

My cheeks heat. "Maybe I was, maybe I wasn't."

He chuckles, his ego refusing to believe it could be the latter.

"Now go, before I change my mind and carry you up to the bedroom for the rest of the day instead."

My thighs clench, the need to continue this line of conversation tempting. But I need to see my family more than I need to lose myself in this dangerous man.

Ripping myself from his body, I saunter toward the open doors, ensuring I put a little extra sass into my steps.

His attention has my skin covered in goosebumps and my nipples trying to break free of my tank. And when I glance back over my shoulder, I find that he's spun around on his stool and his dark eyes are locked on me.

Heat pools between my legs as I drop my eyes down his body, finding his boxers barely containing his desire.

My mouth runs dry, and I have to force myself to keep moving in the opposite direction.

It really should be illegal to be that tempting.

Think of Blake and Zay, horny bitch.

The moment I round the corner and leave his sight, I'm able to suck in the breath I so desperately need.

At the opposite end of the deck to the swing seat, I find a huge sunbed with cushions already sprawled across it. Seems that Alex already had our plans set for the day.

Crawling onto it, I roll on my back and stare up at the clear blue sky above me.

The sun warms my skin, and I can't help the contented sigh that falls from my lips.

It's the Alex effect.

Those silver eyes, his touch, the roughness of his voice... it's hypnotising, and everything I need to leave my worries at the door. Or at least, most of them.

Closing my eyes, I give myself a few minutes to soak up our peaceful surroundings. I've dreamed about this kind of place so many times over the years that I have every intention of making the most of it.

His footsteps against the deck are my first clue that he's about to join me, quickly followed by the dip of the mattress and then his warm breath rushing over my lips.

"You look hot out here in the sun," he says before planting a kiss on my lips.

"Mmm, it is pretty warm."

"Not the kind of hot I mean, but yeah. It's lush. Here," he says, forcing me to open my eyes.

His big body blocks the sun so I'm able to see what he's holding out for me.

"Are they there?" I ask in a rush when I find a tablet with a FaceTime call set up and ready to go."

"Yep, just hit ca—" His laughter cuts off his words, because I hit that little green button long before he's told me to.

It only rings twice before it connects and an image of Blake and Zay appears.

"Evie, oh my God," Blake cries, wrapping her arms around Zay in relief.

"Evie?" he says like he can't believe I'm actually here.

"Hey, bud. How's it going?" I say, focusing on him for now.

"It's good. You should see the house we're staying in. It's like a hotel." To anyone else, he might just look excited. But I know him well enough to recognise the confusion in his eyes.

I hate it. Hate that he's forced to have his life turned upside down because of all this. Although, I'm not sad that he's managed to get away from Dad. That man was toxic to a young, innocent mind like Zay's.

"Is that right?"

"Yeah, it's even got a gym. And my bedroom is the size of our entire flat."

Ripping my eyes from the screen, I glance at a blank-faced Alex. I narrow my eyes in silent question.

What have you done?

He shakes his head, a coy smile playing on his lips.

"I've still got to go to school tomorrow though," he pouts. "And Blake says that Josh can't come to play here. He needs to see it though; he won't believe it otherwise."

Blake sighs in exasperation.

"Back to school?" I ask. "Is that—"

"Normal," Blake cuts me off. "We might not be at home

right now because of the gas leak," My brows lift. Are we seriously pulling the gas leak story? "But life has to continue as normal, right? Just because you've been whisked away on a fancy holiday." She might be smiling, but her eyes show her pain, her confusion, her concern.

"Is it amazing?" Zay asks me. Although we've never made him any promises, he's always talking about going on a holiday. One day, I hope to give him the best holiday to make up for all the shit he's had to endure.

"It is. We're in the middle of nowhere," I say, grateful that I don't know anything about our location so I don't have to lie.

He screws his nose up in disgust.

"You mean, there's nothing to do?"

"Exactly. It's relaxing."

He grunts in disapproval. "Is there somewhere to skate?"

"Sorry, bud. Just trees."

"Not the kind of holiday I had in mind," he mutters.

"Zay, there are those milkshakes you love in the fridge. Did you want to go and pour us one each? And make them dirty."

"Dirty?" Alex asks in shock, his voice quiet enough that Zay won't hear him.

"Make those scoops of ice cream extra big," I tell Zay while answering Alex's question.

"I will. Love you, Evie," he calls as he scrambles from the chair.

My heart clenches. It won't be long now until he's too old to say things like that to his big sisters, so I need to make the most of it.

"Love you too, little man," I say.

Once the door slams behind him, Blake leans closer to the screen, a deep frown forming on her brow.

"Are you okay?" she asks in a rush. "Fuck, Evie." A sob bubbles from her throat, her eyes filling with tears. "I've been so worried about you."

"You knew I had her safe," Alex says before I get a word out.

Moving from behind the camera, he comes to sit next to me.

"Well, excuse me for not wanting to believe you," Blakely snaps. "The last time you saw her, you left her crying outside our building."

Alex tenses beside me.

"Blake," I snap, not really wanting him to know that little embarrassing nugget about me.

"Sorry. Fuck, Eve. Is it really true?"

"Depends on what you've been told." I risk a glance at Alex, unsure what line they spun my sister.

"That Dad put you up for sale?" Okay, so the truth then.

"Yeah, so I've been told."

"Jesus. I knew he was a twisted fuck, but that's... I don't even know."

"Be glad you whored yourself out all those years ago, I think it saved you," I blurt. She didn't know that tidbit from how her eyes shoot up.

"Jesus," she mutters, dropping her head into her hands. "Is this actually real?"

"Sadly," Alex grumbles.

"Where are you?"

My lips part, but he beats me to it again. "Safe. You don't need to worry about her. Just look after you and Zay."

"Who made you the boss?" Blake snaps.

I shake my head. Trust her to backchat the mafia. I bet she'd be no different if their boss was sitting in front of her.

"The one who saved your sister's arse, that's who."

"What are you suggesting exactly?" Blake hisses, anger descending.

"Nothing. Just reassuring you that she's safe."

"Good. And just know, if you fuck this up, you'll have me to deal with. And I promise you, I'll make every enemy you've ever faced look like a pussy cat."

I expect Alex to burst out laughing, but fair play to him, because he manages to keep a straight face as she glares at him through the screen.

"I'll keep that in mind," he says as if he's taken the warning seriously. "And while we're at it. Make sure you behave yourself."

"I've got it covered. Don't you worry about me."

"It's not you I'm worried about," Alex mutters quietly.

"Anyway," Blake says, turning her attention back to me. "You're really okay?"

"Yeah," I confirm as Alex takes my hand and lifts it to his lips, kissing my knuckles.

Blake rolls her eyes at his over-the-top show.

"For a while, I didn't think I was going to be, but then this one turned up and, well..."

"I can imagine. When are you coming back?"

"When we know it's safe. For all of you," Alex says.

"Are you sure that Zay should be going to school if we're in danger?" I ask, terrified for him.

"We have everything in place to ensure his safety."

Reading between the lines of that statement, I blurt, "You can't send him into Lovell Academy with a freaking security guard."

"We can and we will. We're not risking anything right now. If you hear anything from Derek, or any man you think might be involved in this, you tell us, you got it?"

Lifting her fingers to her brow, she salutes him, making me snort. "Yes, sir. And enough about me being good; can you please ensure that my little sister doesn't return pregnant?"

"Blakely," I shriek.

"What? I'm not blind, Evie. Is he even wearing any clothes right now?" she asks, leaning forward and peering down as if it'll allow her a better view.

"He is," Alex confirms, snatching the tablet from my hands and letting my sister see him. All of him.

"Hot damn. You did good, Sis."

"Okay, can we please get back to the seriousness of the situation?"

"I think the most serious issue is sitting right next to you."

"Whore," I hiss.

"If I knew withholding would get me in your position right now, I might have considered it."

"Blakely," I sigh.

"What? This whole situation is stressful as fuck. What's wrong with focusing on something a little more... pleasurable."

"As long as you're not doing that where you are," Alex warns, making my eyes narrow at him.

Where exactly is my sister right now?

"Jeez, you worry too much. We're good here. Safe, looked after. Even if I do have to clean a fucking mansion."

"Here you go," a familiar voice says before a milkshake appears in front of the camera with more ice cream than I'd have thought possible on the top if I couldn't see it with my own eyes.

"Oh, wow," Blakely says, watching as the milkshake runs down the side of the glass, pooling on the table the tablet is sitting on. "Looks like I've got more to clean."

"Oh, stop complaining. Shit could be worse right now," Alex mutters.

I look between the two of them, wondering how they've managed to form some weird sibling relationship already.

"Language," Zay chastises. "You'll need to put a pound in the swear jar."

"Uh..." I can't help but laugh at the confusion on Alex's face. "Y-yeah, you got it."

"Hi, I'm Zay. Are you Evie's boyfriend?"

It's only as he says that that I remember Alex is still in shot, and practically naked.

"Uh... we're... uh... just—"

"Yes," Alex states happily. "She's my girlfriend."

My eyes pop open in shock. I expect Blakely's to have done the same, but when I glance at her face, she just looks smug.

"Have you been fighting?" Zay asks, bringing me back to reality.

"Uh... just messing about with friends. Things got a little out of hand, you know how it is," Alex says with a wink, and Zay nods, a smile curling at his lips.

Great. Now he has both of them wrapped around his little finger.

"Okay, well, we're going to let you go and... relax," Blakely says, wiggling her eyebrows at us.

She really is about as subtle as a rhino at the ballet.

"Please be safe and look after each other."

"You got it, Eve. And you enjoy yourselves."

"We'll do our best," Alex confirms. "Sleep is for the weak, right?"

"Damn right," Blake agrees. "Talk soon. Love you, Eve."

"Love you, Evie," Zay adds before the call cuts.

12

EVIE

"I like them," Alex says after placing the tablet on the end of the sunbed and rolling on his side to study me.

"They're all right, I guess," I mutter teasingly.

Reaching out, he wraps his large hand around my hip and rolls me so we're face to face with only a couple of inches between us.

"Your sister really wants us to hook up, huh?" he teases, his eyes alternating between my eyes and my lips.

"She just wants me to grab life with both hands and enjoy myself. She was worried I'd turn into a friendless recluse who only talked to her sketchpad."

"I'm sure that's not true." His hand begins to rise from my hip and drips down to the curve of my waist, his fingers inching under my tank. The heat of his skin makes my body burn up.

"It kinda is. Just ask Emmie; I wasn't exactly the life and soul of Lovell Academy."

"Good," he states. "It means none of the arseholes of Lovell has had a taste of you."

"Careful, you're starting to sound awfully jealous."

"Nothing to be jealous of when you've only been mine," he growls. "When you're only going to be mine."

"Is that right?"

His fingers climb higher, brushing over the ridges of my ribs, his thumb grazing the underside of my breast, making my breath catch.

"It is," he confirms, leaning forward and closing the space between us.

My breath hitches as I think about where this could lead.

"Alex," I murmur before we collide, knowing that he'll steal all my thoughts the second that happens. "Where are Blake and Zay staying?"

His eyes find mine.

"My dad's."

I rear back. I was not expecting that.

"Y-your dad's?"

"Yeah, didn't she tell you about her new job?"

"No," I say with a frown. Blakely doesn't keep secrets from me. And she certainly doesn't tell my not-boyfriend before me. Or at least, I never expected her to.

"Don't look so offended. She probably didn't get a chance, and she was only meant to start this week."

"Explain, please," I demand.

"She's my dad's latest housekeeper."

It takes a couple of seconds for his words to register, and when they do, my chin drops.

"Housekeeper?" I ask, unable to keep the amusement out of my tone. "My sister? How the fuck did she swing that? She's the world's biggest slob."

Alex shrugs. "I wasn't a part of the whole thing."

"But... Derek gets her work. That means your dad must

know him. Have contact with him. He uses Derek for his parties."

Realisation slams into me like a truck, and I push up onto my elbow in such a rush that Alex's hand slips from my top.

"If he knows him then—"

"Then he'll do everything in his power to find him and get the answers we need," Alex assures me.

"But what if he's working with him? What if—"

"No, Evie. My father is a lot of things, but he's not a traitor. His life is the Family. He wouldn't do something like that. This is a good thing, not bad."

He slips his hand around my waist once more and puts a little pressure on it.

"Trust me, Dad's on our side. Come back. We're relaxing."

I let him pull me back down and don't miss when he shifts a little closer.

"I'm not sure what you're thinking about right now can be considered relaxing."

"Maybe not, but I guarantee that when it's over, your muscles will be like jelly and you'll be totally blissed out."

"So full of yourself."

"Have I given you reason yet to doubt my skills, Vixen?"

Slipping his hand around my back, he tugs me closer, pressing our bodies together.

"I guess not."

"You should have said yes, really given me a chance to prove myself."

"Feel free to prove me right," I tease.

His nose bumps mine, his breath racing over my lips.

"I might have to do that. I know this situation is shit and that your life is upside down right now, but I just want you to know that being here with you, having you to myself, it's everything."

He doesn't give me a chance to reply, to agree, because his lips brush mine and I quickly lose myself to his kiss.

It starts sweet, so freaking sweet as his fingers trace circles up my spine, but before long, his tongue is searching every inch of my mouth, he's hooked my leg over his hip, and he's slowly grinding into me, making me gasp and moan into his kiss.

"Addicted to those sounds, Vixen. Wish I could record them and listen forever," he groans, kissing down my throat.

When he gets to the strap on my shoulder, he pushes it off and continues across my chest.

Rolling me onto my back, he climbs between my legs and tucks his hand under my tank.

"Off," he growls before dragging it from my body and throwing it to the side.

"Yes," I moan, my back arching when he cups my aching breasts in his large, calloused hands.

"Jesus, Vixen. You're so fucking perfect."

"Alex," I moan when he pinches my hard nipples between his fingers.

"Fuck, I missed you," he growls before flicking my peak with the tip of his tongue.

"Yes," I cry, not caring about how loud I am. There is no one for miles. No one but us. It's a heady feeling.

His hot mouth surrounds me, and I melt for him.

Rolling my hips, I grind myself against his length, desperate for more than he's giving me.

"Vixen," he groans. "You're addictive."

He switches sides, driving me crazy with kisses, licks and little nips of my sensitive skin that ensures my knickers are ruined.

"Please," I moan when I can't take it any more. It's like I'm being tortured, but in the best way possible.

"What do you want? Talk to me."

His eyes find mine as he peppers kisses down my stomach.

"I-I want—" My words are cut off when he drags his tongue along the waistband of my shorts.

"You want?"

"I want your mouth."

"My mouth where?" he growls.

"On me." His eyes flash with desire, and it gives me the confidence to keep going.

This really isn't any different to camming.

It's very different, a little voice says. *It's real. It's real and intense and everything you didn't realise you wanted.*

Sucking in a deep breath, I channel my inner vixen, knowing that hearing the words will drive him as wild as he is me.

"I want you to eat my pussy."

"Damn, Vixen," he growls. "All you gotta do is ask and I'll do it all fucking day."

His fingers tuck under my shorts, dragging both them and my knickers down my thighs.

Warm summer air rushes between my legs, making me shudder with need.

"Oh my God," I gasp when Alex lifts the fabric to his nose and inhales deeply. His eyes close as if it's the most delicious scent he's ever smelled.

I'd probably be hiding in my hands if I weren't frozen in shock.

But. He. Just. Smelled. My. Underwear.

"I wish I could have taken this with me," he confesses, his eyes locked on mine.

"My underwear?" I ask, confused.

"Your scent, your underwear. You."

"Oh," I gasp as he throws my clothes aside in favour of the real thing.

With his hands on my knees, he forces my legs wide, exposing me to him.

"So fucking pretty," he mutters to himself, making my cheeks burn.

He stares at me for long seconds, almost as if he's memorising every inch, just in case he has to go without again.

"Fuck, Evie. I can't wait to make you mine."

I gasp when his fingertip collides with my clit, my thighs trying to close from the intensity.

Any response I might have gets stuck in my throat when he presses harder and begins circling with the most dizzying accuracy.

How, after only a few times together, can he touch me as expertly as I do myself?

Meant to be, a little voice floats around in my head.

I never really thought much about fate or higher powers which control our lives, but I can't help feeling that we were meant to meet. And not just so I'd give them a missing piece of this trafficking puzzle they're trying to put together.

"Alex," I cry when he pushes that single digit inside me, curling it to find my G-spot. "Yes."

"You're not coming on my fingers, Evie," he warns before dropping to his front, wrapping his hands around my hips and dragging me closer.

I scream when he latches his hot mouth onto my clit.

It. Is. That. Fucking. Good.

My fingers twist in his hair, holding him tighter, not that

I actually think he's going to go anywhere. He seems entirely too addicted to my pussy to leave me hanging.

His tongue is relentless as he teases me, working me up until I'm teetering right on the edge, and then letting me down again before I fall.

It's heaven and hell all mixed into one.

I suck in greedy lungfuls of air when he releases me in favour of kissing and nipping down my inner thigh.

"You're a tease," I moan, still writhing as if he's right there.

"I know. You love it really. Delayed gratification is hot as fuck." His eyes roam over my body, tracking the little bite marks he's left, the hickies, and the evidence of how much I need him.

My hips continue to grind even though there's nothing to find any friction on.

"You'll regret that the next time I'm sucking your cock," I cry when he begins getting closer to where I need him once more.

His eyes flash with heat. "Will I?" he asks coyly. "That's assuming I allow you enough power to take charge, Vixen."

Fuck. Why is that so fucking hot?

"You like that?" he asks, able to read my reaction. "You want me to take charge? To tell you what to do and take what I need?"

"Yes."

"And you'll be a good girl and follow orders?"

"Yes."

"Good. Let's start now then. I want you coming all over my face."

I don't get to agree, because his mouth is back on my sensitive skin and he's eating me as if his life depends on it.

"Alex. Alex," I chant as he builds me back up in seconds.

Before I know what's happening, he's shoving me right over the edge, sending me free-falling into the most intense orgasm I've ever experienced.

And he eases me through every second of it.

My body convulses, shudders and erupts like a firework as his tongue continues lapping at me, his finger slowly fucking me.

"Holy shit, baby," he groans. "You're so beautiful, but when you come for me? Fucking mind-blowing."

He climbs to his feet and shoves his boxers down his legs, kicking them to the side.

In a heartbeat, he's back between my legs with his cock in his hand. The thick head glistens in the sunlight, showing me how desperate he is.

My core clenches as I try to imagine what it might feel like when he finally pushes inside me.

I've used toys before, but never anything as big as him. And add the power he holds in those hips... A shudder rips down my spine. I'm half impatient to feel it and half terrified he'll rip me in two.

"Evie, fuck," he groans, his eyes locked on mine as he works himself.

I'm mesmerised by the way his muscles pull and ripple, by the hard set of his jaw, the excitement that makes his eyes glitter in the sun.

Dragging my eyes down to his dick, I watch him pleasure himself, heat pooling in my core once again from the sight alone.

"Mine, Evie. You're fucking mine."

There's a loud bang, then footsteps and then—

"FUUUUCK,"

"Well, it's safe to say Alex has cheered up," an amused voice announces loudly as the man in question unloads all over my stomach.

How. Fucking. Mortifying.

Everything happens in a blur. Alex jumps to his feet and grabs a pillow, shoving it at me to cover my nakedness from prying eyes.

He isn't as concerned by his. But then, why should he when he's rocking a dick like that?

"What the fuck are you doing?" he barks, swiping his boxers from the decking and tugging them up his legs in frustration. "I thought you were on a fucking plane."

Thankfully, when I risk a look up, I find both Emmie and Theo are looking elsewhere to give us some privacy. Although, I can't help thinking it's too little too late, really.

"We were. Landed a couple of hours ago."

"But I spoke to you like..." Alex looks around as if he's trying to find a clock.

"We were on the plane."

"But—"

"We brought Evie's things," Emmie says, meeting my eyes and holding a bag up, as if that excuses them barging in at the worst possible moment.

Shuffling from the bed with the pillow pinned to my front, I walk over and take it from her.

"Thanks. I think," I add quietly before slipping into the cabin, leaving Alex to deal with his friends.

I don't turn around until they're out of sight. They've already seen enough; they don't need a shot of my arse as well.

I bolt up the stairs as if the hounds of hell are snapping at my heels, and I don't stop until I'm in the master bedroom.

I throw both the sticky pillow and the duffel bag on the bed before unzipping it and rummaging inside.

"Yes," I cry when my fingers brush over the rings of a notebook. Ignoring everything else, I slide it free along with my pencil box and glasses.

My need to curl up on the sofa and lose myself in a sketch while they deal with whatever they need to deal with downstairs almost gets the better of me.

But then, I remember that I'm standing here naked, covered in Alex's spunk, and I think better of it.

Abandoning it all on the bed, I take myself to the bathroom, closing the door behind me and leaving reality on the outside.

Turning the shower on, I step under the spray, tip my head back and roll my shoulders, letting the tension go.

13

———

ALEX

My eyes follow Evie as she shimmies sideways into the cabin, every inch of my body yearning for her.

Silence dances around me, but they're watching. My skin tingles with their attention, and I just know that when I turn around, I'll find them smirking at me like smug arseholes.

"You have the worst fucking timing. Isn't it enough that I've been forced to endure watching all of you fuck on every available surface for months? Now I've found a girl, you fucking cockblock me."

"We never said you needed to stop," Emmie offers up.

"Fucking hell." Combing my fingers through my hair, I turn my back on them in favour of collecting up Evie's discarded clothes.

"So I guess you're planning on hanging about for a bit?" I ask, assuming that I'm now expected to play host, seeing as I've taken over Nico and Calli's woodland cabin while the hunt for the traffickers continues in the city.

"A bit. We've got to be at school tomorrow and we're jet-lagged as fuck, so we can't party late," Theo says.

"There will be no partying," I mutter.

"I'm joking. You want drinks?" he asks, but he's gone before either of us get a chance to answer.

"So," Emmie starts, "you're smiling again."

"Really?" I ask, placing Evie's folded clothes on the table.

"We were worried about you last week."

I glare at her as I fall back into one of the loungers and stretch my legs out.

Honestly, I feel like an entirely different person from the one they dragged to Vegas with them. Such a waste of such an incredible place while I was drowning in misery and missing my vixen. All my own fault, of course. And I'm not just saying that because I spent almost an hour eating her out before coming all over her perfect skin.

My lips kick up in a smile just thinking about her. Without knowing I'm doing it, my hand lifts and I run my finger over my bottom lip, remembering how incredible she tasted, hearing her mewls and cries for more.

"You are so fucking gone for her," Emmie says happily, reminding me that she's still there.

Dropping my hand onto my lap, I focus on her.

"Tell me you're here with good news," I demand.

Her expression softens. "You're asking the wrong person there, A. I've no idea what's going on, other than both Theo and Toby have spent every second either on their computers or their phones since you left. They've got the entire Family, the Marianos and the Riveras on this.

"They will find whoever is responsible, and they will serve them the kind of painful punishment they deserve."

I nod, more grateful than I can put into words that they're working so hard on this.

I mean, I've done it for all of them repeatedly in the past, but knowing they've got my back—Evie's back—means fucking everything.

"Is she okay?" Emmie asks softly.

I let out a heavy sigh as I slump lower in my chair and look up at the huge master bedroom windows.

"Yeah, I think she is. She's stronger than she looks."

"I know," Emmie says confidently. "She wouldn't have survived Lovell if she weren't."

"She... uh..." I rub the back of my neck, not really wanting to confess what's about to fall from my lips.

"Here you go," Theo says, passing Emmie a can of Coke before throwing one at me.

"Thanks."

"Could you give us a minute?" Theo asks Emmie.

For a second, I think she's going to refuse. She doesn't usually take too kindly to being left out of important conversations, but she doesn't even try. Instead, she pushes from her seat, gives him a peck on the lips and moves toward the cabin.

"We'll finish this another day," she warns, looking at me.

"Great," I mutter, rolling my eyes at her.

"What was that about?" Theo asks, taking the chair closest to me.

"I think... Evie thinks I've bought her."

He's silent for a beat before he shocks me. "Probably for the best."

"That I'm lying to her?"

"Well, no, obviously not. But she's been through enough in the last few days. Not having to worry about who really owns her arse is probably a good thing. She can relax here with you, which we see you've already started doing."

"It was all going swimmingly until you interrupted," I mutter, cracking my can open and swallowing a couple of mouthfuls.

"You taken her yet?" he asks casually.

"You just walked in on me jizzing on her stomach, what do you think?"

He shrugs. "I dunno, maybe you were pulling out so she didn't end up in the same state as Calli."

"Oh yeah, because that will make this whole situation less complicated. There will be no more Deimos babies in the near future."

"You say that now... You do know she's not on birth control, right?"

"How the fuck did you— You pulled her medical records," I sigh. I hate that he has the power to invade her privacy like that, but also... "Anything I need to know about?"

"So quick to judge until you realise it can benefit you," he mutters teasingly.

"Fuck off. I'm just curious. I don't want you knowing more about my girl than I do."

He shakes his head at me.

"Oh don't give me that. You knew every single thing about your wife long before you were tied to her. I bet you were pulling her records less than ten minutes after you met."

"Give me some credit. We were in school. It was at least a couple of hours later," he deadpans.

"So?" I ask.

"Nothing to tell. She was on the pill for a few months, came off it because of the side effects. That's it."

"Good. That's good," I say, nodding.

"We haven't got any closer to finding anything else, though."

"How is that possible? You have guys on the inside."

"We had one guy for a brief moment. Then he misdelivered your girl, and now they're all on high alert. They've gone to ground, and we can't get in touch with anyone."

"Fantastic."

"We'll get them, A. We always do. We're not going to let anything happen to Evie. Even if we have to play a little dirty."

I wince. I'm not sure I like the dark look in his eyes right now.

"What do you mean by that?"

"That they might need tempting out of their hiding places."

"Tell me what to do, and I'll make it happen. Anything to ensure that whoever bought her pays for it."

"Of course," he confirms. "Which is why you're both not at the centre of this. Just stay here, keep your heads down, and let us do our thing. And while you're hiding, make her yours. Take her off the market."

"I've got exams, T. I can't just—"

"There will always be someone outside keeping watch. Just keep it to exams only and be smart."

"Great. Sound advice," I mutter.

"What do you want me to say? Go back home and flaunt her around town? You're safe here, the internet is secure, you've got burner phones. Just... keep her off that fucking camming app."

The sip of Coke I'd just taken sprays from my mouth.

"Tell me you haven't watched."

"What the fuck, man?" he asks, sounding totally offended.

Really, I'm not surprised he knows. He knows fucking everything.

"As far as the world knows, she's MIA. We don't need her online, letting her sugar daddies know she's still about."

"She doesn't know I know," I admit.

"Probably time you confessed if you want to keep her safe."

"She wouldn't get on it with all this going on," I say confidently.

"You willing to risk her life on that?"

Silence falls between us as the weight of that question presses heavily on my shoulders.

No, I'm not willing to risk her life for anything.

Theo watches me closely as I lose myself in my thoughts.

"Did it scare you?"

"What?"

"Falling for Emmie."

"Pfft. I didn't fall for her. I can't stand her, really," he jokes.

"Funny."

"Honestly," he says, sitting forward and resting his elbows on his knees. "Most fucking terrifying thing I've ever done. But," he counters, "also the easiest. Falling for her. It was... inevitable, unstoppable. Easy. It was everything else that was hard work. Accepting it. Understanding it."

"Were you worried about how fast it happened?"

He dips his head and rubs the back of his neck, clearly not comfortable with these deep kinds of conversations.

"It was too late for that. We were already married."

"Yeah, I guess the situation is a little different."

"I'm just lucky we discovered we actually liked each other and one of us didn't end up dead."

"You know it would have been you, right? She'd have shanked your arse in your sleep."

He laughs, but there's no bitterness there. It's pure love. The sound of it makes something deep in my chest ache.

"Too fucking right." He sits back. A wide smile pulls at his lips as he thinks about his wife.

"So what did I miss in Vegas? Anyone else get married?"

He chuckles. "Not that I'm aware of. But I wouldn't put it past Seb and Stella to sneak off."

"I'm with you there." They were the exact couple I had in mind.

"Everything calmed down once we discovered all this shit. Emmie went to visit the artists in Rebel Ink Vegas with the girls. Brianna got a permanent reminder of her time in Sin City."

"She got inked?"

"Yep, another little surprise Nico organised. Apparently, Emmie drew her something while she was in hospital and she's had it put over her scars."

"Wow, that's incredible."

"It looks amazing."

"You weren't tempted? You could have got matching Mr. and Mrs. ones."

"Emmie will get me under the machine, I've no doubt."

"So whipped," I quip.

"Takes one to know one."

"Yeah," I breathe, thinking of my girl upstairs. "I think she's it, you know."

"What about all that shit from before Vegas?" he asks curiously.

I shrug. "I dunno. Right now, this is more important.

Keeping her safe and putting an end to it all. I guess... I dunno. I'm going to have to tell her. Talk to Dad about changing my job. Fuck knows. All I know right now is that I'm not letting her go again."

"Thank fuck for that. You were a right miserable fucker without her."

"Sorry if I put a downer on Vegas. I shouldn't have come."

"Too late for regrets, man. She's safe. She's here with you. That's all that matters. And hey, now you know how much life sucks without her. I think it might have been the reality check you needed."

"I still think we're crazy. I barely know her."

"You know enough. Trust that."

"Who are you and what have you done with our cold-hearted future mob boss?"

"Fuck you, man. I'm right here. But there's more to me than just that future. I want it all."

"Aw, you're quite the romantic at heart, aren't you?"

"Just don't tell the others." He winks before yawning.

"You should get back, get some rest. You got an exam tomorrow?"

"No, Tuesday. Then only one more to go."

"I can't fucking wait. We need to do something epic this summer once this is all over. Just the twelve of us, no stress and plenty of sun and sex."

"Sounds like a plan, man."

"We could take Stella back to Florida. I've always wanted to meet Mickey."

"Of course you have."

"And her friends seemed cool."

"Oh, you noticed. Thought you were too busy sulking."

I shake my head. "We could teach them how to play real football."

"Yeah, maybe. Reid came back with us," Theo says, surprising me.

"Oh, shit must be hitting the fan," I chuckle, trying to make light of the situation.

"He's on a mission. And I think he wants to spend more time with Bri. He's been fighting this ring for a long time. He wants to finally see it crumble."

"It will," I say confidently.

He nods. "It will. This is our city," he says, sitting back and spreading his thighs wide. "And any fucker who tries to take it from us will live to regret it."

I squeak in surprise when I pull the bathroom door open and find someone sitting on the bed I shared with Alex last night with my sketchpad in her lap, pencil moving furiously against the page.

She stills and looks up, her dark eyes locking on mine. "Sorry, I got bored waiting. I hope you don't mind." She flashes me a quick look at what she was working on, but it's gone before I get a chance to see it. "How are you doing?"

"Um..."

"The guys wanted to chat business, so I thought I'd come and check on you. All of this, it can't be easy."

A laugh tumbles from my lips.

"Sorry, that—"

"It's okay," I mutter, walking toward the bed with one towel wrapped around my body and another on my head. "It's... I don't even know. I'm having a hard time telling myself that it's real and not just some bizarre nightmare."

She scrambles across the bed to sit next to me. "I get that. Trust me, I do. I've been in some fucked-up situations.

We all have. But if I've learned anything from this life, it's that Lovell was the perfect place to get us ready for it."

"Easy for you to say. You embraced Lovell and its darkness. I just hid from it all."

She shakes her head. "Nah. You're more resilient than you realise. Plus, you're not alone." Her hand twitches on her lap as if she's going to reach for mine, but she thinks better of it. I'm not sure if I'm relieved or disappointed. I could do with some extra strength right now.

"I meant what I said when we walked in on you. Sorry about that, by the way."

I shake my head. She rode her husband right next to me in the back of a car last weekend; I think we might be beyond that kind of thing now.

"Don't mention it," I whisper, my cheeks burning bright as I think back. "And, what did you say?"

She laughs. "Fair enough. Not sure I'd have heard anything either if the situation was reversed. I said something along the lines of, 'Hey look, Alex has cheered up'." When I narrow my eyes at her, she goes on to explain. "I've never seen him as down as he was on our trip. Seriously, it was pathetic."

My lips part to respond, but I quickly find that I don't have any words.

"He really likes you, Evie. Like, *really* likes you," she repeats to nail her point home.

"Then maybe he shouldn't have left me." If you'd have asked me if I was over it before I said those words, I'd have thought I was. But the whole statement came out sounding bitter and angry.

"He was freaking out, Evie. He went and fell for you, and he didn't know how to handle it," Emmie explains.

"He said that?"

"Hell no, he's a guy. They don't very often say shit like that. But I know him. We all do. He's the last single one of his childhood friends, and he's been lonely for a while. We've tried to keep him a part of the group, but I think he's felt pushed aside more than he's allowed us to see."

I sigh, hating that he's been hurting while his friends have been moving on with their lives.

"He'd have got over himself and come back. I know that for nothing."

"Or he could have bought me on the dark web and given me little choice."

Emmie stills, and I lift my eyes from my lap to study her.

"Y-yeah, or that."

Her voice and the expression on her face gives nothing away.

"Pretty sure that's the least of what he'd do to protect you."

"Maybe," I mumble. "All of this"—I gesture to the room around us—"is so much to take without all of the talk about trafficking rings and the mafia and..." I blow out a long breath, letting my words trail off. "I'm just the girl who hides in the background, dreaming of the day she and her family get to embark on a better life," I confess quietly.

"You are embarking on that better life, Evie. This could be it, everything you've ever wanted."

"It's all been taken out of my hands," I argue.

"Would you have chosen Alex if it weren't for all this? Would you have given him a second chance if he came back from Vegas and turned up at your front door?"

I don't answer straight away, my head and my heart battling each other.

Emmie chuckles to herself, obviously reading something in my silence.

"You know, I never in a million years would have thought that at seventeen I'd be a wife. A wife to the future leader of the Cirillo Family. I knew I was connected to some dangerous men. What my pops and my uncle Cruz were involved in wasn't anything Mum ever kept from me, despite my dad's intentions. And while her intentions might have been questionable, I can't regret anything that I've been through.

"Like this, like what you're dealing with right now, it was messy, and painful, and at times deadly. Nothing about this life is easy or straightforward, but that is part of its beauty. We can wake up each morning and have no idea how the day is going to end. It's exciting and exhilarating. But it's also full of love and a family that will literally do anything for each other. The bond we all share runs so much deeper than blood. It's something that I hope I never, ever take for granted.

"You're a part of that now, Evie. It might not have been by choice, but I like to think that there's something out there that decided we all needed each other and found a way to bring us together.

"And in case you need to hear it... something tells me that no matter what, Alex would have always chosen you. He's gone for you, Evie."

I lift my hand up, swiping away a tear that escaped as she finishes her little speech.

Everything she just said about her family... I might not have met them all yet, but I know it's true. I feel it, see it, in the way Alex talks about them.

It's the same kind of unconditional love I feel for Blake and Zay. And they have that, all of them.

I'd be lying if I said I didn't want to experience what that was like after living almost in solitude all my life.

Blake has been my best friend for as long as I can remember, and I know just how sad that sounds. What would it be like to have other girls on my team?

"All of this... I think it's just a way to show you where you were always meant to be. With Alex. With us. Lovell kids don't always have to be Lovell kids, thank fuck."

I can't help but laugh.

"You deserve better. Let Alex give it to you."

Silence falls between us until she finally reaches for my hand and squeezes supportively.

"I'll leave you to get dressed. Theo and I really need to go home to sleep. Jet lag on top of a wild five days in Las Vegas is no joke."

"Did you have an amazing time?"

She nods. "Yeah, it was... well, it was Vegas. I've never experienced anything like it. You can come next time," she says, pushing to her feet and walking to the door. "They'll fix all this, Evie. Trust everyone around you to do their jobs, and it'll be over before you know it."

"Promise?" I ask, thinking of Blake and Zay.

I might have been reassured that they're okay earlier, but seeing them through a screen and being able to hold them is entirely different.

"Yeah, I do. What I can't promise is that it'll be simple and easy. It's likely to get messy and bloody. But you're just going to have to roll with the punches with that and trust us."

I suck in a breath. I want to believe she's joking, but something tells me that she's not.

"Take your time. He'll wait." She winks before slipping out of the room and closing the door behind her.

I fall back on the bed with a sigh.

Closing my eyes, I think over everything she said.

Am I exactly where I'm meant to be right now?

Is all of this fate?

The new life, the new start Blake and I have spent years praying for?

I think about Dad. About where they might have taken him, what they might be doing to him. Whatever it is, he deserves it.

He was a pathetic excuse for a human before this. But selling your own daughter... that really takes the fucking biscuit.

I've no idea how long I lie there contemplating everything, but my skin is dry and I'm at risk of falling asleep.

Pushing myself up, I rummage through my bag for something to wear. I can only assume Blake packed it for me, because it has all my favourite things inside. My heart swells for her but aches in equal measure. I miss them both something fierce. We've never been apart for an extended period of time. And I didn't even get to give them a hug goodbye.

Pulling out my bikini, I glance at the huge windows that showcase the beautiful summer day outside.

Without second guessing it, I pull the red two-piece on and then finish it off with a black cover-up. Not that it actually covers anything, it's so sheer. Makes me feel a little less exposed, though.

I scrunch my hair into messy curls and keep my face clear of make-up. Before I leave the safety of the room, I walk over to the windows. For a few seconds, I focus on the trees and the solitude, but movement beneath me soon distracts me.

Emmie has joined the guys and is sitting on Theo's lap, her hand wrapped around the back of his neck, her fingers playing with the short hair there as he talks.

I shift my eyes to Alex just as he throws his head back on a laugh.

My heart fractures, seeing his happiness. His wide smile, his sparkling eyes.

It feels right, being here, being with him.

As if he can sense my attention, he looks up, those mesmerising eyes landing on me.

My breath catches as something crackles between us.

Lifting his hand from the arm of the chair, he gestures for me to join them, and without thinking about it, I spin on my heels and walk out of the room.

With each step I take, my heart pounds harder as my need to be closer to him grows.

It's a weird, mind-boggling feeling after never needing to be close to anything—not physically, anyway—for eighteen years.

My skin heats with his attention long before I step into the doorway.

His eyes eat me up. They begin staring deep into mine before they drop down my body. The silver darkens as he sucks his bottom lip into his mouth.

From the way he's reacting to me, anyone would think I walked out here naked.

"Come here, Vixen," he demands, and my legs take off across the decking without instruction from my brain. It's like my body has a mind of its own, and it's screaming to be pressed up against his.

The second I'm in touching distance, he drags me into his lap and wraps his arms around my waist.

"You look sinful in that bikini, Evie," he whispers in my

ear, making every hair on my body stand on end. "But I think it would look better on the floor."

"I've no idea what he just said, but I think it's definitely our cue to leave," Theo says, placing Emmie on her feet and pushing to stand.

Alex's lips brush down my neck, stopping at the curve of my shoulder.

"Don't leave on our account," he murmurs against my skin.

Theo laughs. "I think we've seen more than enough for one day."

"My girl likes an audience. Don't you, Vixen?"

I instantly still at his words, my blood turning to ice.

"I've seen you dance, the way you feed off the eyes on your body. Gets you hot, doesn't it?"

"Okay, we're out. Call if you need anything," Theo says, but I'm too lost to my panic to pay attention to where they are.

"What's up?" Alex asks, his warm breath washing over my skin. "There's nothing wrong with enjoying having eyes on you."

"I-I know, I just—"

My words are cut off when he grips me around the waist and twists me around so I'm straddling him.

He moves me as if I'm nothing more than a rag doll for him to play with. I love it.

I love how his fingers almost meet around my waist. I love that he's so strong that he makes me feel weightless in his arms.

"I don't have an issue with people watching you, if that's what you're worried about," he says sincerely, searching my eyes.

I want to close them for fear that he'll find whatever he's searching for within them.

Just tell him about the camming, Evie. It's not a big deal.

My lips part to respond, but I don't get a chance to form any words when his lips find my throat and his hands slip up to cup my breasts.

"I'll watch you dance, or do anything you need an audience for, any day of the week, Vixen. All you need to do is ask."

His lips leave a burning trail as he kisses my collarbone and over the swell of my breasts.

"W-what did Theo have to say?" I force out, trying to not to lose myself all over again to this incredible man.

"That they're working on it and to trust them. We've just got to hang out here and find a way to keep ourselves entertained."

"Sounds terrible," I gasp when he pinches my nipples through my bikini.

"I thought the same thing. How ever are we going to fill our time?"

"Well," I practically moan, "I saw a bookcase inside. We could read. Or... can you draw? If you can't, I could teach you. Don't you have exams, m-maybe I-I should..." I swallow as he tugs my cover-up and bikini aside and flicks my nipple with the tip of his tongue. "T-test you," I breathe.

"You're testing me right now, Vixen," he groans, thrusting his hips up to ensure I can feel how hard he is beneath me. "My restraint."

It would be so easy, too easy to let this continue.

I want to, hell knows I do. But there are other things I want.

"Alex," I say, my voice raspy with need. "Stop."

Twisting my fingers in his hair, I pull his head back so he has no choice but to look up at me.

"Stop?" he asks, his brows pinched in confusion while his bottom lip pops out in a pout.

It's too fucking cute.

"D-don't you want this?" he asks, something dark flashing through his eyes.

My heart pounds as realisation slams into me.

I stopped what was happening so we could talk, continue to get to know each other better, not just drown in each other's bodies and the desire that burns red hot when we're together.

But if I want him to open up, then I need to do the same.

And hell, after all his confessions since I opened the dressing room door and found him standing there, I think I owe him this truth.

"Yes, Alex. I want this." His entire body physically relaxes at my words. "But—"

He sighs. "There's always a but."

"It's a good but," I promise him, cupping his rough jaw in my hand, smiling when he leans into my touch.

"Is there ever a good but?" he asks, his hand gliding down my body, coming to rest around my hip.

"Sometimes."

Releasing his jaw, I trail my fingers over his shoulder and to what looks like a fairly recent scar on his upper arm.

"How'd you get this?" I ask, figuring that it's a good a place as any to start.

His eyes drop to where I'm brushing my fingertip over the reddened skin.

"Were you in Lovell the night of the riot?"

I nod. Where the hell else would I have been? I barely go anywhere.

"It was that night. I got shot."

I freeze. "You got shot?"

"The guys will try and argue that it was just a graze and that I was being a pussy, but I totally got shot, and it really fucking hurt."

I can't help but laugh at the serious look on his face.

"I'm sure it did. Did you freak out?" I ask, remembering his admission earlier.

"A little. I refused to go to the hospital. My mum patched me up."

"Aw, you went running to mummy."

He glares at me. "She happens to be a—"

Unable to hold my amusement in any longer, I burst out laughing.

"Oh, you think you're funny, do you?" Alex laughs, his fingers tickling my sides, making me squeal as I fight to get away from him.

I manage it, but I'm not naïve enough to think that it was for any other reason than him letting me.

"No, enough. Enough," I plead with my hands up in surrender. "I'm ticklish."

"So I just discovered." He prowls toward me like a lion closing in on his prey. "Take the black thing off."

"We're talking. Getting to know each other better," I say, backing up.

"I got that. But I want to do it without that offensive thing blocking my view of your body. That bikini deserves to be shown off."

His eyes roam over my body just like they did when I first returned, making me feel as naked as the day I was born.

"Alex," I warn, my own wandering eyes unable to stay locked on his.

His body is insane. A well-toned weapon. Not just against opponents in the ring, but female hearts all over the globe, I'm sure.

Images of the kinds of things that happen in Vegas that I've seen on TV over the years flicker through my mind.

"What?" he asks, able to read my expression. "What are you thinking right now?"

"Did you party in Vegas?"

"Yes. Two of my best friends got married. There were celebrations."

"Did you pull?" I don't even know why I ask, but the words just spill from my lips, my own insecurities getting the better of me.

My question catches him by surprise as well, because it takes him a minute to register.

"What? Did I pu— No, Evie. I didn't pull. I barely even looked at anyone who wasn't a part of our group."

My entire body sags in relief and I curl my fingers around my cover-up, dragging it up my body and giving him what he wants.

"Emmie wasn't joking. I was a moody fucking bastard the whole time we were gone. I missed you so fucking bad, Vixen."

"But you were surrounded by dancing girls. I've seen them on TV walking up and down the strip wearing no—"

"They weren't you," he says, moving closer. "No one mattered because the only person I wanted, the only person I want is you."

I gasp when I bump against the railing and discover I have nowhere else to go.

"M-me?"

"You." He steps right into my space, his eyes holding mine. "I'll answer any question you throw at me honestly, I promise. Even if the answer isn't pretty. But you do not need to doubt this."

My entire body jolts from the spark that shoots through me when he wraps his fingers around the side of my throat.

"I want you, Evie. You. No one else. No one in Vegas. No one in London. No one anywhere. Just you."

I nod, trying to swallow down the lump that's blocking my throat.

"I'm sorry, I— ALEX," I scream when the world disappears from beneath me when he throws me over his shoulder and marches across the deck.

I kick and punch for a few seconds, but I soon discover that despite the unpleasant feeling of having all the blood rushing to my head, the view of his arse in his tight boxer briefs is more than worth it.

As he gropes my arse, I take the opportunity to do the same, shoving his boxers down and taking his firm cheeks in my hands.

"Fuck," he grunts as I squeeze hard, although I doubt it comes anywhere close to hurting. "You're perfect."

His words warm me from the inside out, but I only get to enjoy the buzz for a few seconds before he pulls the rug from beneath me once more.

One second, I'm tucked against his body, and the next I'm flying through the air.

"Alex, what are you—" My words are swallowed as I'm plunged under warm water.

No sooner have I gone under do I burst through the surface, sucking in deep lungfuls of air as if I'd been submerged for much longer.

I find Alex standing at the edge of the sunken hot tub

with his arms crossed over his chest and a smug grin on his face.

"You wanker," I hiss, wiping water from my face.

"Guilty," he says happily, cupping his junk. "And I'm always thinking about you when I do it."

I shake my head as I get myself comfortable in one of the moulded seats. When in Rome and all that.

"Damn, you look good in there," he says, his eyes flicking over me. "You want the jets?"

"Hell yeah."

Dropping to his haunches, he presses a button, making bubbles erupt everywhere.

A filthy moan rips from my lips as the powerful jets hit my back.

"Christ," he mutters, scrubbing his hand over his mouth as he stands. "I'm going to get us something to drink and then I'm joining you. Think about your questions, Vixen."

"Questions?" I call as he begins walking off.

"I thought you wanted to know more," he shoots over his shoulder. "Do your worst." He winks before he disappears into the house.

Sucking in a deep breath, I rest my head back as the jets massage my tight muscles.

Yeah, life could definitely be worse.

With Evie relaxing back in the hot tub, I head inside to grab us some drinks before joining her.

Just thinking about how slick her skin will be from the water, how relaxed and pliant her body will be has my dick aching for her.

Reaching down, I readjust myself in my boxers. The thin fabric doesn't leave much to the imagination, not that I care. I want her to know how much she affects me. I also love the way her eyes take me in. The way the blue hue of her irises darkens with interest and she sucks her bottom lip into her mouth as she imagines a whole host of dirty things involving my body that I am more than interested in.

I'm halfway to the kitchen when a duffel bag on the island catches my eye. Theo said that he'd stopped by my place to grab me stuff, including everything I'll need to attend my last few exams.

It's been easy to push them to the back of my mind over the past few days, but now I'm back here and Evie is safe, the pressure of them is starting to hit me once more.

I've never been academically gifted like some of our group. I've had to actually work, force myself to sit my arse in a chair and study for these exams, for a chance to get the grades I need to get into uni. And I've neglected them since I found the perfect distraction.

Something sitting in front of my duffel drags me from thoughts about the future, and I can't hold in my laughter.

"Fucking prick," I mutter, staring at the giant tub of Vaseline.

My phone is on the other side of the kitchen from when I was making croissants earlier. Snatching it up, I tap out a message.

> Alex: You're funny. *middle finger emoji*

> Theo: Just a little reminder of what you'll be forced to do for yourself if you fuck this up.

> Alex: I'm not fucking anything up. Evie is mine.

> Theo: Prove it.

> Alex: Have you always been this much of a controlling prick?

> Theo: Trying to help, man. Make her yours in every way that counts. Leave the rest to us.

"This is fucked up," I mutter to myself as I lock my phone and continue with what I came in here for.

With armfuls of drinks and snacks, I return to the deck, my eyes on Evie as she rests back and soaks up the power of the jets and the sun that's warming her face.

Perfect.

I place everything on the ledge beside the tub so we can reach it before syncing my phone with the speakers, flooding our little bit of paradise.

Her lashes flick as the sound of Ed Sheeran hits her ears.

"Hey," she says, her voice rough.

"Did you fall asleep?" I ask with a smirk as I step into the tub.

"No, just chilling."

"Sure you were." A loud groan spills from my lips as the water surrounds me.

"Good, right?" Evie says seductively.

"So good," I agree, cutting through the water so I can get closer to her.

Searching out her hand, I twist our fingers together.

She looks over, studying my face before her eyes land on my lips.

The urge to drown in her, to spend the day worshipping her—doing the deed that needs doing—is strong. But there's more to this thing between us than just the burning chemistry. My desire is wider than just pleasure.

I want her. All of her. Her hopes, her dreams, her fears.

Every-fucking-thing.

And the next words that spill from her lips give me a clue that she might be on the same page. And also prove that she wasn't actually sleeping.

"What were you laughing at?"

My lips curl into a smile.

"Theo and Emmie left me a present," I confess, shaking my head at my idiotic friends.

Evie's brows lift, urging me to continue.

"Seb and Stella got together first. She started at Knight's Ridge in September and Seb hated her. Blamed her for all this shit that she had nothing to do with. It was a whole thing. But once they discovered how to channel that hate into sex, well, they were fucking every time someone blinked. To be fair, they still are." Lifting my free hand from the water, I rub it down my face. "I've seen way more of them two than I ever wished to see."

"I want to say I'm surprised, but... The car."

"That was hot," I point out, remembering being able to join in with the antics for once, instead of being left on the sidelines with a hard dick and an empty heart. "But anyway," I say, getting back on track. "Seb was pretty much living with Theo at the time in a coach house on the boss's property. They were at it so much, and he was clearly lusting after Emmie so he became the butt of a joke that involved a tub of Vaseline."

"Why— oooh," she sings when realisation hits.

"We were all very worried about his health and risk of blisters."

She laughs, the sound making the hairs on my neck lift.

"Wait," she says, sobering suddenly. "They left you a tub. Don't they think that I'm good enough?"

"Shit, Evie no," I say quickly, feeling like a dick for telling that story as I did.

Reaching out, I pluck her from her seat and place her on my lap.

"He's just teasing me because he knows we haven't gone all the way yet."

Her eyes narrow on me, fear and confusion warring within them.

"You talk about that stuff?" she asks meekly.

"Uh, yeah. We're all pretty open. You don't talk to Blakey about sex and stuff?" I ask. From what she's said and knowing their jobs, I kinda assumed that—

"Yeah. I do. She knows where we're at too. I'm not angry you told him, I was just... I dunno. I'm out of my depth here, Alex."

"Why do you think we're taking it slow?" Her soft, appreciative smile makes my heart pound a little harder. "There's no rush here." Liar. "And trust me, you are more than good enough, Vixen. Your touch alone makes me burn."

"Same," she whispers, resting her head against my shoulder and brushing her lips against the underside of my jaw.

A shudder rips down my spine and I hold her tighter.

"Tell me more about them. How did Theo go from pretending he didn't want Emmie to being her husband?"

A laugh falls from my lips.

"You want all their dirty secrets, Vixen?"

"Hell yeah," she laughs. "Something tells me that it's going to be wild."

"You've no idea."

Sinking lower in the water, I set about talking through everyone's stories. There are a few things I keep back, but mostly, I tell all. And she eats up every word of it.

"Sounds like something that should be on TV," she says when my story comes to an end with us in Vegas last week.

"We don't live normal lives."

"That riot night in Lovell was terrifying," she says, going back to something she can understand. "I can't believe you were in the middle of it."

Under the water, her fingers find my scar, tracing it absently.

"It's the kind of thing we've trained all our lives for. We knew what we were doing."

"People died, Alex. There are kids I went to school with

that will be forced to live the rest of their lives with the fallout from that night."

"I know. Jodie's best friend is still recovering," I say sadly. I haven't heard an update on Sara for a while, but the last time Jodie spoke about her, things weren't good. Medically, she's recovering as they hoped. But mentally, not so great. "All that is over now, though. Archer has that place under control and them, us, and the Reapers are finally working together."

She shakes her head in disbelief.

"Tell me something about you, your friends, family, anything."

"You already know all the important stuff. I don't live the kind of life that could be turned into a movie."

Releasing herself from my grasp, she pushes to the other side of the tub and reaches for a drink.

"Let's play a game," I suggest.

She shoots a look over her shoulder. "Sure. What have you got?"

"Favourite food?"

"Ice cream," she answers instantly. "Or pizza," she adds when I laugh.

"You?"

"Anything, as long as I get to eat it with people I love."

"Cute," she says, sinking into the seat opposite me.

It's fucking ridiculous, but I miss her.

"Seriously though, if you have your choice of anything, what would you pick for dinner?"

"Pizza. Boring, I know, but I've never had a bad one so..."

"Fair enough."

"Favourite childhood memory?"

I regret the question the second her smile falls.

"Any that involve my mum."

"Shit, I'm sorry. I—"

"It's okay. What about you?"

Multiple memories flicker through my mind. Times with Daemon as young kids. Times at our grandparents' beachside home, running around in the sand and being the carefree boys we were never able to be in London. Then I think of my boys, my brothers.

"The day we stepped up to be a part of the Family. It's what we'd all dreamed of since we were old enough to understand what we'd been born into. Donning our suits for the first time, standing side by side, knowing that for the rest of our lives, we'd have each other's backs. It was pretty epic."

"You're all close, huh?"

"Yeah." I scratch at my rough chin. "This year has been hard. Until Stella and Emmie crashed into our lives, it's been us. Sure, there had been girls come and go, but no one ever stuck. Then all of a sudden, these two girls were everywhere. They slotted in so easily, like they were missing pieces of a puzzle none of us knew were ever gone.

"I watched Seb fall in love, and then Theo. Toby, Nico. Even my brother who'd personally tell you he didn't believe he had a heart to give to someone else is now shacked up and expecting a kid." My smile grows once more as I think about Calli and D.

"You're going to be an uncle?" she asks.

"Yeah. He's due at Christmas. My brother... we're... different in many ways. Where I'm light and laughter, he's dark and moody. But since he got with Calli, I've never seen him smile so much. She's incredible too. She's Nico's little sister. She'd always been kept on the sidelines, and seeing her become a part of us..." I shrug. "It's right, you know?"

"Yeah," she agrees softly, her eyes locked on mine. "I think I do. I can't wait for the day Blake finds herself a decent guy. She deserves it."

"She had some bad ones?" I ask.

"There have only been a handful. Her lifestyle doesn't really blend well with serious dating. But when someone catches her eye, she falls hard and fast, and ultimately gets her heart ripped out. There aren't many men out there who are secure enough to have a girlfriend who is a sex worker." She eyes me closely. If I didn't know her secret, then I probably wouldn't even see it. But I do.

"I can imagine. So she's more than just a dancer, then?"

Evie deflates, sinking lower.

"Blake had little choice but to step up and be Mum to me and Zay when our mother died. Dad, well... putting me up for sale is probably the most effort he's put into anything other than drinking in as long as I can remember. Blake had to start making money or we'd all be out on the streets.

"Blake had barely finished school. She had no prospects. She was meant to be going to uni, but even that was a push, but Mum wanted her to have the chance to do anything. She never had the opportunity, so she wanted to do everything in her power to ensure we had every chance in life. Only if we wanted it though; she wasn't pushy or anything.

"Blake was the wild child. For years, she'd stumble in drunk in the middle of the night after hanging out with the Wolves getting up to God knows what. She knew the power of her body by then, and the second she had the offer to use it to make money, she took it."

"Where does Derek factor into all this?" I ask.

Evie pauses, thinking back. "I've never really thought about it before. Sometime after the accident, he just...

started coming around more. I remember thinking that he was a creep the first time I met him, and that never changed. He used to make my skin crawl. Especially when he insisted we start calling him uncle."

Evie visibly shudders as she says the words.

"Do you think it could have been Blake's new career choice that brought him deeper into your lives?"

The question rocks through me. He had always been about but never as much as he was in the years since Mum died.

I just assumed that he was being a good friend, trying to do his bit to help. He used to bring us food, and sweets sometimes. But was there an ulterior motive with Blakely?

The answer is obvious. And it makes me sick to my stomach whenever I think about it.

We stayed in the hot tub until my skin was pruned and the sun began sinking behind the trees.

Despite the pull I felt toward him and the desire to have his hands on me, I stayed at the other side of the tub as we fired questions back and forth at each other, getting to know each other in the way we probably should have done the first few times we were together. But hey, too late to take it all back now. And despite all of this, I wouldn't want to if I were given the choice.

We showered the chlorine from our skin, hands and lips everywhere as we shared the huge shower cubicle, but neither of us took it any further. It was the perfect blend of frustrating and comforting.

I won't lie, I freaked out a little when he told that story about Theo and the Vaseline earlier.

It's obvious that he has way more experience with this stuff than I do, and the fear that I'm not good enough, that I'm too hesitant and naïve, got the better of me.

But I believed the words he said to reassure me. And, yes, despite the fact he was hard from the second he pulled me from the hot tub until he dragged a pair of boxers up his legs, he didn't try for more. He didn't push me to try to take more than I was willing to give. Not that I was unwilling. If he'd pushed me up against the wall and wrapped my legs around his waist, I'd have been all in.

I squirm at the image of us tangled together with the water raining down on us.

"What are you thinking about?" Alex asks, his deep, rumbling voice dragging me from my dirty little fantasy.

I blink, forcing the image away as he steps between my knees and places floury hands on my cheeks.

"You," I confess.

After we came down from the shower, Alex announced that we were making pizzas and lifted me up onto the counter right next to where he set to work making us fresh dough for the base.

If I thought the croissant situation earlier blew my mind, then I'm not sure what the sight of him kneading fresh dough did for me. I knew exactly why he'd stayed shirtless for the event, though. He was purely thinking of me and my enjoyment. And did I freaking enjoy it.

"That's what I like to hear," he murmurs before leaning in and stealing my lips.

"Have you ever cooked for another girl?" I ask when he pulls back.

"Not outside of our family, no," he confesses honestly.

"What about you?"

I can't help but laugh.

"What's so funny?"

"Well, firstly, I wouldn't even invite my worst enemy into our flat. Even if it meant I could poison them with my cooking."

"I'm sure it's not that bad."

"Says the boy who grew up in a mansion and now has his own two-bedroom fancy-pants apartment all to himself. Yeah, I can see how you'd come to that conclusion. How many times do you have to kick used needles aside on your stairwell to stop your little brother from standing on them?"

Alex winces before squaring his shoulders.

"You're not going back there. Ever."

As much as I love the promise of his words, I can't latch onto them.

"It's our home, Alex. And what would I do instead, move in with you?" I joke.

"Yes."

I rear back at the confidence in his voice.

"You're crazy. I can't just move into your flat. We... we barely know each other."

"It's working okay for us right now."

"Yeah, but we're like... on holiday or something. I'm not invading your life here."

He shakes his head as if I'm the one who's lost my mind.

"You're overthinking it. I want you to invade my life. My life sucked before you." I lift my brows. "Okay, it didn't entirely suck, but I was lonely and—" He sighs. "You being here... It makes everything better."

Reaching up, I mimic his position, cupping his jaw in my hands.

"You're something else," I whisper, searching his eyes in the hope of discovering more about who this dangerous Cirillo soldier really is.

He shrugs one shoulder. "You're everything."

He kisses me again, and when he eventually pulls back, he rests his brow against mine.

The timer he set on his phone to let the dough prove dings and he steps away, leaving me cold without his touch.

"You okay?" I ask when he drops his hand to his crotch.

"Never better," he says with a teasing wink over his shoulder.

"So, no ex-boyfriends I need to worry about?" he asks, getting our conversation back on track.

I laugh. "Well, there was one."

His spine stiffens at my admission.

"Yeah, Liam and I were tight. We even talked about marriage and how many kids we wanted."

"W-what?" he breathes in disbelief.

I fight to keep my face straight. I really, really do, but after a few seconds, my smile breaks free.

"What?" he asks, although it comes out entirely different from the last time he asked.

I snort unattractively. "Yeah, it was serious," I say, now unable to hide my amusement.

"Evie," he growls, throwing a cloud of flour at me. It covers my bare arms and black tank and shorts.

"Year four. We were going steady for all of two hours before he stole my favourite pink pencil and snapped it."

"What a knob," Alex hisses. "Well, his loss is my gain."

Reaching for the bag of flour, I throw my own handful back. "Is that right?"

"Oh, you're in trouble now."

The next handful gets dumped on the top of my head before I hop off the counter and throw one of my own back.

In only minutes, we're surrounded by a massive white cloud, both covered, rolling around on what must look like snow since he took me to the floor in what I can only describe as an expert wrestling move.

With my wrists pinned above my head and my hips trapped between his muscular thighs, I can't move an inch.

"Look what you did, Vixen," he says, not looking anywhere but in my eyes.

"Me?" I gasp. "I think you'll find that you threw the first handful."

"Prove it."

Dipping his head, he runs his nose along my jaw before licking down my throat.

"Ugh," he complains. "I fucked up."

"Oh yeah?" I moan, tilting my head to the side to give him better access.

"Should have thrown icing sugar. This shit is gross." But the second he says the words, the heat of his tongue is back.

"Doesn't seem to be stopping you."

"Nothing will when it comes to you."

His burning kisses move across my chest before he works his way back up again, taking my lips.

"Ew," I complain when his tongue tangles with mine. "Gross."

"Careful, Vixen. Offend me too much and only one of us will get a happy ending here."

"You wouldn't," I hiss as he sits up.

His chest is covered in flour, his tanned skin pale.

Unable to stop myself, I reach out and draw through the dust.

EVIE.

His chest heaves as I slowly write each letter, his eyes boring into mine as I focus.

"Mine," he whispers.

"Yours."

The air between us crackles with electricity, and the current only grows stronger when my hand slides from his thighs in favour of rubbing his length that's once again straining against the fabric.

"Evie," he groans, a thick swallow making the column of his neck ripple in the most delicious way.

"What? Did you want me to stop?"

His eyes flare, the silver turning dark grey when I squeeze him a little.

"I—" He rolls his lips between his teeth. "I'm trying to be good."

"Good is sweet, and I like sweet Alex, I do. But right now, I think I want bad Alex."

A deep growl rumbles in his chest as his length thickens even more in my grasp.

Releasing him, I tuck my fingers under his waistband, and when he helps me out by lifting his arse, I pull them down, exposing him to me.

The second my fingers wrap around his shaft without the barrier of the fabric, he sucks in a sharp breath.

"Evie, fuck," he groans, his dick jerking in delight.

Slowly, I start working him, my eyes darting around his body, watching his reactions.

His eyes are dark pools, his full lips are parted, but his jaw ticks as he clenches his teeth. The muscles of his chest and abs tense and relax as I work him. Then his dick... I've seen a handful through a screen. Never any other in real life. But none of those compare to his. Is it possible for a cock to be pretty? If it is, then Alex definitely has one of them.

It's perfect. The skin smooth, long, and thick with veins running down the length that makes my mouth water to run my tongue down them.

"Jesus. That feels—" He swallows again, cutting off his words. "I think I need to return the favour."

"What favour?" I breathe, my voice raspy with desire. It doesn't sound anything like the shy, timid girl I know myself as. I love it.

I love the confident and brazen woman I turn into when I'm with Alex.

It's almost as addicting as he is.

Reaching out, he drags my tank down, exposing my breasts.

"I'm going to leave my mark on your chest like you did me."

He shifts, looming over me like a terrifying wall of strength and muscle. He makes me feel tiny and feminine and breakable. I love it.

"Like that," he praises. "Keep going."

I stroke him, spurred on by his words and the deep rumbles in his chest until his cock jerks. He throws his head back, my name falling from his lips as his hot cum hits my bare chest.

I don't stop. I can't. I'm too enthralled by watching him lose himself to even realise I'm still working him until his fingers wrap around my wrist, stopping me.

Spinning that arm to the floor, he lifts the other one and continues with his favour.

He dips his finger into the mess he's left behind and begins writing.

ALEX.

My chest heaves, my breathing beyond erratic and my knickers soaked as he claims me in such a carnal, raw way.

"Please," I whimper.

"We need to get you on birth control, baby. I need you, I need you so fucking bad, but there's no way I'm putting anything between us."

His confession knocks the wind right out of me.

"I—" I swallow. "I can't go on the pill. I hated it. The side effects."

"I know," he says, making me frown.

"We'll figure out a way. It's either that, or we're going to be having a lot of kids."

Before I can even attempt to formulate a response to any of that, I'm lifted from the floor and spun around.

My back hits the cold counter and I cry out in surprise. But the second his knuckles brush my hips, grasping my shorts and dragging them down my thighs, I forget all about it.

The moment one of my legs is free, he abandons the fabric hanging from my other foot and stares at what he wants.

"Fuck the pizza," he mutters, diving for me.

"Alex," I scream, gripping his hair.

Unlike earlier, he doesn't tease me, doesn't build me up and then pull away. Once his tongue is on me, he doesn't stop until I'm screaming, writhing on the counter as my body trembles with the strength of the release.

He works me back down and then stands to full height and wipes his hand across his mouth.

"I change my answer. If I could choose anything for dinner, I'd choose you."

"How are you so perfect?" The words are out of my mouth before I realise I've even thought them.

Something dark passes through his eyes and his jaw tics.

"I'm not, Vixen. I'm so far from perfect, and I'm terrified you'll find out and turn your back on me.

I shake my head. "Not going to happen."

"We'll see," he mutters sadly, helping me down from the counter.

"Go clean up." He swats me on the arse, gently pushing me toward the stairs. "I'll sort this out and follow."

I want to argue, but the expression on his face stops me, so I do as I'm told and climb the stairs on shaky post-orgasm legs.

17
———

ALEX

I don't think I've ever cleaned a kitchen so fast in my life. No, scratch that. I've never cleaned a kitchen so fast, full stop. I might be able to cook to a point, but that doesn't mean I do it all that often.

My own kitchen is usually limited to cereal, toast and reheating pizza. It's certainly never seen a flour storm quite like we created.

Honestly, my clean-up job probably sucks, but the image of Evie upstairs naked in the shower again was enough motivation to keep it short and sweet.

Better things awaited, and I could still taste her on my lips.

"I know you're watching," she says, keeping her back to me.

"I wasn't hiding," I confess from where I rest against the doorframe, still covered in flour.

If I step into that shower with her, then I'm not sure I can be held responsible for my actions.

I have a job to do. But this isn't like any I've ever had before.

Because I care. I care so fucking much it hurts, and I know I'm going to fuck it up.

How can I not?

Just because we're here, because I've opened up to her and accepted that I need her in my life, it doesn't rid me of the fears that forced me to drive away from her on Monday evening.

I'm still not good enough for her. I still believe that she'll turn her back on me when she knows the truth. But I'm powerless. I walked away once, and look where I ended up.

For whatever reason, someone wants us together. And as long as it keeps her away from whatever sick fuck purchased her, then I'll be right here beside her, doing everything I can to be the man she deserves.

"Not joining me?"

My dick jerks at her words.

"I want to," I confess.

"So why are you still standing over there?"

Finally, she turns. The sight of her makes my breath catch.

So fucking beautiful.

"Not sure I trust myself right now, Vixen."

Her eyes run down my body, locking on the tent in my pants.

"Again?" she asks coyly.

"With you, always."

She smiles at me as she slowly shakes her head. She has no idea how beautiful, how breathtaking she is. But I do. I see all of it.

"I trust you," she finally says, throwing me for a loop.

"What?" I ask when she starts laughing.

"Nothing, I just like that look on you. It makes you look like a cute, confused puppy."

A groan rumbles in my chest.

"I'm not cute," I argue, pushing from the doorframe and shoving my boxers down my legs. "And I'm not a puppy."

Stepping around the shower screen, I pause a few feet from her, letting my eyes eat up her bare skin.

"But you are confused?"

"Huh?" I ask, the proximity of her naked body frazzling my brain cells.

"Nah, you're definitely a cute puppy," she muses before I pounce on her.

"Then I guess you won't mind if I lick you all over," I growl in her ear as I pin her against the cold tiles.

"Now what?" I ask once we settle onto the huge sunbed outside, Evie with her sketchpad and me with a stack of revision.

After our shower, we finally made it down to roll out the dough and make our pizza.

It was good, but I've tasted something better on that counter now, and nothing could ever compare. Even my favourite dishes.

Her frown softens as she looks from my books to my face.

"Just shocked, that's all."

"Why? Did you think I was all beauty and no brains?" I ask lightly.

"Not at all. I just... I dunno, didn't have you down as a law student."

"Well then, I guess it's good we have this uninterrupted time to get to know each other better. If this all goes well, I'll be starting a criminology and psychology degree come September."

Evie rears back a little.

"You're joking, right?"

"Uh... no. I'm deadly serious." I keep my expression blank despite desperately wanting to smile. I know what she's thinking. It's exactly the same as everyone else does when I confess my interests.

"B-but... don't you like, run around the city and kill people for a living?"

"What are you suggesting, Vixen?" I say, swerving to answer that question directly.

She shrugs. "Just seems crazy that a guy who spends his life breaking the law should want to study it."

"Is it? The way I see it, if I know the laws, then I know how to get around them," I deadpan.

"Well, I guess when you put it like that..." she says, getting herself comfortable with her legs crossed in front of her.

A pair of glasses rests on her sketchpad beside her, and I'm almost desperate to demand she put them on. Something tells me I'm going to like nerdy Evie very much.

"That's not the reason I'm doing it, though. It just interests me."

"Fair enough. And I guess your organisation can never have too many lawyers, huh? It's a good job, even if it is dodgy as hell," she jokes.

"Our lawyers are the best. They have to be for obvious reasons. I'm not sure I'll be good enough to join them."

She gives me a double take, and I regret the words instantly, wishing I could suck them back into my mouth and swallow them as if they never happened.

"Don't be silly. You can do anything."

Reaching up, I rub the back of my neck awkwardly. "It's... uh... it's not exactly the role that was laid out for me from before I was old enough to make any decisions for myself." I don't look at her. I can't.

"Okay, so is there some law in place that stops you from changing your role? Surely, it's not set in stone. People change what they do all the time."

"I've had years of training to do what I do now."

"Which is?" she asks.

The question hits me like a fucking bullet, knocking all the wind out of me.

"I... umm..." I hesitate, and I fucking hate myself for it.

I should never have said anything. Stupid fucking insecurities.

A warm hand landing on my forearm gives me pause.

"It's okay if you can't talk about it. I get it... I think. I mean, all I know about crime families has come from Netflix but—"

"Intelligence," I blurt.

"Wow, okay. Not what I was expecting," she confesses.

"What did you think I was going to say? Torture?"

Risking looking at her, I lift my eyes, finding hers soft and full of understanding.

"No, that's more my brother's thing."

"Well, now I'm even more intrigued by your dark sibling."

I smile conspiratorially. I should tell her that looking at Daemon is like looking at me on a dark day, but for some reason, the words still don't find their way out. Maybe I am just a bit of a sadist, because it will be amusing as hell the day she discovers it.

"Trust me, you got the better end of the deal." I wink, making her laugh.

"If his ego is as big as yours, I'm surprised you both fit in the same house growing up."

"We found a way to make it work."

"So," she says, giving me a hard look. "You need to get to work if you're going to be the Cirillos' next kick-arse lawyer."

She throws a book into my lap and finally picks up her glasses.

"Holy shit," I blurt once they're on her face.

The thick black rims make her look so much more feminine and dainty.

"What's wrong?"

"N-nothing. Everything is very, very right. Do you know how hot you look right now?"

Heat rises on her cheeks.

"I look like a geek."

My smile grows. "Exactly. A sexy nerd who needs teaching a lesson or two."

"Well, I can confirm that I'm definitely learning a lot with you."

Reaching out, I tuck a lock of her dark hair behind her ear. "Same, Evie."

She covers my hand with hers as I cup her cheek softly.

"Work, Alex."

Releasing my hand, I salute her and flip my book open on the chapter I need.

I read about five sentences before she distracts me again. I mean, it's really not hard. She's sitting there braless with a loose-fitting top covering her and a pair of tiny shorts that apparently aren't underwear, according to her. They might as well be, for how little they cover.

"What's wrong?" I ask after her shocked gasp has filled the air.

"I-I forgot that Emmie had this."

"Had wha— holy shit."

"She was drawing in it while you and Theo were down here," she says, gently running her fingertips over the artwork. "She's seriously talented."

Evie's eyes are glued to the sketch, but mine are locked on her.

"The cage," she whispers. "It's as if she knows—"

"Oh fuck, I forgot," I blurt, throwing the book to the end of the sunbed and rushing into the cabin to find my carry-on bag.

I locate it and run back outside.

"You okay?" Evie asks, studying me.

"Yeah, I got you something."

"Oh?"

Crawling back onto the sunbed, I pass the simple black box to her.

Her eyes dart between us and me as her hand trembles.

"Don't worry, I didn't get *that* inspired in Vegas."

"Okay, good."

"I was stuck in the airport. My flight had the longest delay in the world, and all I could think about was getting back to you. Calli, my brother's girl, she... she suggested I go shopping to stop me from going stir crazy. She told me to find something I could give you when I had you safely in my arms. So..." I nod to the box, encouraging her to open it.

She studies me for a few seconds before doing as she's told and lifting the top off.

I know the second she sees it, because her eyes go impossibly wide and she gasps, "Oh my God."

"Do you like it?"

"Alex, it's... beautiful."

"Just like you."

She shakes her head. "This... I don't even think you can fully comprehend how much this means, what it represents to me."

Taking the box from her, I pluck the bracelet free and gesture for her to hold her arm out.

"I'm hoping that maybe you'll trust me enough to tell me."

I clip it into place and then sit back to watch her while she studies it.

Her finger trails over the small birdcage just like she did on Emmie's sketch as the diamonds and rubies sparkle in the evening sun sinking into the trees behind us.

She sucks in a shaky breath before looking up at me with watery eyes.

My heart knots.

"I didn't mean to make you cry, baby."

"They're good tears. I love it so much. Thank you."

It takes a while, but eventually, I refocus on what we're meant to be doing, and with the sound of her pencil scratching across her page, I lose myself in my books with thoughts about the future filling my mind.

Maybe there is a way. With Evie beside me, I feel invincible. Like I could do everything, be everything she deserves.

Maybe. Just maybe.

18

———

EVIE

I moan as a loud bell rips through the air.

"What is that?" I groan, rolling over and curling around Alex like a koala.

Laughter makes his body jiggle. "The doorbell, Vixen."

I groan again. "Who?"

"I called in a favour for the birth control situation," he confesses.

"Firstly, do you know how desperate that makes you sound?" He laughs, but it's pained, proving just how desperate he is. Cracking my eyes open, I look down at his body, and just as I suspected, tented sheets greet me. My mouth waters, but I stay on track. "And secondly, who the hell turns up at this time?"

"It's almost midday," Alex points out.

"Oh."

He chuckles again, pressing a kiss to the top of my head.

"And yes, I am desperate. But only if you are, too. No pressure, okay? I just want to get this sorted in case we slip up."

"Slip up?" I ask teasingly. "Or slip in?"

"Oh, baby. There will be no slipping in. When I push inside you for the first time, you'll know about it."

My thighs clench and my core pulsates, impatient to know exactly how it does feel.

The bell rings again, making Alex jump into action. "I'd better go let them in before they change their minds."

He slips out of bed before tugging on a pair of boxers and stalks out of the room, my eyes watching his every move.

"Keep looking at me like that, Vixen, and we'll be testing this out sooner rather than later."

"I can't wait," I whisper, but he's already gone, racing down the stairs to let whoever he's invited in to help with this little situation. All I can hope is that he's managed to sink his boner before he greets them.

Hello, the woman I own needs birth control, and as you can see, I can't wait a second longer.

I laugh at my own ridiculous thought before swinging my legs over the edge of the bed.

I might be about to talk to these strangers about something very intimate; I don't need to be in bed and naked for it as well.

I've peed, brushed my teeth and pulled on a tank and pair of shorts by the time there's a knock on the bedroom door.

"Hey," Alex says, his boyish smile making my stomach flip-flop wildly.

"Hey."

I stand awkwardly in the room as he walks inside with two older ladies behind him.

Both of their eyes land on mine, soft smiles playing on their lips.

"These two are the best nurses in the city. Whatever you need, they've got you covered. Promise, Vixen." He winks, his smile growing wider. Two such simple moves shouldn't make me relax as much as I do, given the circumstances.

I smile nervously at both of them.

"Okay, I'll leave you to it. Be nice," he warns, looking at the two of them before he slips from the room.

"Hi Evie, it's so good to meet you. I'm Gianna."

I expect her to walk over and shake my hand or something; the last thing I'm expecting is for her to pull me into a hug.

"Oh... uh... hi. It's good to meet you too."

"Evie, I'm Elen. We're here to talk about birth control, right?" she says, getting down to business.

"Uh..." My cheeks burn red hot. "Y-yeah."

"Shall we?" she says, gesturing to the sofa.

The three of us sit down. Elen is still all business while Gianna looks a little more relaxed.

"I understand that this situation is a little... unique. And I just need to ensure you understand what is happening here. My patient is my priority, and I want to ensure that you're not being pressured into anything you're not ready for. I—"

"Elen," Gianna hisses.

"What? I'm just checking."

"It's not necessary," I say. "I know what I'm doing, and we're just being sensible."

"See," Gianna says confidently.

I study her as she glares at Elen, recognition niggling in the back of my mind, but it's not strong enough to grasp.

"Okay, so I understand that you've already been on the contraceptive pill and didn't get along with it."

"No, not at all. If possible, I don't want any extra hormones in my body. It screws me up."

"Okay, that doesn't leave us with many alternatives. Have you considered an IUD?"

The next hour is filled with more information than I can even try and compute before I agree—because what is the other option: condoms for life or a baby?—and find myself in a seriously compromising position with two strangers.

Elen does the dirty work while Gianna holds my hand in support.

I repeat over and over in my head that they're both professionals and have probably seen more vaginas and cervixes than I've had hot dinners. But that is not the point, because right now, Elen is staring at mine while Gianna gives me encouragement because FUCK, it hurts like hell.

I was not prepared for that.

"Okay, sweetie. You're all done." Elen finally says, sitting back and pulling her gloves off. "You'll probably experience some cramping and spotting for the next few hours, but it should settle down. If you have any questions or concerns, my number is here. Call me anytime." She places a business card on the end of the bed before she begins packing her things away.

"C-can I get up?"

"Of course." Gianna helps me, although it's not necessary. "Any pain?"

I shake my head. "Just cramps. Nothing I can't handle." Honestly, the embarrassment is worse than anything.

"All done," Elen says, lifting her bag over her shoulder.

"We'll leave you to clean up."

"Thank you," I say. "I'm sure these calls aren't exactly every day."

"Sweetie, when you live lives like we do, anything is

possible. I'd take this any day over some of the other things those boys have brought us."

My mouth opens and closes, the need to tell them that they're welcome dancing on the tip of my tongue.

Thankfully, they both disappear before I say anything that will make all of this worse.

With a sigh, I pull the towel from my waist to give me some modicum of dignity. I swear to God, Alex better know what he's doing and make it mind-blowing after having to go through that.

Why do men have to have it so easy?

I'm still going through all the things that women have to suffer and men manage to escape when I walk through the bedroom to try and find the man I suffered through all that for.

The second I hit the bottom step and see him lounging on the deck, still only in his boxers with a steaming mug of coffee in his hands, I realise that it was totally worth it.

He looks over and finds me standing there watching him, and he pushes from the chair. Abandoning his coffee, he stalks toward me looking like a freaking model.

"You okay?" he asks, running his eyes over every inch of me.

"A little sore but yeah."

He steps closer, wrapping his hand around the back of my neck. His lips brush my ear, his warm breath making me shiver when it washes down my neck. "I promise I'll make it worth it. Over and over again."

"You'd better. That was no joke."

"I'm sorry, baby. Let me take care of you, yeah?"

"Let's see what you've got," I challenge.

"Well your coffee is already waiting, and I found a hot water bottle in case—"

"Wait, how do you know what I need?"

His arm wraps around my shoulder, and he leads me to the deck without answering my question.

As we round the corner, I discover something—or someone—sitting on the opposite lounger with her own coffee.

"Vixen, meet my mum, Gianna."

My chin drops as the world falls out from beneath me.

My eyes dart between the two of them. That niggle of recognition I felt upstairs is now more than obvious, making me feel like an idiot.

"You arsehole," I hiss, elbowing Alex so hard in the stomach he grunts in shock and bends over.

"Ohh, Pup. I like her," Gianna teases, her silver eyes sparkling all too familiar.

"Great," he grunts. "I'm starting to change my mind," he says, still faking his injury.

I make a beeline for the mug of untouched coffee sitting on the table. I need something to get me through this. Although, I think alcohol would be better.

"Oh no, you don't," Alex says from behind me, wrapping his arms around me and dragging me back into his warm body.

"Evie, I'm sorry," Gianna said. "Alex didn't want you to know beforehand because you would have been freaked out. Rightly so. But that's my job. The version of me you got upstairs was nurse me, not mum me."

Alex lowers us to his lounger, refusing to let me up from his lap.

"Even still," I mutter, dropping my head into my hands.

"My boys," Gianna starts. "Their hearts are in the right place. Their heads, however, sometimes need a little support."

Alex huffs while I laugh.

"I guess I'm owed a few secrets after what I went through," I say teasingly. "Do you have any mortifying baby pictures for me?" I ask Gianna, barely able to look her in the eye.

"Not with me. But when you're able to, come to my house and I'll dig out everything I can find as payback."

"Feel free. I've got nothing to hide," Alex offers, although from the loaded look Gianna shoots him, I have to wonder how true that is. "And anyway, what's the big deal? Mum would rather us be safe than sorry, right? She's too young to have a whole tribe of grandkids already."

"Alex," I gasp. "Your mother doesn't need to know what we're doing."

"Oh sweetie. I know my boys better than they know themselves. I know exactly what they're up to. And yes, I'm glad you're being smart. I might not know the details of what is going on here, but I do know that you're not in a position to be reproducing."

"I hope you said that to D and Calli," Alex mutters.

"Was too late by the time I found out."

"Fair point."

"So, Evie. My son has kept you very much a secret, and I want to get to know you better."

"Uh…" I stutter. "There's not really much to tell."

Gianna smiles at me before diving into questions that thankfully have nothing to do with the reason she was invited here in the first place.

That will have to go down in the record books for the most mortifying way to meet your mother-in-law. I mean, assuming this lasts long enough to… ugh.

I could kill him.

Gianna stays for about an hour. She's lovely. The kind of mum I wish I still had in my life. And despite the obvious awkwardness, I found myself liking her more with every second that passed. Her love for Alex was clear as day in her eyes. So was her exasperation with him.

And the way she called him Pup... The cutest thing ever. It only solidifies my comments the day before about him being a cute little puppy.

But after checking that I was okay after my... procedure, she gave us both a kiss on the cheek, told us to look after each other and have fun, which made me want the ground to swallow me whole.

"I can't believe you did that to me," I shriek the second Alex closes and locks the door behind her.

"What? Mum's cool. She doesn't care."

"Alex, she... she saw... Jesus. No one wants their first meeting with their boyf—" I cut myself off before the word spills from my lips.

"Boyfriend's mum?" he fills in for me.

"Yeah. No one wants *that* to happen while they're naked from the waist down and have their legs wide open."

"Best to get all the awkward shit out of the way at the beginning. And we don't have anything to worry about now," he says, his hands wrapping around my hips as he pulls me into his body.

I stare up into his eyes, seeing not an ounce of embarrassment about the fact that his mum blatantly knows that we want to fuck like bunnies all over this cabin.

"But she knows that—"

"My mum is a normal person, Evie. She and Dad were

young parents. And while I know she doesn't regret it, she's also aware of how hard it is. And she's also aware of what we get up to when we're alone. She's not naïve."

"This is fucked up."

"Welcome to my world, baby. Never a dull day."

"I'd like to agree, but it's my fault we're even here. And I thought I had the world's most boring life."

"Mmm," Alex moans as he dips his head, kissing down my neck, making me shudder in desire. "How are you feeling?"

Honestly, I'm totally fine, but after this morning, he doesn't need to know that.

"A little sore. I'd love a massage followed by some more croissants followed by a massive tub of chocolate ice cream."

He chuckles against my skin.

"Well, lucky for you, I can deliver on all those things. And maybe just a few more, if you're a good girl."

"I'm always a good girl," I counter.

"Hmm, well, I can think of a few times that you've been on your knees being very, very bad."

"Must be your imagination. I don't remember such things," I tease.

"Then I guess we'll just have to do it again to remind you."

I shriek when he steps back and swats me on the arse.

"Get out there and relax. I've got you covered, Vixen."

With a sly smile over my shoulder, I walk toward the open doors, more than ready to indulge in a bit of pampering from my man. It's the least of what he owes me for what I've done today.

19

ALEX

I start, my heart thundering in my chest, my muscles tensing, ready to fight, when a set of warm hands land on my bare shoulders.

My eyes shoot to the bed, recognising her gentle touch instantly, and I find exactly what I'm expecting. An empty bed.

One AirPod is plucked from my ear before she leans over the back of the sofa, her hot breath dancing over my skin and making it erupt in goosebumps.

"Have you slept at all?" she whispers sleepily in my ear. Her voice is raspy, and it hits me right in the cock.

Despite her now being protected, we didn't dive straight into bed yesterday. When Mum came back down from seeing Evie yesterday morning, she gave me the CliffsNotes of what they'd done and warned me quite sternly to be good. It wasn't necessary. Despite the ticking clock over making her mine, I still didn't want to rush her.

So instead, I did exactly what I promised Mum I would do, and I looked after her like she's the most precious thing in my life. Which of course, she is.

Mum saw it the second I opened the door for her and Elen yesterday morning. She didn't even need to meet Evie to know what she meant to me.

"I got a couple of hours," I groan, abandoning the textbook in my lap in favour of her.

Reaching behind me, I manage to grab her beneath her arms and lift her over the back.

"Alex," she squeals.

"Missed you," I murmur, cradling the back of her head and lifting her lips to mine.

Her fresh minty tongue brushes against mine, and I forget about my almost all-nighter and impending law exam and lose myself in her for just a few minutes.

"How long until you need to leave?" she asks, blinking up at me with big, hungry eyes.

Grabbing my phone from the cushion beside me, I check the time.

"Just under an hour."

"Perfect," she purrs, allowing me to indulge in one more kiss before rolling off my lap and sinking to her knees before me.

"Evie," I growl as she slides her palms up my thighs.

"We want you nice and relaxed going into that exam. You need to smash it so you can be the Cirillos' next hotshot lawyer."

"Fuck, Vixen," I groan as she rubs me through the fabric of my boxers.

My hips lift from the sofa involuntarily, my cock desperate to sink into her hot little mouth—almost as much as it wants to sink deep inside her pussy.

"Fuck," I bark. Just the thought of finally getting to do that, getting me closer to the release I'm desperate for. "Yes, baby. Fuck."

She pulls my boxers down my thighs and sits between my feet as her fingers wrap around my shaft.

I watch her tiny hand move up and down, enthralled by the way she touches me.

Every time she does, she gets a little more confident. I can't wait to experience what it'll be like in weeks', months' time.

Sitting up, she looms over me before lowering down and licking the precum that's beading at my tip.

I growl, sliding my fingers into her hair, desperate for more.

Unable to hold back, I push her down.

"Yes," I hiss as the wet heat of her mouth and her velvet tongue surround me.

My hips jerk, my need to get deeper all-consuming.

"Fuck, you suck me so good, Vixen."

Releasing my grip on her hair, I force myself to calm down and let her do her thing.

It's so fucking beautiful, watching her pleasure me.

Tilting her head a little, she looks up at me.

Her dark blue eyes are watery, framed by dark lashes. But they're nothing compared to the sight of her lips wrapped around my cock.

"Gonna come in your pretty little mouth, baby. You good with that?"

She nods eagerly before picking up the pace a little, never averting her eyes.

In only a few more seconds, I blow, my release crashing into me like a fucking steam train.

She takes it all, swallowing me down like a pro before releasing me with a pop.

Her cheeks are flushed red, and her lips swollen.

Fucking perfect.

Reaching for her, I lift her onto my lap and claim her lips again.

"Can't you taste yourself?" Evie asks into our kiss.

"Yeah. It's fucking hot."

"Really?" she asks, pulling back to look at me. "I didn't think guys would be into... that."

"I'm not just any guy. Come here, I've got ten minutes and I'm not getting up until I've heard you screaming my name."

"Alex," she moans when I push my hand into her knickers and find her soaking for me.

"Are you in pain?" I ask before pushing inside her.

"No. I need you, please."

"Any-fucking-time, Vixen."

"You need to leave," Evie says, pressing her palms to my chest and shoving me toward the door.

"I know. I know. I just—"

"I'll be fine. I'll keep all the doors locked while you're gone and just sketch, okay?"

"Still don't like it."

"You have to go to your exam, Alexander," she says firmly.

"Shit. I know," I groan, shoving my fingers through my hair.

"And Theo is waiting for you."

He told me there would be a ride for me this morning, but I wasn't expecting him to pull up on his bike two minutes ago. Right now, he's patiently waiting outside, but I know that isn't going to last long.

"Okay, okay. One more kiss, then I'm going."

I pull her in and steal a filthy kiss full of promises of all the things I'll give her when I get back.

"Later," she whispers against my lips.

"Keep your phone on you."

"I promise. Now go."

She shoos me toward the door. The thought of leaving her alone does not sit right with me, but I need to go.

I have to go.

I could have asked one of the others to come and babysit her, but I knew she'd hate it. And everyone has exams and classes. We've already missed more than we should.

She'll be safe here. No one knows where she is, and we have the place secure.

With one final look in her direction, I pull the front door open and slip out.

"About fucking time."

"Shut up," I mutter, glaring at Theo where he's resting against his bike with a spare helmet waiting for me.

A part of me is looking forward to the ride, but there's another part that was hoping for a car so I could continue studying.

I don't feel prepared for this exam in the slightest, and I can't afford to fuck it up.

I need this A to get into my top uni choice. And now I know Evie's plans for next year, that is more important than ever.

"Well, seems someone hasn't got laid yet."

"Fuck. Off."

Snatching the helmet from his hands, I drag it on my head.

"Touchy."

"Can we please just go? I can't be late, and I want to get back here as soon as physically possible."

"She's going to be fine. We've got this place surrounded."

I wince as I think of our guys being out in the wilderness, watching us chill out on the deck. I know better than to think they're creeping on us, though. We're all trained better than that, and they should also know that should I find out any of them are, then I'd set Daemon on them. And no one in this city wants that.

"I know," I mumble, waiting for him to climb on so I can do the same. "Any closer to finding the cunts who did this?"

His silence doesn't fill me with much hope. "Hasn't her dad squealed yet? Is D losing his touch?"

"He's squealed plenty, but none of it is any good. If he knows anything, he's a fucking good actor."

"He alive?"

"Barely. Now, did you want to get to this exam, or are we going to chit-chat out here all morning?"

"And you think I'm the grumpy one."

He rolls his eyes at me but throws his leg over his bike. The second he's settled, I follow, sitting comfortably on the back as he brings the engine to life.

He shoots off like a rocket, and as the warm summer morning air whips around me, I discover why he brought the bike.

I really fucking needed this.

By the time we pull up into Knight's Ridge College car park and come to a stop next to Emmie's bike, my head is clearer and I'm feeling a little more prepared for this exam.

Pulling my helmet off, I hand it to Theo.

"Ready for this?"

"Fuck yeah," I say, adjusting my bag that's hanging from my shoulder. "I got this."

"Good. I'll meet you after. Good luck."

I nod in appreciation and take off toward the exam hall.

A few people nod in my direction, but no one tries to stop me to talk, and I'm grateful.

Once I get to the closest bench, I lower my arse down and pull my textbook out. I've got twenty minutes before I need to go in, and I plan on making the most of it.

But before I do that, there's something else that's more important.

Pulling the burner from my pocket, I message Evie.

> Alex: Just got to school. Exam starts in 20 so I'm gonna cram. You good?

Her response is immediate. It's as if she was sitting with her phone, waiting for me to message.

> Evie: Yes, I'm good. You've got this. I believe in you. x

A smile pulls at my lips, her faith in me melting my heart.

"Well, let's hope that's good enough, because right now, I feel like I need all the miracles I can get," I mutter to myself.

20

EVIE

With my fingers gripped tightly around my phone, I wait for him to reply. But he never does.

I might know where he is right now, but I've never stepped foot on Knight's Ridge College grounds. It's not exactly a place where people like me ever go. And while our schools might only be a few miles apart, it's not like we've ever been invited there. Knight's Ridge is probably too scared that the Lovell kids will burn their fancy old buildings to the ground should they be allowed inside.

No, the two schools keep their circles very separate. Probably for good reason.

I can't help wishing for once that they didn't, though. That I could have had a chance to meet Alex before all of this.

Although, really, if it were for a football match, I wouldn't have been anywhere near it. Organised sports aren't exactly my thing. And let's be honest, with all the Knight's Ridge girls lusting after him and the rest of the players, I can hardly imagine that he'd ever have looked twice at me.

He only did it because I was up on a table, dancing in my underwear.

A pained sigh rips from my lips as images from our recent history play out in my mind.

Lowering my phone, I look around the vast cabin I'm sitting in and wonder once again how I ended up here. I dread to think how much this place is worth. Not only is it massive, but it's in the middle of nowhere on the outskirts of London—I think. I'm pretty sure the price tag has more zeros on it than I could ever comprehend.

Nothing but silence greets me as I sit alone on the huge sofa. It reminds me of those first few hours I had here alone. And without Alex's presence now, this place feels too big, too vast, too... cold.

After making another coffee and staring longingly at the decking that's bathed in sunlight, I do exactly as I said I would and curl myself into the corner of the sofa and pull out the sketch I started the other night.

It's safer in here. All the doors and windows are locked. No one can get me.

Or at least, that's what I keep telling myself.

"It's just a couple of hours. You've got this."

With that little pep talk out of the way, I somehow manage to lose myself in my sketch.

Time seems to fly past, and when I finally reach for my coffee, it's cold.

With a huff of annoyance, I put my pad down and head for the kitchen.

My eyes land on the window that looks out the front of the house, but just like it's always been since I got here, the blinds are closed.

I'm not sure why—I assume for privacy. With Alex taking up every inch of my headspace, I haven't really thought about why the house is the way it is.

Turning my back on the window, I set the coffee maker to work. As I twist around and resting my arse on the counter, the window taunts me once more.

And that's when I see it.

A shadow moves on the other side.

My heart jumps into my throat and my hand flies up to my mouth to smother the scream that threatens to rip from my lips.

My knees give out and I drop to the floor as the suspicious person-shaped shadow moves once more.

I've no idea how I manage to move with my body trembling so hard, but I somehow tuck myself into the corner of the kitchen, totally out of sight if someone were to storm through the front door.

With trembling hands, I unlock my phone and hit call on Alex's number.

I've lost track of time. I've no idea if he's currently in an exam or if it's finished already.

There's a little voice at the back of my head that tells me that he'd have messaged me if he were out, but the rational side of my brain upped and left the second I saw that shadow.

I don't even really know why I'm scared. Alex has kept the details of what's happening around us so vague that I don't really know who the enemy is right now. Derek? The men they took me from? But if Alex bought me, then he had every right to take me. Or was I promised to someone else and he beat them? Or...

"You've reached the voicemail service for—"

"Shit," I hiss, disconnecting the call and trying to think

of my options.

Pretty sure I only have one.

"Evie. Is everything okay?"

"I-I-I don't—"

"Shit. I'm walking out of my revision session now. Are you in danger?" His voice is so calm and collected, it somehow manages to settle my panic.

"I don't know."

I hear a door open then close down the line before he talks again.

"Okay, tell me what's happening," Theo demands.

Sucking in a breath, I will my heart to stop racing so hard I fear I might just pass out right here.

Don't make it that easy for whoever is outside.

"I-I saw a shadow move past the blinds. I think someone is out there. What if they saw you leave and—"

"Evie," he says calmly. "I need you to get yourself together, okay? Panicking will get you nowhere."

I nod despite the fact he can't see me.

"Okay?" he says, wanting confirmation that I can handle this.

I suck in a breath and hold it for two seconds before releasing it.

"Yeah. I got this," I confirm, putting as much confidence and strength into my tone as possible.

"Right, I'm just checking a few things. Sit tight for a second, okay?" When he speaks this time, his voice sounds different, farther away. I can only assume he's put me on speaker. But despite what he's doing, he doesn't stop talking to me, reassuring me that everything will be fine. "Can you move toward the window for me, Evie?"

"What?" I hiss.

"Trust me. I won't let anything happen to you."

I nod again, trusting him with my life just like I know Alex does.

Slowly and silently, I crawl toward the window. It's awkward as hell with my phone still pressed to my ear, but I make it work.

"I'm here," I whisper, suddenly terrified that someone outside will hear me.

"I need you to look out of the window and tell me what you see."

My heart pounds, all kinds of gory, terrifying images of my untimely end flashing through my eyes. "You want me to—"

"Look out, Evie. Tell me what you see."

Fucking hell.

Doing as I'm told, I lift the blind from the window and risk a look, wishing that whoever is standing on the other side has his back turned.

"Oh shit," I gasp, stumbling back when I find a man dressed in black staring right at me.

"Don't freak out. How many fingers is he holding up?"

"What?" I hiss. "I don't care how many fucking—"

"Do it," Theo growls dangerously.

"Okay, okay." I look back out again. "Three."

"Do you know why he's holding up three?"

"Is that a trick question?" I ask after a few seconds of confusion.

"He's holding up three fingers because I asked him to, Evie. He's protecting you."

"Oh," I breathe, all the fear that was previously flooding my system rushing out of me. "Well, why didn't you just tell me that?"

"Would you have believed me?"

"Um..." Honestly yes, I would, but he doesn't give me a chance to say that.

"You're safe there, Evie. I know it feels like you're in your own bubble, but everything is in place to protect you. Both of you."

"Shit. I know. I'm sorry. I freaked out. Being alone here, it's—"

"It's okay. You don't need to explain yourself. I know this situation is... intense."

Silence fills the line for a beat.

"Theo?"

"Yeah."

"Do I have reason to be this worried about something happening?"

"With our protection, no."

"I'm not talking about that. I mean..." I'm not entirely sure what I mean, but something isn't quite adding up here. "I mean, why do I even need protection? The deal has been done, right? I've been... bought. What's the issue?"

The fact he takes a second to formulate his answer doesn't fill me with joy.

"Let's just say, we didn't exactly follow their rules. They had other plans for you, and we stormed in where we weren't wanted and caused a bit of chaos."

"So surely, they want payback from you, not me?" Honestly, I have no idea how any of this works, but that makes sense in my head.

"Yes and no. By taking you like we did, we proved that you're an important asset to us. Which means—"

"To hurt you, all they need to do is get to me," I finish for him.

"Exactly."

"But you're all at risk too, right? Emmie, the others?"

I don't need to be able to see him to know he just swallowed thickly at the mention of his wife.

"Yes, but that's pretty much a standard in this life, Evie. Our surnames alone put a target on our heads."

"Right. Isn't that exhausting?" I ask, twisting away from the window and resting back against the wall.

"Some days. But it's the life we were born into. Well, almost all of us. The others have been brave enough to choose it."

"Why do I feel like there is a challenge in there somewhere?"

"No challenge. I trust that you'll do the right thing when this is all over," he says confidently.

"And what is the right thing, exactly?"

He lets out a breathy chuckle. "I don't think you need me to tell you what Alex feels for you, Evie. You're no idiot."

My chest tightens at his words.

"Thanks. This whole thing, it's been such a whirlwind. One minute I'm dancing in Paradise and the next..." I trail off. He knows the rest.

"Maybe it was just meant to be?"

"Hmm, you don't strike me as a man who believes in fate or coincidences."

"Maybe, maybe not. All I know is that, whirlwind or not, if it feels right, then it probably is. Trust your heart, Evie. And let Alex trust his."

I shake my head, a smile playing on my lips. "Does Emmie know you're so romantic?"

"Hell no, and don't you dare tell her either," he half warns, half laughs.

"I can't make any promises," I tease.

"You going to be okay there?"

I look out the window once more. The guy is still standing there watching, and the second he sees me, he gives a little salute.

"Yeah," I say, any fear I had when I made this call evaporating. "I think I'll be okay."

"I'm here if you need me. Alex will be out of his exam soon. He won't be back for a few hours, though. I need him. But, I'll send you some entertainment to keep you distracted."

"That sounds ominous."

"You've no idea," he laughs. "Call me if you need me. I'm here. We all are."

"Thank you," I force out through the emotion that clogs my throat.

"Any time. Talk soo—"

"Wait," I call. "Am I okay to call my sister?"

"As long as it's on her burner, or Wi-Fi if you video call."

"Thank you," I say again, a rush of excitement shooting through me at the prospect of having uninterrupted time with Blake.

The second I hang up, I push from the wall, grab my fresh coffee and find my tablet.

I've no idea if she's home. I can only assume she's under house arrest like I am, so I'm banking on her answering.

It rings a handful of times before the call connects and butterflies of happiness explode within me.

"Evie," Blake squeals, leaning her forearms on the kitchen counter and giving me a close-up shot of her impressive chest.

"Jesus, Blake. Put the girls away."

She laughs before pushing the table back a little and giving me a better view of her.

"Better?" she asks, showing me that she's actually wearing a fairly modest tank.

She drops a cloth on the side and hops up onto a barstool.

"Much. Are you... cleaning?" I ask, my eyes darting to the cloth.

She barks out a laugh. "I'm meant to be. But I'd much rather talk to you."

"I don't want to get you into trouble."

"I'm sure I can handle it," she says, wiggling her eyebrows mischievously.

21

ALEX

The second I step out of the exam hall, I find Theo leaning against the wall with his hands deep in his pockets and a frown on his face.

Fear turns my blood to ice while regrets over leaving Evie slam into me.

"What's wrong? What's happened?" I demand, pulling my phone from my bag where I stashed it for the exam.

"Nothing. Evie freaked out, thinking someone was watching the cabin, but she's okay."

"What?" I roar. "Why the hell are you here if there's someone—"

I race toward the car park, but he's faster and stops me with a firm grip on my upper arm.

"She's fine. It was just Bas."

"Oh," I breathe, my body instantly relaxing.

"She knew the place was being watched, right?"

"Uh... yeah. I told her that we had protection and..." I scrub my hand down my face. "Shit. I guess I didn't lay it out in detail."

Theo rolls his eyes at me. "The sooner you get inside her and restart your brain, the better."

"My brain is fine, thank you. And I'm not exactly lacking over here."

"Good for you. But while we're here scrambling around to dig up intel on them, they might already be on to us. On to her. And if they so much as suspect she's still—"

"All right, I got it," I mutter.

"How'd the exam go?"

I shrug. "I dunno. It wasn't terrible, but I'm not sure it was great either."

"Could be worse."

We come to a stop at a bench and I lower my arse down, letting the sun warm my back.

"I told Evie about uni."

"Okay," Theo says, his brows pinched in confusion. "Why is that so bad?"

"She thinks I can be Cirillos' next hotshot lawyer." I can't help but laugh.

Theo doesn't, though. Instead, his unwavering attention remains on the side of my face.

"And why can't you?" he asks, as if it's that simple.

"That's not the role that's been carved out for me. It's not what I've been trained for."

"So?"

"B-but—"

"But nothing, Alex. Things can change, jobs change. Just because your cunt of a grandfather thought you'd be good at what you do now—hell, you are good at what you do now—it doesn't mean that's the only thing you can offer the Family."

"But I can't be a lawyer. Our legal team are the best, they're—"

"They'd be lucky to have you."

"What?" I blurt.

"Fuck me, man. For someone who has the ego and confidence the size of the Pacific, you're sure fucking insecure."

I frown, really not fucking liking that.

"I'm not, I—"

"Alex, the only person who can carve out your future is you. You want to keep using your body to get us intel, then please, carry on. You want to pick up a pair of pliers and join your brother in his torture chamber, then go for it. You want to join the legal team, then get your arse into the best fucking uni you can and do whatever it takes to get there."

"You really think—"

"No, I don't think, Alex. I fucking know. And anyway, one day I'll be in charge, and you can have whatever the fuck you want."

My lips open and close as I try to formulate words.

"All you need to do is be honest with yourself, with Evie, if you're serious about her, then find a way to move forward. Will your dad still want you to do jobs? Probably, but it's up to you how you handle that."

"I don't know, I—"

"I know," he says, slapping me on the shoulder. "And your girl does, too. Trust us, we're smart."

"Smart-arse is more like it," I mutter.

"Come on. We need to talk properly, and we're not doing it out here."

"Has something happened?"

"No. And that's the fucking problem."

Together, we make our way back to his bike. My attention is firmly on my phone as I message Evie to check in. Then, after a quick stop at Burnt Coals for takeout, we're pushing into my flat.

I look around, trying to remember the last time I was here.

At the arse crack of dawn before Nico whisked us all off to Vegas. That's when.

Walking to the kitchen, I throw the window open, then pull out one of the stools and plop my arse into it, immediately ripping into the paper bag containing my much-needed burger and chips.

"Start talking," I mumble around my mouthful.

"All the leads we've had have been dead ends. We can't get to these cunts. They've covered their tracks too well."

"Fuck's sake."

"I know."

"They'll fuck up eventually."

"Yeah, they will. But how long are you willing to wait and risk them finding us first?"

"It's already been too long," I state. "I'm not letting them find her and take her from me."

"Then we need something to nail their arses."

"D hasn't got anything?"

"He's got plenty out of her dad, but none of it has led them to us. Seems him and his best friend aren't as close as Jeremy believed."

"Brilliant. So what's next?"

"We've managed to hack into the camming app Evie uses."

Every muscle in my body tenses with the thought of having access to every motherfucker who's ever watched her online. My body burns up as bloodlust threatens to take over.

"We've managed to get everyone's details but a handful that we're still working on."

"What are you suggesting? That it's one of her clients?" The final word tastes bitter, like ash coating my tongue.

"I don't know. But it's worth looking into, right?"

"Seems like you've got fuck all else," I hiss.

"Trust me. We're doing everything we can. But getting her out like we did showed them that someone can get into their ranks. They've locked down and are refusing to poke their heads up."

"So this is Evie's fault?" I bark, my hackles rising.

"What? No. We did what we had to do to ensure her safety. It just would have been nice if we could have been a little more discreet."

"They don't know it was us, though? It could have just as easily been Riveras, or Hawks, right?"

"Right. But they'll turn to us eventually if they haven't already."

"And what are Luciana and Reid saying about all this?"

"Same as we are. Reid is out for blood. Luciana is as terrifying as ever."

"Crazy bitch," I mutter under my breath, making Theo laugh.

But that humour only lasts so long.

"You're going to need to talk to her about her clients, Alex. Try and get some intel on the men she spoke to. Anything. The fact we can't just pull some of the profile's account details rings massive alarm bells. No one covers shit up that well for no reason."

"Great," I mutter, rubbing the back of my neck.

"It's about time you came clean, anyway. Tit for tat, if you know what I mean." I groan, my half-eaten burger now less than appealing as I consider how that conversation will go. "Hey, just think, if it is them, you two could tag team in bringing them in. Hell knows she possesses the same kind of seduction skills you do. You'd be like Bonnie and Clyde or some shit."

"Huh."

Suddenly, the thought of walking into a restaurant toward a mark or two doesn't seem so bad.

"You'd be unstoppable."

"I'm not dragging her into this shitshow, Theo," I state. It doesn't matter how good it would feel to work together. She deserves more than to be my partner in this shit.

"Okay," he says, but when I look up and see the mischievous glint in his eyes, I know he doesn't believe me.

"I mean it," I growl.

"I know." When he grins at me, I almost can't stop myself from punching him in his smug-as-fuck face.

"Did you need me for anything else, or am I free to return to my girl?"

He laughs. "You're free to return. But I should warn you, you might not want to."

"Why? What have you done?"

His previous smirk only gets wider. "Sent the girls to keep her company."

"Oh, for the love of God. They'll tell her worse shit than my mum."

"She's met Gianna? How don't I know this?"

"Because, oh fearless one, contrary to popular belief, you don't actually know everything," I tease, making him press his lips into a thin line. "I called her out to get Evie on birth control."

Now, it's not often anyone aside from Emmie can shock Theo, and I can't help but feel a little victorious when his chin drops.

"You called your mum for— Jesus, Alex. She must have been mortified."

"Oh, you don't know the half of it," I say before explaining the whole story.

"You should be grateful that she's not Emmie or Stella. They'd have both killed you in your sleep."

"If you've sent them over to hang out with her, then they might just convince her to do it tonight, and it'll be all your fault."

"I'm sure you can handle it. You good driving yourself back? I've got to head over to Empire to see the boss with Nico."

"Sure thing. I'm going to drop in on the devil and my father before I head out. Make sure he's behaving himself with Evie's sister."

Theo snorts. "You've met your father, right? There's no way he's not already fucking her six ways from Sunday."

"If he is, and I find out, then his life isn't going to be worth living. He's been warned."

"Haven't we already had enough parental killings recently?" Theo asks with a smirk.

"Not if he's broken his promise."

"You really love her, huh?"

"Get the fuck out of my flat, Cirillo," I growl, throwing his empty can of Coke at his head.

"Jeez. I just think you need to be a bit more realistic. You got your skills from somewhere, you know, and the apple never falls far from the tree."

"Get the fuck out," I bellow before he finally fucks off, leaving the sound of his laughter behind him.

"Hello?" I call after letting myself into Dad's house.

Little boy laughter fills the hallway, making my steps falter. It's been a long time since I've heard anything like that in this house.

I follow the sound, intrigued to find out what's happening at the other end of it.

Coming to a stop outside the den, I lean my shoulder against the doorframe, my smile widening at the sight before me.

"Look out," a familiar voice says. "He's hiding behind that crate. Take him out and I'll go inside."

"You got it," the other voice says.

Together, they slay their enemies like pros. The sight takes me back to years gone by when me and the boys would innocently be doing the same thing.

"You two are pretty good," I say, making my presence known as I stride into the room.

"Hey, Alex," Atlas says, his eyes lighting up at my arrival.

"Hey, man. How's it going?"

"It's good. Have you met Zay?"

"Not in person, but I have heard a lot about you, man."

I hold my hand out to shake his, and Zayden's eyes almost pop out of his head.

"Umm... hi... it's... nice to meet you. You're like... real."

I can't help but laugh. He's looking at me as if Cristiano Ronaldo just strolled into the house.

"Are you really like... in the mafia?"

"Atlas," I groan. "What tales have you been telling?"

"No tales. Just the truth about what bad-arses you all

are. Gonna be us one day, bro," he says, nudging Zay's shoulder.

I lift my hand just in time to hide the smile that pulls at my lips. I shouldn't be encouraging it. Evie would kill me. But also, it's so fucking cute.

I saw it the night in The Empire when I opened her purse and found the photo of the three of them, and then again the other day through the tablet. But he is just a miniature, male version of the woman who's stolen my heart.

"Atlas," I warn again. Much like Zay, he's the spitting image of his older sibling too. He's just cheekier than Theo. And something tells me he's going to get into a hell of a lot more trouble, too. "Good day at school?" I ask them both, seeing as they're still in uniform.

"Meh, it was all right," Atlas mutters.

"I go to Lovell Green Primary. Is there ever a good day?" Zay asks seriously, his expression a little darker than before.

"Uh..." I rub the back of my neck awkwardly. "I guess not."

"I told you," Atlas says. "You need to talk to your sister about coming to Knight's Ridge in September. It would be epic."

Zay visibly winces, a little more aware of how it's not quite as easy as Atlas makes it out to be.

It's a massive reminder of the differences between how we've grown up compared to Evie, Blakely, and Zay.

"Yeah, it would," Zay confesses sadly. He glances at me and I smile. My heart aches for him. I'm desperate to tell him that I'll do whatever I can to make it happen. But I'm aware that I could be overpromising and definitely overstepping.

"Boys, I've got snacks," a female voice calls through the house.

"Yes. Your hot sister has food," Atlas barks, jumping to his feet and running from the room.

Zay groans but follows. He's slower, and when he gets to the chair I'm sitting in, he pauses and looks at me.

"Is Evie really okay?"

"I swear to you, Zayden, man to man, she's fine. And, I promise I will do everything in my power to ensure it stays that way."

"Good," he says, accepting my words with a single nod. "Because I can't lose her."

"Me either, bud," I say honestly, pushing to my feet and trailing after him to find the snacks that are up for offer.

My legs stop moving the second my eyes land on Blakely standing in the middle of Dad's kitchen in a black tank top and a pair of ripped jean shorts. I can't see the back of her, but I'm pretty sure they're obscene. And not something appropriate for cleaning a house.

One thing is for sure. My dad is either going to break his promise, or he's in literal hell.

A wicked smile pulls at my lips. Is it wrong of me to hope for the latter?

22

———

EVIE

The second the sound the biometric scanner releasing the door locks hits my ears, excitement explodes within me.

I know it's not Alex. And while a part of me wishes it was, I can't help but be excited by the prospect of some more girl time. Chatting to Blake showed me how much I missed it.

I've no idea who Theo has sent, I assume Emmie and Stella, but when loud laughter hits my ears, I get the feeling it's from more than just the two of them.

"Hey," Stella says, surging into the room first, making a beeline straight for me. She pulls me in for a hug. "You holding up okay?"

"Yeah, I think so." This morning's freak-out aside.

"Sorry, we haven't been out before. Alex wanted all your attention. Selfish prick," she says with a smile.

"I don't think she's complaining," Emmie points out happily.

Stella releases me, allowing me to see the others who have joined us.

"Evie, this is Calli, your one-day sister-in-law, and Jodie, Toby's girl. We wanted to bring Brianna too, but she's old and has a job."

"Boring," Stella says while I say hello to the girls I've heard so much about but never met.

"So, you're really growing your future queen here, huh?" I ask, glancing at Calli's cute bump.

"Ah-ha, so Alex is on team pink, huh?" Emmie laughs.

"Seems that way," I agree.

"Knew we'd turn him to our side eventually," Stella adds.

"You have alcohol, right?" Emmie asks, marching toward the kitchen.

"The whole place is fully stocked," Calli says before focusing back on me. "It's so good to meet you at last. We've all been waiting for someone to steal Alex's heart."

"You two are close, yeah?"

She nods. "Yeah. He's... amazing. Best brother I could ask for."

"Why is this place locked up like it's winter?" Jodie asks, walking toward the wall of windows.

"I promised Alex I'd stay inside, just in case."

"Screw that," Emmie says. "This place is better protected than Buck Palace right now. Plus, you have the baddest bitches in all of the city at your disposal."

"Evie, just so you know, not all of us have egos the size of the guys'," Jodie says with a smirk.

"Oh pipe down, Walker." Jodie flips Emmie off before she steps outside.

"Are you sure we should—"

My words are cut off when Stella produces both a gun and a knife from fuck knows where.

"We're sure. I'd love to see someone try. Now come on, I need to top up my tan."

Stella starts stripping off her school shirt as she and Calli join Jodie out on the deck.

"You okay after earlier?" Emmie asks, studying me closely.

"Yeah. It was stupid. Being here alone messed with my head."

"It's normal. Don't beat yourself up over it. And anyway, we're here now. And only really stupid motherfuckers would ever dare mess with us."

With arms loaded up with glasses, vodka and cans of Coke, we make our way outside.

"I have good memories of that hot tub," Jodie confesses when we join them.

"I hope you had it cleaned before Alex and Evie got here," Stella says to Calli.

"Don't worry," Calli says, looking at me. "It's perfectly clean and hygienic."

"Well..." I confess.

"Oh oh oh, have you been getting jiggy in the hot tub?" Emmie laughs.

"I don't kiss and tell, so..."

"That's not what I hear," Jodie pipes up. "I have it on good authority that you've joined the exhibitionist club we seem to have going on around here."

"I... uh..."

"Girl, it's totally cool. Anyone told you where I work yet?"

"Um..."

"You heard of Hades?"

"Not in the way I think you might be referring to," I confess, getting comfortable on a lounger.

"It's a sex club," Emmie supplies.

"A what?" I ask after spraying Coke from my mouth.

"Alex failed to mention that, huh?"

"Maybe he wanted to surprise her with a visit. You have a thing about cages, right, Evie?" Emmie asks.

"Umm... I danced in one, if that's what you're referencing. Not sure I have a thing about any cages that might be in a sex club."

"Hey, don't knock it until you try it."

All eyes turn on Jodie.

"Oh, now this sounds like a story that we all need," Stella muses.

"Isn't Toby your brother?" I ask, frowning.

"Yep, but honestly, it's best to try and forget it. I do."

"It's okay. We haven't tested out the cage, but I've seen couples using it."

"You get to watch... stuff?" I ask.

"If the occupants keep the windows clear, then yeah, they're inviting an audience," Jodie explains, reminding me that I'm just that naïve little nerd from Lovell again.

"And you've all been to this club?"

"I haven't," Calli says.

"Only because Bri and Nico are the first through the door," Stella laughs.

"And unlike some," Calli pins her friend with a deadly look, "I'm unable to watch my brother thrusting into his girlfriend."

"Wife," Emmie corrects.

"Yeah. That doesn't make it any better."

"Aw, it's cute how much he loves her."

"It is. And I am more than happy to appreciate that while they're clothed."

Everyone laughs as Calli's top lip peels back in disgust.

"Well, colour me intrigued. I want to see this place," I announce.

"When this is all over, I'm sure Alex will be more than happy to oblige."

Heat stirs in my lower stomach, and it only gets harder to ignore as they continue telling me about this club.

I'm also wondering if they'll give me a job, because it sounds a hell of a lot more interesting than just dancing at Paradise. With Derek MIA, I can only assume that my employment has been brought to an abrupt end.

The conversation morphs to school and exams, and I lose myself in their easy friendship.

I've never had this. Blakely has always been my ride or die. But what these four have... Well, I'm jealous.

They're so open and honest with each other about everything. It's so refreshing. So pure.

The alcohol flows and the conversations get wilder.

Stella and Emmie happily lie out on the big lounger that Alex and I have spent so much time on in just their bras and school skirts, while Calli stays tucked into the shadows, sipping on orange juice. But even with her lack of vodka, she's still just as fun and animated as the others, happily talking about Alex's brother Daemon like he literally hung the moon for her.

I can't wait to meet him. After everything Alex has said about them being polar opposites mixed with the love Calli obviously has for the dark knight, I'm more intrigued than ever.

Jodie excuses herself to the toilet and I get up to make everyone a fresh round of drinks, but unsurprisingly I find the bottle of vodka empty.

"Whoops," I say, holding it up for Stella and Emmie to see.

"We'll be in trouble when the boys get here," Stella says, a slur to her voice that wasn't there when she first arrived. Probably has something to do with the shots she and Emmie were doing.

She's right. They are freaking trouble.

Collecting up the empties, I carry them all through to the kitchen and set about finding more, along with some snacks to soak it all up with, when Jodie rejoins me.

"Hey, you okay?" she asks, hopping up on the stool and taking one of the packets of crisps I've found to help me.

"Thought they needed food," I say, glancing out through the door.

"They're something, huh?" she says fondly. "I thought Brianna was crazy until I met them."

"Sounds like she might fit in well then."

Jodie laughs softly. "She does. It's the family she never knew she needed but always wanted."

"And they say blood is thicker than water."

"Nah, that's bullshit. Blood just makes people think they have a right to fuck with you. You get to choose the water for yourself. They're what's really important." Although her words might be fierce, there's a sadness in her tone.

"Alex said you were in Lovell the night of the riot."

"Yeah," she sighs, putting the empty packet back down before picking at her nails.

"I'm sorry about your friend. I can't imagine how hard it's been."

"Watching it is tough, but it's nowhere near as hard as it is for her. She's... I don't know. She's still Sara, still my childhood best friend, but she's... broken. Something within her is broken, and I'm scared she's not going to be able to get past it."

Reaching over, I squeeze her hand, needing to do something to comfort her when she's quite clearly hurting.

"Shit, I'm sorry. I shouldn't be loading all of this on your shoulders. You've got enough of your own crap."

"It's okay. It's a nice distraction. Not that your friend's issues are... shit. Stop talking, Evie," I chastise.

"I get it. You don't need to apologise." I smile at her, relaxing again. "So your dad's a scumbag, huh? I had one of those too."

"Oh? What happened?"

"We killed him." She says the words so seriously and without even a flicker of emotion, and it somehow makes me choke on my own breath.

"You're kidding?" I say once I've finally recovered.

"Nope. Sent him to hell, exactly where he belongs. You can do the same, if you want. There will be no judgement from any of us."

My lips open and close like a fish as I try and come up with something to say. "I'll... uh... remember that."

"No matter what happens, we've got your back."

"I appreciate that," I say, studying her.

"What?" she asks suspiciously.

"I... um... when all this is over, do you think there's any chance of getting a job at your club? I'm a dancer and I—"

"Girl, when this is all over, you can have whatever you want. I'm always down for torturing any of the boys in whatever way possible, and putting you up on stage would make Alex's head explode."

I can't help but laugh.

"He'd love it," I argue.

"Oh, I don't doubt that for a second. You'd likely have the best night of your life."

"Is that a promise?"

"Hell yeah."

"Foooooooood," Stella sings when Jodie and I join them back out on the deck. She sits up and makes little grabby hands until I pass a bowl over, stealing a handful of crisps and stuffing them in her mouth.

"I know, I've no idea what Seb sees either," Emmie says with a laugh.

"Fuck off. I'm hot and you know it," Stella mumbles around a mouthful.

"Yeah, full of hot air."

The banter between the girls continues as I take my seat.

My eyes catch on Calli's, and she smiles softly at me. I have so many questions I want to ask her about Alex, seeing as she seems to be the one who's closest to him. But with Stella and Emmie cackling like a pair of drunken witches, it doesn't seem like the right time. And that thought is only confirmed a few minutes later when the front door opens and a loud booming voice bellows, "Honey, I'm home."

My stomach explodes with butterflies and I'm out of my seat and rushing toward him before I've even registered that my legs are moving.

The second he's in my sights, I run faster, slamming into him so hard he grunts with the impact.

"Hey, Vixen," he manages to get out before I find his lips and kiss him like he's been gone for a year.

"Well, that's the kind of welcome home everyone dreams of," an unfamiliar voice says from behind him. But I pay it zero attention as I sweep my tongue into Alex's mouth, drowning in his taste.

A deep groan rumbles in his chest as he kisses me back with as much passion as I am him.

"Missed you too, baby," he groans without breaking our connection.

"I need to get laid," the voice says before heavy footsteps move away from us.

The girls' voices filter through as they greet whoever it is, but I'm too lost.

"How was your exam?" I ask when we finally come up for air.

"Yeah, it was okay. Are you okay?"

I shake my head, hating the concern I see in his eyes.

"It was nothing. I just freaked out."

"I'm sorry I wasn't more explicit about there being men here. I should have—"

"It's okay. It's okay." I take his hand when he puts me back on my feet. "Come on, the girls are here."

"I'm surprised this place is still standing," he mutters as he trails behind me.

"Ah good, I was worried she was going to suck your face off, man," the unfamiliar voice says with amusement.

"Evie, this is Ant. He's Italian, and his invitation to hang can be pulled at any time."

"Like you would," Ant quips, getting himself comfortable on the lounger beside Calli that I'd vacated.

"Oh, I totally would."

"Evie," he says, turning his eyes on me. "It's nice to finally meet you." His eyes run down the length of me in appraisal, but there's no heat or interest behind it. He's clearly just baiting Alex. "When you're ready to trade up to a real man, you know where I am, darlin'." He winks, and I can't help but giggle when Alex growls like a wild beast.

Pressing my hand to his chest, I look up at him. His dark eyes are laser-focused on his friend.

"Hey," I say, sliding my hand up to cup his cheek. "He's joking. I'm not going anywhere. Least of all to your friend."

"I know," Alex says confidently, finally looking down at me.

I gasp the second his eyes land on me. They're burning with something that has the power to utterly consume me. But before I get to ask, he slams his lips down on mine, evaporating all my thoughts.

"See," one of the girls pipes up. "Evie likes to put on a show just as much as the rest of us."

"Speak for yourself," someone else—I think Calli —mutters.

Before we break apart, the front door slams closed and a voice booms, "Let's get this party started."

Alex groans before he whispers, "I love my friends, but I just want to be alone with you."

My heart beats wildly in my chest at his confession.

"You've got me the second they leave."

"That's awfully presumptuous to think they'll ever leave."

"At some point, Calli will have to have a baby, so..."

He laughs, and a warm blast of breath covers my face and rushes down my neck, making my nipples pebble and my stomach clench.

Yeah, I really want to be alone right now, too.

"Here you go, lovebirds," someone says, and when I look back, I find they've carried the swing seat over.

By the time we drop into it, all the guys have found their girls, bar Daemon.

"Where's your brother?" I ask Alex, but he just shrugs as he pulls me onto his lap and wraps his arms around me.

"He's busy playing with a new toy," Theo says.

"What is he, five?" I ask, frowning.

Alex chuckles beneath me, the others quickly following.

"No, Vixen. By toy, Theo means a person."

My eyes shoot to Calli as my breath catches. Surely, he's not—

"He's torturing him," Calli says, reading my mind.

My chin drops. "Like... actual torture?"

"Yep. See, Vixen. We're like night and day. I'm all about the loving and D is... well, he's into that too, obviously." He tilts the beer that someone has given him in Calli's direction.

"So he's like... beating him up? Or..."

"To start with, maybe," Alex agrees. "He was heading down there hours ago, though. He's probably pulled teeth and cut off fingers by now."

I gawp.

"You're not joking, are you?"

He takes a pull on his drink, letting me have the perfect view of his throat when he swallows.

Damn, I really shouldn't want to lick him so bad when we're in the middle of a conversation about cutting off fingers, but...

"Nope."

"Evie, this is Brianna, Nico, and Toby," Emmie says, changing the conversation and introducing me to the newest members of the group.

I find the couple who are tangled together on a lounger that looks like it's about three seconds from collapsing onto the floor and smile.

"Congratulations," I say, glancing at the massive rock on Brianna's finger.

"Thank you. Shame you couldn't make it."

"Sorry, I was busy being sold," I deadpan, the alcohol in my veins loosening my lips.

Some laugh, but Alex doesn't even come close as his body tenses beneath me.

"Not funny," he groans, tucking his face into my neck.

"I'm here, aren't I? You saved me. You're my hero."

"I'm no hero, baby."

Grabbing his face so he has no choice but to look at me, I stare him dead in the eyes and state, "To me, you're everything."

23

———

ALEX

Laughter fills the air as my girl wiggles her hips on my lap, ensuring my dick remains hard and desperate.

Right now, I have everything I've ever wanted. Okay, apart from Daemon leaving his torture chamber to join us. Calli might have helped ease him out of his anti-social lifestyle, but some things still die hard. All I can hope is that the prick who's on the other end of his special techniques tonight will get us some answers we so desperately need.

The drinks are flowing and everyone is buzzing, apart from Calli and Theo, who are driving back. But to my surprise, everyone is mostly well-behaved.

I mean, from where we're sitting, we can't really see what Seb and Stella are up to. But from the noises I've heard, I'd say it's easy to guess.

"Alex, I just sent you something," Nico says. "Can't believe you fucking missed it."

Without removing Evie, I pull my phone from my pocket to find a photograph of Nico and Bri in Vegas. Their eyes are alight with happiness, and they've got the widest smiles on their faces.

Seeing things like this used to make my chest ache, but right now, all I do is hold Evie tighter and pray she won't force me to let go anytime soon.

I show her the photo, and she smiles.

"I've never even left London," she confesses quietly so only I can hear.

"You have," I state. "You're out of London right now."

"Oh?" she asks, making me realise that she really has no idea where we are.

Her trust in me blows me away.

"Yep, consider this your best holiday ever."

"Best?" she asks, her brows arched.

"Hell yeah, because you're on it with me."

"Not because it's my first then?"

I nuzzle her neck, desperate to get that sadness out of her eyes when she thinks about her life compared to mine.

"Fucking love taking your firsts, Vixen," I confess, peppering kisses down her neck. "Shit, I really need to take a piss," I groan when she shifts on my lap, making the situation unignorable.

Swiping out of the photo, I throw my phone onto the cushion beside me, then lower her next to it.

I'm on my feet and about to take a step toward relief when Evie's gasp cuts through the air.

I spin to look at her.

"What's wrong? What—" My words cut off when I find her holding my phone and staring down at the apps on it.

My heart jumps into my throat as one single app seems to glow like a beacon on the screen.

"Evie, it's not—"

Ripping her watery eyes from it, she looks up at me.

I've no idea if everyone else has noticed that something is going on, because every one of my senses is focused on her.

"You knew," she breathes.

Her hand trembles so bad that she drops my phone, and before I figure out the right thing to say—if there even is a right thing—she's on her feet and running into the house.

"Shit, Evie. Come back, I— FUUUUUCK," I bellow before dropping my head into my hands.

Silence surrounds me as my world crumbles in on itself in a way I'm not sure I've ever experienced before.

"What happened?" Emmie asks, breaking the tension.

Dropping my hands, I risk a look over at my friends before my eyes find Theo's.

"Just go explain. Everything," he urges.

"What don't we know?" Emmie demands.

"Things that don't concern you, Hellcat."

"She's my friend, and he just sent her running off crying. I think that concerns me." She's on her feet before Theo can stop her and storms to me. "What did you do? You're meant to be protecting her."

Her fists curl at her sides and I wait for the blow to land.

"Stand down, Em," Calli says. "Theo's right though, you need to go and talk to her."

I glance around them all once more, the weight of my lies pressing down on my shoulders.

"You all need to leave," I demand before marching to the house. I want to run straight after her, but I need to fucking pee.

I swing by the downstairs bathroom, and when I emerge, everyone is making their way to the cars.

Each of them gives me sympathetic looks, but the only person who pauses is Ant.

"You okay, man?" he asks, studying me closely.

"Brilliant. I've probably just done the inevitable," I confess.

"What's that?" he asks as if it's not obvious.

"Fucked up the best thing that's ever happened to me."

"Nah, man. Whatever you've done, she'll forgive you."

I shake my head, rubbing the back of my neck as I try to believe what he's saying.

"You don't know—"

"I don't need to, Alex. Whatever you've done, you had a reason. You're a good person, and she knows that."

"Does she?" I ask.

"She's here right now instead of being..." A shudder rips through me as I mentally finish his sentence.

He reaches out and squeezes my shoulder.

"You've got this," he says confidently. "And if you need anything, I'm at the end of the phone."

I nod, accepting his friendship while being really fucking relieved we didn't screw it up that night, and he walks away, disappearing out the front of the cabin.

"Be honest. She can handle it," Theo says, letting me know that he watched that exchange.

"I don't doubt that. I just wish she didn't have to."

"That's life, bro. Good luck, yeah?" He ducks out of the cabin and closes the door behind him. The locks engaging echo through the silent space and I blow out a long, slow breath.

It does little to calm me or help me figure out what the fuck I'm meant to say to her.

The truth...

Taking the stairs two at a time, I race toward the back of the house and the closed bedroom door.

Every inch of me wants to storm through it, take her in my arms and force her to forgive me. Maybe throw in an orgasm or two for good measure.

But I can't. I know I can't, and it kills me.

Lifting my hand, I rap my knuckles on the solid wood.

Silence.

"Evie," I call.

Nothing.

"Evie, I'm sorry. Please, can we talk about this?"

The only sound that can be heard is my heavy breathing and the loud bang of my forehead colliding with the door.

My heart thunders in my chest.

"Please, Vixen. It's not a big deal. It doesn't bother me that you do it." *So long as no one else touches you...*

Still nothing.

I should probably leave her. She clearly doesn't want to talk to me. But despite knowing that, my hand lifts to the handle and I twist it open.

The room is in darkness as I step inside, and initially, I don't see her. But then, her dark form appears in front of the windows.

She's sitting on the floor with her arms wrapped around her legs, staring up at the dark night sky.

"Evie," I whisper, terrified that I'll scare her.

The only sign I have that she hears me is in the sharp rise of her shoulders.

"Please, baby. I fucked up, I know. I should have told you that I knew. I—"

"I don't want to talk about," she says so quietly it would be easy to think I imagined it.

"Okay," I say, walking toward the window and lowering my arse down beside her and mimicking her position.

"What are you doing?" She balks, her eyes burning into the side of my face.

"Not talking."

"It wasn't an invitation to join me," she hisses.

"Well, maybe you should have been more specific."

She huffs in frustration.

"Being cute won't get you anywhere," she warns.

Finally, I look over, and what I find makes my breath catch and my chest ache.

The moonlight reflects off the wetness coating her cheeks, and her bottom lip is swollen from where she's been chewing on it.

"Shit, Evie. I never meant to upset you. I just—"

"I said I don't want to talk," she snaps.

"You don't have to. You just need to listen."

"Alex, no. I—"

"Please?" I beg, dragging my eyes away from her profile to look at the darkness before us.

When she doesn't respond, or get up and walk off, I take it as agreement.

"It's okay that you do it. I understand."

The last reaction I expect to that comment is for her to laugh.

"How is it okay? How can you possibly understand?" she asks, her voice a few octaves too high.

"Because it is and... I do. You want to explore your sexuality in the safety of your own home and make some money while doing it. What's wrong with that? Gotta be better than being out in the street selling either your body or drugs, right?"

Her lips open and close as she tries to find the right words to say.

"All the men in the world could watch you, Evie. But there's only one who gets you."

"I get naked for them, Alex. Pleasure myself for them. How could you—"

"I know what you do, Vixen. It's hot as—"

"Oh my God," she gasps, jumping to her feet and covering her mouth with her hand as she backs away from me.

"Baby," I say, standing to full height and following her.

She shakes her head in disbelief. She looks so small and vulnerable as she comes to a stop against the wall and curls in on herself.

"You watched me," she sobs, her tears spilling over once more.

"Vixen, you are the sexiest, hottest, most incredible woman I have ever met. You undo me with just one look, with the simplest of touches. You're beautiful and kind, the most incredible sister. You have absolutely nothing to be ashamed of."

"I'm not ashamed," she cries. "I'm mortified. And here I was thinking that having your mum hold my hand while—" She cuts herself off with another shake of her head. "You watched and you never so much as mentioned it. When?" she demands.

I dip my head, scrubbing my hand over my jaw.

"The afternoon before the party in Lovell," I confess quietly.

All the air leaves her lungs in a rush. She stares at me as if she doesn't know me, and it fucking wrecks me.

"Th-that was you. The private chat?"

"Baby." I reach for her, and she tries to make herself

even smaller, as if she wants the wall at her back to swallow her whole.

"No, don't *baby* me," she says quietly. "You paid to watch me? Do you not see how fucked up this is?"

"I fucking loved it."

A bitter laugh falls from her lips. "I bet you did. Fucking hell, Alex." She stands a little taller, finding some strength from somewhere.

"I was at work. We were on security at The Empire, and I got a notification telling me that you were online. I watched on silent as you put your make-up on. I was mesmerised. Fucking captivated. Before I knew what I was doing, I requested that private chat. I needed you. I needed your sole attention.

"I made my excuses and locked myself in the disabled toilet." I shake my head, not proud of what I did in the confines of that bathroom. "I was so hard for you, Evie. Everything I said, everything I did. It was true."

"Y-you asked me why I did it?" she whispers. "You asked... Jesus, Alex, you were asking about yourself, digging for information. You said you didn't mind sharing me with... what? Yourself? What were you hoping for? That I'd confess to falling in love with you and promise to stop camming?"

Her eyes are hard, the complete opposite to how I feel. Hearing those little words falling from her lips made my heart skip a beat, and it's still racing like a motherfucker.

I don't think I ever realised how much I wanted to hear them. And while she might not have said it properly, the fact she even went there gives me something at least.

She put me and love in the same sentence. It's only a short skip and a jump to being in love, right?

"No, that wasn't what I wanted. I just wanted to hear

your voice, and they were the first questions that popped into my head."

"Bullshit."

I close in on her a little more, holding her eyes, praying to anyone who will listen that she can see the truth within them.

"No, Evie. Not bullshit."

She gasps when I lift my hand and trail my finger over her cheek, tracing the lines of her tears. Her skin is so warm and soft, it's a battle not to pull her into my arms to feel every inch against me.

"I want to know everything there is to know about you. I want every inch of you. This is your body, Evie. You're the one who gets to decide what to do with it. Not me, or society. If camming makes you happy, then there's nothing wrong with that. Same as dancing, stripping, anything."

My finger trails over her bottom lip and my mouth waters with the need to lean forward and suck it into my mouth, tasting her.

"I want you, Evie. And I want you happy and confident in your own skin."

"You need to stop," she whispers, her bottom lip trembling.

"It's the truth," I say, finally getting close enough that the heat of her body burns into mine.

"But you lied to me. You sat on the other end of the call and pretended to be someone else."

"I fucked up, Vixen." Her eyes shutter, cutting off our connection. "You called me that, in our chat. I should have known."

"It's your username. A username I like to think I inspired."

She sucks in a quick breath. It's all the answer I need.

She opens her mouth to speak, I assume to confirm my suspicion, but what comes out isn't what I'm expecting.

"You changed me," she says. "I was never meant to be a dancer, to be doing any of this stuff. I was never meant to be at your dad's that night. Blake was sick, and Derek was losing his shit, so I agreed to stand in.

"I had never done anything like that before in my entire life. I was terrified. How I didn't drop every tray of drinks I was carrying is beyond me. My entire body trembled with fear. It was embarrassing.

"But then, I saw you. There was something in your eyes that made all the creepy guys who were leering at me bearable.

"I don't know what it was, I still don't understand it to this day. But there was something there, some kind of—"

"Connection," I finish for her. "I felt it too."

"That must explain why you were so warm and welcoming," she deadpans.

"Most of those girls, I wouldn't trust them with a barge pole. I judged you like I do them because of your presence, and I was wrong. I'll admit that. And I'll spend forever apologising for it, if you'll let me."

"Didn't stop you beating that creep to a pulp for me though, did it?"

"Seeing his hands on you..." I grit my teeth, picturing that exact moment I saw red. No different from fight night when I caught sight of him with Evie over Xander's shoulder. "Fuck. I lost my mind."

"Would you do that for all the girls?" she asks.

"If they obviously didn't want it, yes, I'd have stepped in. Not sure I'd have gone quite as far as I did for them, though. But you—"

"Then you caught me trying to steal your watches, and you thought I was just like one of them."

I swallow, hating where my mind went I found her that night.

"I should have hated it when you shoved me to my knees and pushed into my mouth."

"I shouldn't have done that," I whisper regretfully.

"Maybe not, but I'm glad you did. It changed everything for me. Opened me up to things I didn't realise I wanted before. I wouldn't have started dancing or camming if it weren't for you. And while most wouldn't understand, having those jobs and the money that came with them did incredible things for my family."

"You're incredible," I say honestly. "And I'm sorry for not telling you that I knew. I just... I didn't want to—"

My words are cut off when she leans forward and closes the space between us.

"I get it," she whispers before slamming her lips against mine.

No, Vixen. You really, really don't. But like a pussy, I'll take this out while you're offering it.

I shouldn't be kissing him.

I know that. I really, really do.

But that look on his face. The anguish, the sorrow.

I might be wrong, but I believe his apology. And I understand why he wouldn't have said anything.

It doesn't make it right. But then... wasn't I lying by not telling him something so important about my life? Wasn't I just as guilty?

Isn't a secret that withholds such vital information when we're building a relationship the worst kind of lying by omission?

My stomach knots as he hungrily sucks my tongue into his mouth, easily putting this behind us in favour of more pleasurable things.

I gasp when he wraps his hands around the back of my thighs and lifts me up the wall.

Instinctively, my legs wrap around his waist, and he groans when his hardness lines up with me.

He rolls his hips, and the next groan filling the air spills from my lips.

"Tell me something," I demand into our kiss.

My fingers are in his hair, holding him in place as he teases me relentlessly with his hips.

He moans, letting me know that he heard me, but he doesn't break the kiss.

"Tell me something you've kept hidden. Even the score."

He stills, but his lips don't leave mine.

Tightening my grip in his hair, I drag his head back.

"I know there's probably loads of stuff that you can't tell me. I might not really have any understanding of the kinds of things you do for work." He swallows roughly, his Adam's apple bobbing. "But I understand there will always be things you can talk about."

"Evie," he groans, resting his brow against mine and letting his racing breaths rush over my face.

"Tell me something important to us that you've held back. There must be something. The number of notches on your bedpost, or past girlfriends. I know I'm not your first so—"

"I'm bi," he blurts a second after closing his eyes.

"W-what?" I stutter, shocked by his confession.

He keeps his eyes closed as he rolls his lips between his teeth.

"I've never said those words out loud before," he confesses, making my chest ache. Then, his eyes open, and I find those usually glittering silver eyes shadowed by uncertainty. "It's not because I'm ashamed. Or because I'm worried about what people will think. I just... I fucking hate labels. But I don't know how else to admit it."

"Okay," I whisper, sensing that he doesn't need any

words from me right now. But that doesn't mean my mind isn't spinning. I had no clue, no niggling of suspicion at all. Not that it matters even if I did. The times we've been together, he's given me no reason to believe he's noticed another person on the planet exists. Male or female.

"Anyone I've been with before you... it's been purely physical. I've never met anyone who's made me feel even close to what I feel when I'm with you. I've never pictured tomorrow, next week, month, next year even."

My hands slide from his hair to each side of his neck. His pulse thunders beneath my palms as he waits for my reaction.

His eyes search mine, hunting for a clue about how I'm feeling about all this.

I hate that he's questioning whether I might be okay with this or not.

Suddenly, a memory hits me, and it's out of my mouth before I catch it.

"Ant."

Alex's eyes widen in shock, and he swallows nervously.

"W-we... uh... once, yeah," he finally confesses.

The image of the two of them together plays out in my mind. Their hands on each other's bodies, their lips moving together.

Is it hot in here or...?

"Evie?" he growls.

"Shit, sorry. I just..." Heat burns my cheeks as I hesitate to confess to how hot that little fantasy just made me.

"You were imagining it, weren't you?"

"Maybe," I whisper coyly, his gaze dropping to my lips.

"Vixen," he groans, rolling his hips once more.

My eyes shoot back up to his.

"It doesn't bother me, if that's what you're worried about."

"So I see," he mutters with a smirk. "I should have known better than to doubt my dirty girl."

His hands slide up my sides until he's gently squeezing my breasts.

"I know where your mind is at right now," he confesses, leaning forward to run his nose along the line of my jaw. "But there's only been one person in mind since I saw you at Christmas. Don't mistake me having fun with what I want to have with you."

His teeth sink into my lobe, and a filthy moan rips from my throat.

"It's you, Evie. Since the moment I laid eyes on you, it's been you."

I gasp when he pulls me from the wall and twists us around so fast it makes my head spin.

He lowers my arse to the back of the sofa before his lips find mine once more in an all-consuming kiss that makes my body burn and my toes curl.

His fingers curl around the hem of my tank, and he quickly drags it up my body, only breaking the kiss long enough for it to pass my face. Then he's back again while he unsnaps my bra and throws it away.

"Oh God," I mumble when his hands cup my aching breasts, his fingers pinching my nipples.

His lips move from mine, kissing down my neck, over my collarbone, and down to my breasts.

"Alex," I moan when he swirls his tongue around my peak before sucking it deep into my mouth.

As he switches from one to the other, giving each the same amount of attention, he tucks his fingers into my shorts and drags them and my knickers down my legs. The second they hit my ankles, I kick them free and he drops to his haunches before me.

His gaze starts at my feet and works its way up until he finally finds my eyes.

My heart pounds, my body practically boiling in my veins just from his attention alone.

"I'm in fucking awe of you, Evie." My breath catches. That sincere glint is back in his eyes. "Look up."

"Oh shit," I gasp when I do as I'm told, finding that he's put me right in front of a tall wall-mounted mirror that allows me to see every inch of my naked body.

"Look how beautiful you are." I close my eyes, and when I open them again, I try to see me the way he sees me. The way the men in the club or on the other side of the screen see me.

My cheeks and chest are flushed with desire. My breasts are full, my nipples pert and begging for attention. My waist dips in before my hips flare. I fight not to see my insecurities and just to focus on the good.

Once I've had my fill, my eyes drop to his.

"No," he states, reaching behind him to pull his shirt off. "You're going to watch every second of me worshipping you. I need you to see how fucking beautiful you are. I need you to see how fucking addicted to you I am."

Tucking a hand beneath one of my knees, he lifts it, resting my thigh on the back of the sofa.

"I'd hold on if I were you," he suggests before sitting back a little, giving me the same view he has. "So fucking sexy. And this," he says, running one finger through my folds, "is all mine. Others can look, can wish. But I'm the only one who gets this."

Before I find any words to respond, he leans forward.

The muscles of his back ripple in the most delicious way before the heat of his tongue connects with my clit.

"Oh fuck." My head falls back as my eyes slam shut.

No sooner has the sensation saturated my body than it's gone.

"Watch me or I stop," he warns.

Heat blooms low in my stomach as I pull my head back up and find us in the mirror.

"You good?" he asks, making me want to grab his hair and force him back between my legs.

"Yes," I whimper.

"Good. Now don't even think about looking away."

My agreement is cut off when he leans forward again, sucking on my clit, making me scream.

"How do we look?" he asks.

"Hot," I confess.

"Maybe we should cam together," he suggests. "Oh fuck, you just gushed. You like that idea."

"I... I like anything that involves you," I confess.

"That why you were thinking about me with Ant?" he asks, his lips never leaving my pussy, using his voice to tease me.

"Yes."

"Would you want that?"

He groans, and my cheeks blaze hotter when my own juices run down my inner thigh at the suggestion.

"Fuck, you're perfect," he groans before focusing back on me again.

For a brief second, I realise that he never gave me a clue as to whether his suggestion was on the table or not, but the second his finger finds my entrance, circling at a slow, maddening pace, I realise I don't care.

I don't need anything more than what I have right now.

"Yes," I cry, just catching myself before my eyes fall closed.

"Good girl," he purrs, proving that he's watching me.

He doesn't let up, eating me, finger-fucking me into oblivion. He doesn't even stop when my body locks up with my release and the one leg that's holding me up buckles.

But he doesn't let me fall. He also doesn't let up.

"Another," he demands, slowing his pace so it's not too intense, getting me ready to go again.

I want to tell him that I can't, but my mouth won't work. So, with my eyes still locked on where his face disappears between my thighs, I just let him do his thing.

By the time he eventually sweeps me into his arms and carries me to the bed, my entire body is trembling, my muscles twitching from the powerful orgasms he dragged out of my body.

I didn't even realise I was capable of that many back-to-back.

After stripping out of his trousers and boxers, he crawls in beside me and immediately pulls me into his arms.

"If you were trying to make me forgive you by dragging me to the edge of consciousness with orgasms, then I think you might have just achieved it," I mutter, resting my head above his racing heart.

"I just wanted to make you feel good," he confesses. "Forgiveness is just a happy extra."

I chuckle, so blissed out and exhausted I can barely think.

"I do, though. Forgive you. I was keeping secrets just as much as you were."

"You were entitled to. It's your secret. I know that a lot of guys wouldn't have the same opinion on it as I do."

"You're one of a kind, Alexander Deimos."

He chuckles, the sound making me even sleepier.

"Yeah, you got that right," he confesses quietly.

"Tell me about what happened with Ant," I whisper.

"Shit, Vixen. You really want to know?"

"Uh-huh. I really want to know."

He sighs, and for a few seconds, I don't think he's going to tell me, but then his grip on my hip tightens and he starts talking.

"We were at a party at Theo's. All the couples were hooking up, and Ant, Isla, and I were the gooseberries."

"Isla?"

"She's one of our capo's daughters. Daemon's best friend. She's at uni, so she's not around much, and she and I mostly hate each other," he confesses with a laugh.

"Why?"

"No idea. It's just fun to rile her up. I don't actually hate her; she's a decent person. A good friend to D. Just... don't tell her I told you that."

I laugh with him. "We'll see."

"Oh it's like that, is it?" he jokes. "Anyway, we were drinking and getting high. The three of us were dancing together, and it was just feeling good.

"I was lonely as fuck as all my friends were hooking up. Ant had... well, he was going through a whole heap of shit which meant he couldn't leave our building. He needed the release more than any of us. And Isla, well, she's an up-for-anything kinda girl. A bit like someone else I know."

"Are you calling me a whore, Alexander?"

"Hardly," I scoff. "You're both just fun, up for experimenting. Nothing wrong with that."

"Noted."

"Anyway, when the others were distracted, we

disappeared to the flat Ant was staying in and had a little party of our own."

"What kinda party?"

"Do you really want to know about what happened between me and two others?"

"Do you want to know what I do on a cam call?" I ask innocently.

"Understood," he laughs before he sets about giving me a play-by-play of the night he had a threesome with the enemy and the girl he hates. Not exactly how I imagined my night going... but then nothing since I met Alex has been predictable.

"Would you share me?" I ask brazenly when he's finished explaining how his evening ended with his face between my thighs on his father's desk.

If I knew that he'd already been with two others that night, would I have allowed him to do what he did?

What a stupid fucking question. I'm powerless when it comes to Alexander Deimos.

A growl rumbles in the back of his throat.

"Honestly?" he asks quietly.

"Of course."

"I'm not sure. The thought of another guy's hands on you makes me a little stabby. I'm assuming you could share me?"

I think for a moment. "With the right person we both trust, yeah. Possibly."

"Ant," he breathes, reading between the lines.

"Just the thought of the two of you kissing, touching... it makes me burn."

"Yeah, I've already experienced that," he mutters.

"I want you alone more. That's just... hot, I guess."

"It's okay to have fantasies, Evie."

"What's yours?" I ask, curious to know more about the enigma of a man.

"Uhh… I've spent the past few months watching all my friends hook up right in front of me. Literally. I want to take you in front of them."

All the air rushes out of my lungs at his confession.

Okay, so we've kinda already done it, but in a car in front of Theo, Emmie, Seb, and Stella isn't quite the same as in a room with all of them.

"I want everyone to know you're mine, Evie. And, I want to show everyone just how fucking amazing you are."

"You're pretty awesome too," I say before a yawn consumes me.

"Sleep, baby. Sweet dreams."

He kisses the top of my head, holds me a little tighter, and I sink into darkness with his scent filling my nose and his heartbeat in my ear.

I wake exactly as we fell asleep—with Evie curled around me like a koala.

Pressing my nose to her hair, I breathe her in.

I fucked up with the camming app. I should have told her when we got back here. I should have laid all my cards on the table and explained it all.

But then she looked at me with such love and reverence in her gaze when she incorrectly assumed that I was the one to purchase her and I just... I couldn't do it.

I've wanted someone to look at me like that for so long. It was everything. And I just couldn't bring myself to ruin it. Not yet, anyway.

I told myself that I'd revel in it for a few days and then find a way to come clean. But then things got better. She got better. The life we're living in this little bubble became everything to me. Getting to know her, laughing with her, watching her draw. Fuck. It's all been so simple but so right.

Other than the obvious, I wouldn't change a second of the time I've had with her. I just wish we weren't hiding.

That someone could turn up any second and steal her from me.

Someone out there owns her, and while the leaders of this gang might have gone to ground, that doesn't mean the person at the other end of that transaction has. For all we know, he could be right outside the door, ready to take her from me.

My grip on Evie gets tighter as the fear of losing her drips through my veins like poison.

"What's wrong?" she whispers, letting me know she's awake.

Lifting her head, her sleepy eyes find mine.

"Your heart is racing and you just shuddered."

My lips part to say something. But the truth gets stuck in my throat.

"You," comes out instead of the truth, making her frown.

She pushes up, the heat of her body leaving mine making me realise how that could have sounded.

"I was thinking about you and how amazing you are," I correct in a rush.

Reaching out, I thread my fingers through her hair and drag her back down, pressing our lips together.

She returns my kiss, but she's hesitant.

"I need to brush my teeth," she mumbles into my mouth.

"I don't care." I'm too desperate for her to give a shit about things like that.

"I know but I need to."

I groan as she sits up, but I soon get over it when climbs out of bed naked and walks toward the bathroom.

Pushing up onto my elbows, I watch her every move.

My already painfully hard dick only swells more at the

sight of her slender back, her slim waist, and the sway of her hips.

"Evie," I groan, making her pause in the doorway. Her fingers wrap around the frame before she looks back over her shoulder.

Ho-ly fuck.

I swallow thickly, and when I speak, it comes out all gravelly.

"D-don't move," I state, reaching for my phone on the bedside table.

Holding it up, I snap a quick photo of her.

"Alex," she gasps.

Okay, so I probably should have asked permission. But she puts worse out there on the internet, what's one photo of her arse?

I send it straight to her phone, which buzzes somewhere in the room. "If you ever question how incredibly sexy you are, just look at that photo. And if you ever want to take up modelling, they should probably see it too."

I catch the brightening of her cheeks just before she drops her head.

"Unlikely," she mutters before removing my incredible view and walking into the bathroom.

I give the phone one glance before quickly following her.

She's already got her toothbrush loaded when I stroll in just as naked as she is, rocking the evidence of just how much she turns me on.

She catches sight of me in the mirror, her eyes immediately dropping to my dick, and she drops the toothbrush.

"Shit," she gasps, ripping her eyes from my body to gather it back up.

"That good, huh?" I ask, stepping up behind her, pressing the length of my body to her back as I reach for my own toothbrush.

"You know what you're rocking. You don't need me blowing smoke up your arse."

"Maybe not. But if you're going to mention blowing, I got just the—"

"Alex," she half warns, half laughs as I rub myself against her. "You're insatiable."

Dropping my lips to her ear, I whisper, "I don't think I'm the only one. If I were to push inside you right now, you'd be wet for me."

"Awfully presumptuous, don't you think?" she says, her eyes holding mine in the mirror.

"Anyone would think you want me to test my theory."

Challenge shines bright in her eyes, but she doesn't say anything as she innocently puts her toothbrush into her mouth and begins freshening up.

Mimicking her, I start cleaning my teeth, but after twisting to the side a little, my free hand grazes down her back, my fingertips bouncing off each ridge of her spine.

She doesn't react, but I see everything she doesn't want me to in her eyes.

The blue darkens before getting swallowed by her pupils.

As I palm her arse, her breathing hitches and her brushing slows.

Dipping my fingers down between her legs, I find exactly what I was expecting.

"Vixen," I groan around my toothbrush.

A gasp rips from her lips when I begin teasing her, only pushing my finger knuckle deep. Her body tries to fight me, her muscles clamping down in the hope of sucking me deeper, but I don't.

Dropping my toothbrush to the side, I spit out the toothpaste and focus on her.

She continues to try and brush her teeth as I gently squeeze her breast.

Unlike last night, she watches my actions without me having to say anything.

"You like watching, don't you?"

She nods slowly.

"We should film us together," I suggest, my cock leaking at just the thought of watching those tapes back.

"Okay," she agrees.

"Just for us. No one else."

"Yes," she cries as I slide my hand down her stomach.

I press two fingers against her clit, making her finally give up on the toothbrush. It clatters into the basin as she sags against me.

Working her for a few seconds, I bring her close to release, but before she gets a chance to grasp it, I step away, removing my touch.

"W-what are you doing?" she stutters, spinning around and pinning me in place with a heated glare.

Lifting my hand, I make a show of sucking on the finger that was just inside her.

"You're trouble," she warns.

"Vixen, haven't you realised already? I'm worse than that."

Shaking her head, she moves toward the toilet.

Unable to take my eyes off her, I stand there watching as she hesitates.

"What?" I ask when she doesn't do anything.

"You're not watching me pee," she hisses.

"Why not?"

"Because it's weird."

"I don't think so."

"Of course you don't," she mutters, rolling her eyes.

"Okay, fine. I'll go make us coffee, but I want you back in bed and still naked when I get back."

I spin around and march from the bathroom.

Without bothering to cover up, I jog down the stairs, hoping that the coffee machine likes me and will make our drinks in double quick time so I can be back where I should be before I know it.

The second I step into the kitchen, a shadow moves in front of the window as our security does a perimeter check.

"Fucking moron," I mutter to myself for not warning her properly. It's easy to see why she freaked out yesterday.

I stand there waiting for the liquid gold to fill the mugs, wishing I was upstairs with her body entwined with mine.

My cock bobs in front of me, desperate for some action.

I fell asleep hard as fuck after eating Evie out until she couldn't stand. Even if she wanted to repay the favour, I'm not sure she'd have been able to manage it. Not that I wanted her to. I deserved to go to bed with blue balls after what happened.

This morning, though, all bets are off. I need her.

I need her so fucking badly I can barely think straight. And I need to do that. I've got one exam left. One final push, and then I can focus all my energy on her and getting her out of this shitshow of a situation.

I don't care if the boss still wants us to chill. There is no fucking chilling while my girl is stuck in the middle of this mess. And we're certainly not hiding forever. We've both got lives to live, and as fun as it is being here, just the two of us, there are other things I want to do.

"Yes," I hiss when the second coffee is finally full.

I tuck what I've found for breakfast under my arm and then grab the mugs.

Evie is exactly where I told her to be when I return, only she's got the duvet wrapped around her.

"How do I know if you've followed orders, Miss Moore?" I growl, placing the mugs down and dropping the packet of biscuits to the bed.

"You think I'm brave enough to defy you?" she teases. "Big bad mafia soldier. You could do anything to me in punishment."

Wrapping my fingers around the bottom of the duvet, I roughly tug it. She gasps as it slips from her grasp, leaving her bare for me once more.

The packet of biscuits go flying, but fuck it. There's something I want way more than a sugar hit right now.

"That's better," I groan, running my eyes from her toes to the top of her head.

Unable to stop myself, my fingers wrap around my shaft and I slowly work myself as I watch her squirm.

"You didn't finish what I started while I was gone, did you?"

Biting down on her bottom lip, she shakes her head.

"Show me," I growl.

Sliding her feet up the sheet, she teases me with little hints of what I want before she spreads them wide.

"Fuck," I blurt. I've no idea if she's learned these moves from camming or if she's always been this seductive. If it's the latter, she found herself the perfect job to show off her skills. "I could watch you all day every day, Vixen. So fucking sexy."

"You don't have to watch. You can touch, too."

"Fuck yeah, I can," I bark, reaching for her ankles and

dragging her down the bed. "Every fucking inch of this perfect body."

I start at her feet, kissing, nipping and licking. I've learned all the spots that need attention and I work each, driving her crazy with need.

"Oh God, Alex, please," she moans as I tease one nipple with my tongue and teeth, the other with my fingers.

"Fucking love it when you beg, Vixen."

"Good, because I need you. I need you to make me come. Please."

"Fuck. I'll never get enough of you."

"I hope not, because the feeling is mutual."

"Tell me what you need, Evie."

"Inside me. I need you inside me."

"Which part of me? Fingers? Tongue? Or—"

"Make me yours," she begs, holding my eyes steady.

"You sure? If you're not ready then—"

"I want you, Alex. I want us. Do you?"

With a happy sigh, I drop my head, resting my brow against hers.

"I do, Evie. I want us so bad."

I steal her lips in a filthy yet passionate kiss as I get settled between her thighs.

Resting on one forearm, I move the other to her pussy.

She's soaked for me. More than ready for what's to come.

I plunge my fingers inside her, needing her to be as prepared as possible.

Her back arches as I find her G-spot and she cries out.

"Fuck, I can't wait to watch you do that while I'm inside you."

"Yes. Yes," she cries.

Too impatient to keep this up, I pull my fingers free and use the head of my cock to tease her.

I circle her clit before dropping to her entrance and pushing just inside.

"I promise you I'm clean. I get tested and—"

"I trust you," she cries as her body tries to suck me deeper.

"Fuck, I don't deserve you," I groan, falling over her once more to kiss her, desperate to show her just how much she means to me.

26

EVIE

I stare up into his eyes, my heart pounding like a bass drum in my chest as I wait for him to fully push inside me.

My chest heaves and I fight to keep my body relaxed.

"You do," I whisper, remembering that he said something.

He shakes his head. The movement is so slight that if we weren't pinned together, I wouldn't have felt it.

"Evie."

"Please, Alex. I can't wait any longer."

"Relax, yeah?"

Nodding, I drag my nails down his back, hoping it'll help give him a push.

And thankfully, it does.

His hips thrust forward, filling me in one swift move, stealing my breath and sending a sharp pain shooting through my body.

My teeth sink into my bottom lip as I will it to subside.

"I'm sorry. I'm so fucking sorry," Alex chants. Regret glitters in his eyes, and I swear I also see my own pain reflected back at me, as if he's hurting right along with me. "It'll get better, I promise."

He takes my lips in a searing kiss. No more words pass between us, but as the pain begins to lessen and my need for him to move, to do… something, increases, I hear every silent promise he makes me.

"I'm okay," I whisper as I risk rolling my hips to test things out.

The pain is still there, but it's nowhere near as bad as only a few seconds ago.

"You sure?" he asks through gritted teeth.

I love how hard he's trying to keep it together for me.

"Yeah, I want to feel you."

"Fuck, Evie. You already feel incredible," he says as he slowly pulls out.

"Oh," I gasp as the alien sensation rocks through me.

I've had toys inside me before. I thought I'd know how this felt, but those pale in comparison to this.

The intensity of having him looming above me makes this so much more. So… all-consuming.

But then, could Alex ever be compared to a plastic vibrating toy?

No, probably not.

Slowly, so incredibly slowly that it must push his self-control to its very limits, he thrusts back inside me.

"Oh God," I moan as he seems to hit every single bit of me at once.

It still stings, but there's something so good starting to replace it.

"You're incredible," he breathes, his voice almost strangled as he restrains himself from taking what he needs.

Dragging my fingers down his back once more, I delight in the way his muscles tense and twist for me.

Fuck, I wish I could see us. See our bodies moving together.

"Oh fuck, did you feel that?" he asks through his tightly clenched jaw. I nod, because I sure as hell did. "You just gushed. What are you thinking?"

"About how we look," I confess.

His eyes light up with excitement.

"Yeah?"

Heat blooms on my cheeks. It's freaking ridiculous. He is literally inside me right now. There should be nothing that can embarrass me.

"Want me to film it so you can watch us later?"

I bite down on my bottom lip as he continues his leisurely thrusts in and out of my body.

"Yes," I blurt long before I've allowed myself to really think about it.

Dropping his lips to mine, he drives me crazy with a wet and dirty kiss before reaching for his phone and setting it to record.

My body heats again at the thought of watching it before he gets back to action.

This time, his kiss is more controlled, his hip movements even slower before he kisses across my jaw and breathes in my ear. I feel the shudder his hot breath causes right down to my toes.

"Are you ready?" he whispers, his voice deep and raspy.

"So ready. Show me your moves, playboy," I tease.

He stills for a beat, but the reaction is so fast, I almost wonder if I imagined it when he sits up, giving me the perfect view of his torso, the muscles all pulled tight and ready to unleash.

My eyes drop to the trail of hair that disappears between us, and I swallow roughly.

I'm really doing this. I'm having sex with a Cirillo mafia soldier. And. It. Is. Everything.

For a few moments, everything seems to move in slow motion. His fingers tighten around my hips and he shifts me exactly where he wants me.

"Gonna make you scream for me," he promises.

I'm not stupid. I know that first times are usually awkward, painful, bloody, and mostly a disaster. But being with Alex, a man who clearly knows what he's doing and exactly how to manipulate my body, I have every confidence that this will be nothing like the horror stories.

He circles his hips, hitting some magical deep place inside me that makes me see stars.

"Good?"

"Yeah," I say, licking my lips, desperate to experience it again. "So good."

"It's going to be better, Vixen," he groans before really getting into it.

His movements are smooth, the perfect mixture of soft yet unrelentingly as he works my body.

My breasts bounce as he moves within me, his hands either holding me tight or roaming around my body, adding to the sensation that's building low in my belly.

Eventually, when I'm standing right on the edge, ready to throw myself off, he looms over me once more.

"You're perfect," he whispers before stealing my lips.

He kisses me like he fucks me. Perfectly. It makes my head spin and every muscle in my body tighten.

"Come on my cock, Vixen. Show me how much you love having me inside you."

"Alex," I cry, my nails clawing at his back as he pushes me over the edge with two more of his precise thrusts.

The second my body locks up around his, he groans. It

starts deep in his chest before it spills from his mouth. "Evie. Fuck. I love you."

Even in the middle of one of the most intense orgasms I've ever felt, those words hit like a bat to the chest.

Did he just say...

Tucking his face into my neck, his cock continues to jerk inside me, reminding me of what we just did. His cum is inside me right now.

I really fucking hope that IUD worked.

After a few seconds where only our heaving breaths can be heard, Alex pulls out of me and collapses at my side.

I wince, reminded of the pain I'd manage to forget existed while we were locked together as he leaves me empty.

Is it normal to miss him?

Lifting his hand, he tucks a lock of hair behind my ear before trailing his fingers over my cheek, to my shoulder and down the length of my arm. My skin erupts in goosebumps from his delicate touch as aftershocks from my release still tingle at my nerve endings.

"Are you okay?" he asks softly. "Did I hurt you?" Regret darkens his eyes as he studies mine, searching for the truth.

"A little. But there was more good than bad."

"Yeah," he asks, his demeanour shifting. "I hate the thought of hurting you."

"Trust me, you make it worth it." I smile coyly at him.

"You felt so good, Vixen. You squeezed me so tight when you came. I couldn't hold back."

"Good. I like making you lose control."

"Not sure anyone ever has before," he confesses, making my heart sing.

"Did you... did you mean it?" I ask, unable to keep the words inside.

I need to know if it was a spur-of-the-moment, high-on-oxytocin mistake as he fell.

"I meant it," he confirms. "I've known it for a while. Think I might have started falling that very first night."

I can't help but laugh.

"I'm serious. Just like you said, the second our eyes met, there was something, a connection I'd never felt with anyone else before. You're it for me, Evie. I'm fucking gone for you."

Before I get a chance to reply, he rolls me onto my back and kisses me as if it's the last chance he'll get.

As his lips move against mine, it's like the two of us are the only things in the world. He consumes me on a level I've never experienced before. His tongue slides against mine, and a violent shudder of desire rips down my spine.

"Alex," I groan into his kiss.

It spurs him on. He kisses me deeper, harder, stealing my breath and my heart all over again. His hands are everywhere and my body burns up, needing more. Needing everything.

But despite needing it, he never gives it to me. It's the ultimate tease.

Finally, he pulls back, parting our lips just an inch, and rests his brow on mine.

As he opens his eyes, those dark lashes of his fan his face, making them even more mesmerising.

"Are you okay?" he whispers, his voice deep and raspy. It's so freaking sexy even my toes tingle.

"Yeah," I respond on autopilot.

I haven't stopped to take a minute to consider if I am or not.

"Evie," he growls, as if he can read my mind.

Sucking in a slow breath, I take a moment to think about his question, focusing on my body.

"A little sore, I guess," I confess when something pinches between my legs as I clench my muscles.

He nods, his jaw popping as he grinds his teeth. "It won't always be like that, I promise."

I search his eyes, my heart aching from the equal amounts of love and pain I find staring back at me.

"I know," I whisper.

"I'm going to run you a bath, take care of you."

"Alex, you really don't have—" His fingers press against my lips, cutting off my words.

"Let me. Let me be what you need, what you can't live without."

My chest squeezes so hard, I swear my heart is going to explode inside.

"You already are," I force out through the massive lump that's clogging my throat.

His eyes flare with disbelief, but I don't get a chance to say anything more because he drops a kiss on the tip of my nose and rolls out of bed, leaving me cold.

"Do not move," he warns before turning and running toward the bathroom.

The sound of water filling the bathtub hits my ears before a sweet vanilla scent floods the room.

In only a short few minutes, he's back, filling the doorframe with his big, sculpted body.

My eyes feast on every hard inch of him, but I can't hold back the gasp of shock when I see his dick covered in blood.

His eyes drop to what's stolen my attention as I push to sit up in bed.

"You know what that means, don't you, Vixen?" I'm not sure if it's meant to be a warning, but the heat in his voice does very little to scare me off. "It means you're officially mine now."

I gasp. I'm not sure why. This isn't news to me. Whether he claimed me or not, I willingly handed myself over to the devil in sheep's clothing some time ago. Maybe even that very first night as my knees hit his bedroom floor.

As I push to my feet, he marches forward, eating up the space between us in seconds.

His arms slide around my waist, his palms flattening on my back as he crushes us together.

"Fuck, you're incredible," he whispers in my ear, making tingles rush through my body.

Before I can return the compliment, a shriek rips from my lips when my feet leave the floor.

"Come on, Vixen. It's bath time," he growls, carrying me through to the bathroom where the bubbles are already exploding.

"Wait, wait," I cry before he lowers me into it. "I need to pee."

Placing me down in front of the toilet, he cups my cheeks in his big hands and steals one last kiss before backing away.

"Straight in the bath after. I won't be long," he says before disappearing from sight and pulling the door closed, giving me some privacy.

The second he's gone, reality and the lingering discomfort of what he did begin to set in.

A soft smile plays on my lips as I relive our time together. He was so gentle, so kind. It makes my heart swell even larger in my chest, remembering his tender movements and softly spoken words. Three of them more than any others.

Lifting my hands, I press two fingers to my lips.

He meant them.

He really meant them. I didn't need to ask; I felt them right down to my soul.

Cleaning myself up, I wince at the soreness, cringing when I think about what state the bed might be in if Alex's body is anything to go by.

Unable to follow orders, I twist toward the door.

I don't want to get in that tub alone. I want him behind me, his arms around my body and his breath tickling over my shoulder.

I'm addicted. Utterly freaking addicted.

Wrapping my fingers around the handle, I pull the door open and step into the space it creates. The sight before me makes me still instantly, and before I know it, words are spilling from my lips.

"What the hell are you doing?"

27

ALEX

Coldness washes through me as I step back into the bedroom, leaving her behind. It's the last thing I want to do, but I respect her wishes of not having me watch her pee.

The sight of the screwed-up sheets mostly on the floor ensures my cock stays hard as steel. Images of the two of us locked together not so long ago fill my mind, making me wish we could have immediately fallen into round two.

With a part satisfied, part pained sigh, I walk toward the bedside table and grab my phone.

The camera is still running, capturing every moment of our time together. Stopping it, I stuff down the temptation to watch it straight away, and instead, I focus on something else.

I swallow thickly at the stain of red in the middle of the bed.

One word floats through my head.

Mine.

Something violent and possessive swells inside me.

I might not have handed over any money for Evie

Moore. I would have given the chance to keep her safe. But in every other way, she is mine. Body, soul, heart. I feel it.

This connection between us, this constant pull, this constant need, can't be anything else.

If only it were as simple as a guy meeting a hot girl and making her his.

Lifting my phone, I snap a photo of the mess and use it as a reply to the whole chain of messages I've had overnight from Theo.

> Alex: Deed is done. Evie is officially mine in a way she'll never be his. Let's take those motherfuckers down.

Before discarding my phone on the bed, I take another photo, this time including me, capturing the staining on my dick.

It's wrong, so fucking wrong, but also oh so fucking right.

Until I'm caught.

"What the hell are you doing?"

Her voice cuts through the air like a knife, and I freeze.

There's no denying what I'm doing. She's caught me capturing the evidence of what we did red-handed.

"I thought you were getting straight into the bath," I say, my voice hollow as reality looms.

Time is up, Alexander. Start telling the truth. The whole truth.

Lowering my phone to my waist, I look up to the ceiling for a beat, hoping something or someone up there might be able to help.

"Alex?" she questions, moving closer.

"Evie, I—"

"Don't" she warns coldly. It's so at odds with how she

was in my arms only minutes ago that it's like a slap to the face. "Don't you dare lie to me."

My phone vibrates in my hand, and my arm moves of its own volition, bringing it in front of me.

> Theo: About fucking time, man. Was the thirty seconds you lasted worth it?

All the air rushes out of my lungs.

It's just guy banter. It's normal for us. So why does it feel so wrong, so dirty to be talking about Evie like that?

With the thick carpet beneath her small feet, I don't hear her moving. It's not until the warmth of her naked body washes over my arm that I realise she's close.

No. Not just close.

Too fucking close.

Her entire body tenses the second her eyes land on the screen before she gasps, her own hand lifting to cover her mouth.

She backs away, her eyes still glued to the screen as panic roars in my ears.

Say something, Alex. Make it better.

Tell her you love her again.

Any-fucking-thing.

But I don't.

I don't do any of those things. Instead, I'm frozen. Unable to do anything that might make this better.

Not that I really think that's possible.

"Alex," she whimpers after long, painful seconds of silence. "Please tell me why you sent that."

Her tear-filled eyes lock with mine, and it cracks whatever was holding me motionless.

Throwing my phone onto the bed, I lift my hand to drag my messy hair from my brow.

"Evie, it's not—"

"I swear to God, Alex, if the words 'it's not what it looks like' spill from your lips, I'm going to—"

"Going to what?" I spit, moving closer as she backs up. My emotions swing from fear of losing her to anger in a split second.

"Tell me," she demands. "Who's the him you're talking about?"

My heart pounds wildly in my chest as I continue closing in on her.

She knows. I can see it in her eyes.

She saw that message, the photo, and jumped straight to the correct conclusion.

"Evie," I plead.

"No, Alex. The time for being cute and trying to worm your way out is over. You've already lied to me about the camming app. What else are you hiding from me?"

"I never meant to hide anything," I argue.

"And that's supposed to make it better?" she wails.

"No. Obviously not. But it's a fact. I had every intention of telling you everything when I got back here, but you made up your own story in your head the second you laid eyes on me and—"

"And?" she prompts, nothing but venom in her tone.

"And I preferred your idea to reality, so I let you believe it." I rub the back of my neck as regrets slam into me.

"So you lied?"

"To protect you."

"Bullshit," she accuses. "It had nothing to do with protecting me. You were only thinking about yourself. Trying to make yourself look like this big hero for doing whatever it took. But all this time, you've been lying to my face."

Her chest heaves as we stand barely two feet apart. She's close enough that if I reached out, I could touch her, drag her into my body. But I don't. I can't. And it fucking kills me.

All my fault.

All of this… it's all my fault.

All I wanted was for her to continue looking at me like she was. To know that she felt safe here with me. That I could be exactly what she needs.

It was stupid. I knew it at the time, and I sure as fuck know it now.

"Now's your chance, Alex. Look me in the eyes and tell me the truth about all of this." She holds her arms out from her sides. "Lay yourself bare for me just like I have you, over and over again."

Her tears balance dangerously on her lower lashes, and I will them to stay put. I'm not sure I could cope with watching her cry right now.

All because of me.

Lifting both my hands to my hair, I grip it so hard I'm pretty sure some rips out as I bend over slightly and bark out, "FUCK."

"Tell me, Alex. I can handle it."

"I know. Fuck, I know. I just don't want you to have to," I say fiercely, lifting my eyes from the floor and running them up her naked body.

Fuck, she's so beautiful. Her anger, the fire in her eyes, and the tense set of her muscles only make her more tempting.

She's my fucking kryptonite.

"That is not your decision to make. This is my life, Alex. My fucking life. And I'm stuck here in the middle of God knows where with a man capable of killing me without a second thought who's been lying to me this entire time. Wait—" she says, holding her hand up as a thought hits her.

"Has all of it been a lie? How we met? How you kept finding me?"

"What? No, Evie," I step closer, but her other hand lifts to stop me. It fucking wrecks me that she thinks for even a second that none of this has been real. "I kept finding you because I couldn't stop thinking about you. From that very first night, you wormed your way under my skin, and no matter what I did, I couldn't get you out."

She shakes her head. It's almost as if she's trying to force herself not to believe my words.

But then, she pauses and laughs.

My brows knit together in confusion.

"What?"

"It's just funny," she says, her voice sounding anything but amused. "When Blakely first discovered what had happened between us, she was all for me heading out to find you in our quest to start a new life."

It takes a second for her words to register.

"She wanted you to play me? For what... money?"

Another bitter laugh falls from Evie's lips.

"I'm starting to wonder why I disagreed, seeing as all of this has been nothing more than a game to you. I might as well—"

"No," I roar, spinning around and slamming my fist into the wall beside me.

Pain shoots up my arm, but it's not enough. It's nowhere fucking near enough to squash some of the anger, the irritation, the disbelief that's rushing through my veins.

She gasps, her eyes landing on the blood splatter my split knuckles left behind on the wall.

"None of this was a fucking game, Evie. I fell for you. I

fucking love you," I bellow, my voice echoing around the room.

"Then tell me the truth," she screams, her tears finally falling as her bottom lip trembles.

"I didn't buy you," I blurt. "I was too late. By the time Theo found your listing on the dark web, you were already sold."

All the air rushes from her lungs and she crashes back against the wall.

"We're not just hiding out here from Derek and the rest of them because I wasn't meant to buy you. We're hiding because I've stolen you."

"Oh my God," she mutters behind her hand. "How?"

I suck in a couple of slow breaths to ground myself.

"I put a tracker in your phone the night at The Empire so I'd never have to search for you again. Derek was naïve enough to leave it on you as they took you to their compound.

"The second Theo found your listing, I tracked you, and we sent a team to intercept you."

"The man, the nice one," she whispers.

I nod. "He was working for us, not them. He brought you here for me."

Her hand drops to her stomach, pressing against it.

"I wasn't going to let anyone else have you, Evie. They bought you as an eighteen-year-old virgin. Nothing good comes out of that, and I'd do anything, lay down my fucking life, to stop you from having to endure that," I say honestly.

She stares at me as I cautiously watch her.

"We don't know who he is. But he paid a lot of money for you, Evie. He won't stop until he finds you. The kind of men we're dealing with don't take kindly to being stolen from."

Her tears fall faster, quiet whimpers rumbling up her throat.

"But we'll find him—them—first. We will."

"And what if we don't?" she whispers.

Silence.

"They won't win, Vixen. No matter what happens."

Her breathing increases until I'm sure she's on the verge of hyperventilating.

She doesn't say anything; she just stares through me as she processes my words.

"Blake and Zay are in danger," is what finally spills from her mouth.

"That's why they're with my dad."

"It's not enough," she says in a rush. "Put them on that fancy jet you flew to Vegas on and send them somewhere. Anywhere. If anything happens to them then—" A loud sob rips from her throat at the thought, and I rush forward and pull her into my arms.

"Nothing is going to happen to them. We have them protected."

She sniffles.

"B-but, Zay. School."

"Shhh," I soothe, stroking one hand down the back of her hair. "Trust us."

Wrong thing to fucking say.

One second, she's leaning into my embrace, and the next she's fighting to get away from me.

"Trust you?" she shouts. "Trust YOU? The guy who has been lying to me since you turned up here? Why the hell should I trust anything that comes out of your mouth? Right now, I don't even know if you are who you say you are."

Her doubt in me threatens to break me.

Pain like I've never felt before slashes through my chest and I stumble back, my knees starting to buckle under the weight of her suspicion.

"Evie," I breathe, refusing to let her do this. To push me away when she's crumbling faster than I am. "Please."

"What else?" she seethes.

I stare at her, my pulse pounding so hard I can feel it all the way down to my toes.

"I asked you last night if there was anything else, but you failed to tell me any of this. So... what else are you holding back on?"

I squeeze my eyes closed, and it's as much of an admission as she needs.

"Fucking hell, Alex."

My eyes fly open as her voice gets farther away.

When I find her, she's dragging one of my t-shirts over her head, covering up her beautiful body.

In the next breath, she has my boxers in her hand and throws them at me.

"Tell me," she demands as I catch them without much effort.

"Evie," I warn.

Her eyes narrow on me as I stand there with my boxers in my hand, making no effort to cover up. If she's going to rip open my chest and watch me bleed, she might as well get the full effect.

"No," she spits before pointing at me. "You don't get to tell me that you love me and expect all this not to matter. You lied to me, Alex. You are lying to me. Tell me the truth, or I'm going to walk out that door and hand myself over to fate. Maybe it was where I was meant to be all this time, anyway."

"No," I cry, surging forward ready to physically stop her from leaving.

"Then. Tell. Me. Everything."

She looks up at me, her teeth gnashed together, her jaw popping with anger.

"I'm not some weak little girl who can't handle the hard shit, Alex. You want me to trust you, then you need to trust me too."

We're so close once more that our breaths mingle, the heat of our bodies burning up the space between us.

My fingers twitch to reach for her, to feel the softness of her skin against mine. Her curves against my hard planes. But I don't.

She doesn't want me for my body right now. She wants me for me.

After years of using my body to get what I want, it's going to take some time to understand that anyone could want more than that.

"My job," I confess, closing my eyes as image after image of the faceless targets I've had over the past couple of years flicker through my mind.

"Intelligence," she muses. "That's what you told me you did."

"And that's true," I assure her, still refusing to look into her eyes.

"Okay, so..."

"It's how I get it that you need to know."

She doesn't say a word, just waiting me out. Forcing me to say words that I never have before.

The guys might know what I do, but I didn't exactly sit them down and tell them. It's just a part of my life—a part of their lives. We all have to do things we don't want to. It's something we have to accept if we want to be a part of the world we were born into.

"I... I seduce it out of them," I say quietly.

Evie frowns, her breathing still rapid, but thankfully, her tears have stopped. For now.

"Y-you..." I see the moment the pieces of the puzzle slot together in her head. "You mean you sleep with them to loosen their lips?" she asks. Her voice is cold and detached, and I swear I feel the tether that's been pulling tight between us all this time fraying at the edges.

"Uh..." I rub the back of my neck, shame burning through me.

"I guess that explains how you're so good," she mutters absently.

She stares at the floor, refusing to give me her eyes so I can see how she's feeling.

"Evie, please. Say something," I beg shamelessly.

Finally, she squares her shoulders and looks up. Her eyes cut straight through me, slicing me in two.

It should be the warning I need to prepare me for what comes next. But it's not.

"So you're a whore? You get paid to fuck women for intel?"

My chin drops, words dancing on the tip of my tongue to argue, but none find their way free.

"Oh wait, it's not just women, is it? You fuck the intel right out of men, too. At the same time, maybe?" she asks. The way her brows lift might make it look like she's intrigued, but I see more. I see the dark shadows swirling in her blue eyes.

My jaw pops, my fists curl, but still, no words appear.

"When exactly were you planning on telling me that I

was going to have to share you with… well, who the hell knows?"

"No, Evie. I wasn't—"

"I guess it all just worked out perfectly for you when I said I might be interested in sharing you if it was with the right person."

"No, Vixen. Please, that's not—"

"Get out," she demands harshly.

"What?"

"Get. Out. Either you leave this room, or I leave this cabin and walk straight into the hands of the man who really does own me," she threatens.

As much as I don't want to leave her alone right now, the threat of her doing something stupid is enough to force me into action.

But I don't turn toward the door, not right away.

Instead, I march straight up to her. Gripping her chin, I push her back against the wall and lift her head so she has no choice but to look up.

Unsurprisingly though, she defies me, keeping her eyes locked on the window beside us.

"Evie," I growl darkly. "Look at me."

It takes a few seconds, and for my grip to tighten slightly, but she finally follows orders.

"I'll do as you say, but only because your safety is the most important thing in the world to me right now. But don't you fucking dare think that me walking out of that door means in any way that this is over. It isn't. I don't give a fuck who signed that cheque for you. His money means nothing. His ownership means nothing. You are mine, Evie Moore, and you have been since that first night you got on your knees for me.

"You can threaten all you like—hell, you can even try

and run straight out the front door if you really wish—but rest assured. I will find you, and I will take what's mine."

Her breaths race between her slightly parted lips at my threat, her eyes darkening with heat despite her anger.

I could prove it to her right now if I wanted to. She'd fucking let me too, I know she would. But what we have is more than that. It's more than just me holding power over her. For once, I'm not the one in control, leading the game.

She is.

And I'm nothing but a slave to her needs. And right now, she needs me gone.

"If you need me, I'll be downstairs."

Releasing her, I step back before snatching my phone from the bed and marching from the room.

Just before I swing the door closed behind me, her voice cuts through the air.

"I don't need you, Alex. I never have, and I never will."

I clap my hand over my mouth the second the final word slips free.

I didn't mean to say them, but as the pain of all his lies continues to cut into me like a million tiny knives, my need to hurt him gets the better of me.

I regret it instantly. It's childish and petty, but it all hurts too much to do anything about it, to race after him and take it all back.

He lied to me.

This whole time we've been here, he let me believe that he bought me in some fucked-up way to keep me safe. And while he was busy covering up that he knew about my life as a cam girl, he was keeping his own dirty secrets about what he does for a living.

I shouldn't have called him a whore. That was way below the belt. And very hypocritical.

But the lies. They just kept piling up, and something had to give.

How can he be so sweet, so caring and gentle with me?

How can he tell me that he loves me when he's holding on to all those lies and omissions of truth?

Because it's his job, Evie.

He manipulates and deceives, seduces, and enthrals to get information out of people.

He worked you.

He played you.

And you let him.

He made you fall for him.

Made you love him.

And then, he let you fall and shatter into a million pieces.

With that thought, the world beneath me cracks and my knees buckle, sending me crashing to the floor.

I drop my head into my hands and give in to the pain in my chest and the devastation coursing through my veins.

And to think, only minutes ago, I felt safer in his arms than I ever have in my entire life.

How did we go from that to this?

I sob until my eyes burn and my throat is sore. My entire body aches from what we did this morning, and my nose is full of his scent from the fabric that's covering my body. All of it is a reminder of him, of how stupid and naïve I've been, that I really don't need.

Pathetically, I roll onto my hands and knees before getting to my feet.

My thighs burn as discomfort from having him inside me makes my regrets grow.

I trusted him.

Even after the cam app incident last night, I trusted him. I understood why he'd rather wait for me to confess than spring it on me. But the whole time, he was keeping his own lewd secret.

He knew that if he confessed to knowing mine, he'd have to spill his own.

None of this has been about me. All of it has been about him.

My foot collides with something as I make my way across the room, and when I look down, I find a packet of chocolate Hobnobs at my feet.

Memories of my few hours here assault me.

I had no idea where I was or what was going on. But then he came for me, and everything settled. It all felt right despite everything surrounding us being wrong.

Picking them up, I place them on the bedside table next to our cold coffees.

Desperate for the caffeine hit, I lift one of the mugs to my lips and drain it.

It's not exactly what I'm craving, but I'm so numb I barely taste it.

I drink the second too before padding through to the bathroom.

The bubble bath taunts me, memories of him being so sweet and thoughtful bringing my tears to the surface once more.

My cheeks are streaked with wetness as I lean over the tub to let some of the cooled water out so I can refill it with hot.

Stripping his shirt from my body, I ball it up and throw it at the wall in the hope of dispelling some of the pent-up energy bursting to get out. But it unfolds long before it hits its target and falls limply to the floor.

I need Emmie and Stella, I muse.

Both of them and a punching bag would be welcome right now.

I shake my head, aware that I won't reach out to anyone

except maybe Blake when I'm this broken, as I sink into the lukewarm water.

Keeping my thighs against my chest, I wrap my arms around them and rest my brow on my knees.

My shoulders continue to shake with the strength of my sobs, and I don't even try to hold back.

At some point, the tears will dry up and the pain will lessen. Won't it?

I sit in the middle of the bath, drowning in my own disastrous life until the water is beyond cold.

My teeth chatter and my skin is covered in goosebumps, but I can't summon the energy to move.

Every limb and every muscle seems to be made of stone. But none of them compare to the heaviness of my heart.

The only saving grace in all of this is that I never said the words to him.

If I had, I fear that he wouldn't have listened to me and left.

He'd have continued fighting his corner, using every trick in his playbook to get me to bend to his will and forgive him.

Just like he did last night.

I never should have gone to that poker night in Blakely's place. If I hadn't, then I never would have met him and—

"No," I cry, unable to keep the words inside.

Despite all of this, the pain, the confusion, the unknown, I can't imagine my life now without him in it.

His sparkling grey eyes, his playful smirk, his dirty words and teasing touches.

One thing is for sure; he played his best game with me.

I just hope it was worth it.

Eventually, I can't stand the cold anymore and I push to my feet, letting the water rush over me. I step out, grab a towel and walk to the basin. I do all the things I'd usually do —wash my face, brush my teeth—but it's like I'm not really here, like I'm not really seeing myself in the mirror but some robotic stranger.

Unable to look at myself, I dip my head and make quick work of finishing up.

With heavy legs, I walk across the room and pull open the bathroom door.

My eyes immediately land on the perfectly made bed and the tray full of goodies in the middle of it.

Stepping into the room, I look around, half expecting to find him waiting for me.

But it's empty.

I shouldn't be disappointed, but I am.

Shoving that ridiculous reaction down, I walk toward the dressing room to find some clothes.

After pulling on a tank with a built-in bra and some shorts, I heave the chair from the corner of the room and carry it out to the bedroom. Tucking the back of it under the door handle, I nod to myself.

While I might appreciate the gesture he left for me, I also want the next time I see him to be on my terms. Not because he thinks I need something and lets himself in.

Grabbing my phone where I abandoned it last night, I get into bed, breathing in the scent of the fresh sheets, and survey the contents of the tray—all the while trying to ignore that he did all this for me silently while I was in the bathroom.

Freshly made croissants, a travel mug that I assume contains hot coffee, more biscuits, crisps, fruit, a wrapped sandwich, and two bottles of water. Everything I need to hide out in here all day. And one thing I really don't.

A note. With my name scrawled across the top.

"Shit," I hiss, staring down at it.

There's a part of me that doesn't want to read it, but I can't deny there's a bigger part that does.

But... what if there are more harrowing lies? Ones he never got a chance to tell because I threw him out? Can I cope with any more?

Before I make a decision, I pull up my sister's name and press it to my ear.

It's unusual for us to talk without video unless one of us is working, but there's no need for her to see my face right now. One look and she'll know just how broken I am.

"Evie! How's it going in the middle of nowhere with that hot and sexy man of yours?" she answers joyfully.

I swallow, unable to find any words.

"Evie?"

It's hard to describe the noise that erupts from my throat. Somewhere between a sob and a growl. Whatever it is, it pretty much sums up my life right now.

"Shit, babe. What's wrong? What's happened? Are you okay?" Blake says in a rush.

"I'm okay," I whimper.

"Put video on. I need to see you."

"No, Blake. It's okay. It's—"

"Evie," she warns, sounding uncannily similar to the memory I have of Mum when she used to scold us.

With a huff of irritation, I do as I'm told, and the second the camera shows my face, she gasps.

"What has he done? I'll rip his balls clean from his body for it, whatever it is," she promises, making me smile.

"Maybe don't," I say. "I kinda like them attached."

"Evie," she sighs. "Tell me everything."

"We had sex," I blurt, unable to dive into the deeper stuff yet.

"Yeah?" she asks, searching my eyes. "Was it so bad it reduced you to tears? Damn, I'm sorry. I thought for sure that he'd have moves and—"

"It wasn't bad, Blake. It was..." She stays silent while I try to find the right words. "Amazing. Painful and a little messy, but amazing all the same. He was so sweet and thoughtful. Looked after me, made sure it was good," I confess, my tear-stained cheeks burning up at the memory.

"So why the tears?"

I sniffle, lifting my hand to wipe my nose unattractively.

"He's been lying to me, Blake. All this time I thought he was the one who bought me to protect me, but he didn't. Someone else has, and he intercepted me. That's why we're really hiding out here."

"Shit, Evie. I don't—"

I don't know why, but what he told me about his job doesn't pass my lips. Instead, I spend the next hour on chat with my sister, discussing every possible angle of this new revelation while I eat my way through three croissants and drink the coffee.

When we finally hang up, I'm drained both emotionally and physically, and after shoving the tray aside, I slide farther down beneath the sheets and curl up into the foetal position.

But as much as I might want to pass out and forget about all of this for a few hours, sleep never comes. Instead, I toss and turn, my mind spinning as I think about where he is and what he might be doing.

He should be studying—he's got his last exam tomorrow —but something tells me he's not.

I lie there staring at the door, my eyes locked on the

chair that's keeping me safely locked inside, wishing that things were different.

I guess it just shows how fucked up this situation really is, because I'm disappointed he didn't buy me. I want to be his. I want all of it.

I just don't want the lies.

I can handle the hard stuff, the dark stuff. I've been doing it for most of my life.

***

At some point, I must have finally drifted off, because when I open my eyes again, the sun is low in the sky casting orange shadows all around the room.

The first thought that hits me is that I want to feel the warmth of that early evening sun on my skin. But then, everything comes rushing back, and I remember why I've locked myself in the bedroom to start with.

With a sigh, I throw the covers off, knocking both of the bottles of water from the tray before I pad through to the bathroom.

I don't feel better for the sleep. My body isn't any lighter, and my heart still feels like it's bleeding out inside my chest. And when I walk back into the bedroom and toward the huge windows to look outside, my need to breathe the fresh air and feel the light breeze on my skin gets the better of me.

Pulling my hair up into a messy bun, I hold my head high and drag the chair from beneath the handle. After tucking my sketchpad under my arm, I open the door and step out.

I might not want to see him, or allow him to think for

even a second that everything is okay, but I refuse to stay locked up here like freaking Rapunzel.

I haven't done anything wrong.

Stepping out, I turn toward the stairs, but I don't get very far before I almost trip over something. Or, should I say, someone.

"Evie," he says, jumping to his feet, letting the textbook he has his head stuck in crash to the floor.

I hold his eyes, letting him see exactly how I'm feeling and how little I want to discuss this right now. His lips part ready to speak again, but I beat him to it.

"Excuse me," I force out before stepping over his books and making my way to the stairs. "I'm going to sit in the sun. I don't want company."

It physically hurts me to say it, but I know if I don't that he'll follow me and try to do his best to break me down.

Silence follows me as I pad down the stairs, but it's not long before I hear footsteps. I look back just before I round the corner toward the sunbed on the deck, and I find him on the bottom step with his arms hugging his books to his chest and a totally defeated look on his face.

Good. He did this.

All he had to do was tell the truth.

It really isn't that much to ask, is it?

29

ALEX

I watch her disappear outside with my heart in my throat.

Unlike last night, I knew better than to force myself back into that room so she could hear me out. I knew I needed to wait for her to emerge.

And I thought that when she did, she'd be ready to talk to me.

I never anticipated that she'd basically walk straight past me, barely looking in my eyes as she did.

Her dismissal hurt, just like the comment she threw out about not needing me when I was first banished from the room earlier. It doesn't help that I deserve it.

I do—I deserve it and then some—but it doesn't make it any easier.

My grip on the books pinned to my chest tightens as my need to follow her outside grows.

I want to watch her skin glistening in the sunlight, watch as the loose strands of her hair blow in the wind. I want to study her as she sketches, lose myself in the concentration on her face, on the slight frown as she works on something intricate. But my head won't allow me to join her, despite how much my heart begs for me to.

With a sigh, I fall onto the sofa and find the page I was trying to read outside the bedroom.

I was kidding myself if I thought I was doing anything productive for tomorrow's exam. The reality was I was staring at the page reading the same sentence over and over again while my head was lost in thoughts of my girl and drowning in the depth of my regrets.

If she never talks to me again, I only have myself to blame. I could have corrected her the very first moment I realised she thought I'd bought her. But I didn't, because I was too desperate for her to look at me like I was something special, someone important.

Dropping my head back, I stare up at the ceiling.

The only time I remember feeling anything similar to the uselessness I do right now was when Daemon disappeared.

I knew he was still out there, I felt it deep in my soul. But there was still a chance I'd never get to see him again.

And while Evie might only be on the other side of a wall right now, there's also every chance that what we've found together is over.

Twice in less than twenty-four hours, I've shown her why I don't deserve her trust.

Even I can admit she'd be foolish to forgive me, and I know my reasons.

I never meant to dupe her, not really. But it was selfish of me to do what I did all the same.

I didn't talk to her about the camming, because I knew it would inevitably turn back on me and the life I lead, and I didn't confess the truth about who owned her because I wanted it to be me. I want to be her everything.

She stays hidden outside while the sun continues to sink lower in the sky.

She doesn't even come in for a drink, and while I consider taking her one out more than once, I don't move. I keep my arse planted on the sofa and try to respect her wishes.

My only relief comes when my phone starts buzzing in my pocket.

Seeing my brother's name staring back at me, I swipe and connect the call.

"Have you ever pissed Calli off so much you're worried she'll never forgive you?" I ask by way of greeting.

Evie can probably hear me, but I don't care. Hopefully, she'll hear the pain and regret in my tone.

"Probably," he mutters with a laugh. "She's right here. You want me to ask her?" he offers.

"Nah, it's okay," I concede.

"What have you done?"

"Been a selfish prick," I confess.

"In any way specific or just generally?"

"You're a dick," I mutter.

"I heard congrats are in order," he says. "Finally got your dick we— ow, Angel, what was that for?" he complains.

"Fucking Theo," I scoff.

"I'm happy for you, man. Or I was before you answered my call. What can we do?"

"Turn back time?"

"Ah. No can do, Bro."

"Do you have to be so happy? I think I preferred it when you were the miserable one out of the two of us."

He laughs down the line. "Sorry, that's not possible

while I've got my girl sitting on my lap, wiggling her delicious arse over my— ow," he complains again.

"Was there a reason for the call, or did you just want to piss me off?"

"Just letting you know that I'm heading out later on a lead for a guy who might know a thing or two."

"Yeah?" I ask, sitting forward, suddenly more than interested in what he has to say.

"Yep. Not all these leads will take us to a dead end. At some point, we're gonna hit gold."

"Sooner rather than later would be good," I mutter.

"If the intel is to be believed, I'll get all his secrets by the time the sun rises," he promises.

"Good. I'm ready to get this done."

"It'll happen. Have faith."

I shake my head. What Calli has done to my brother is nothing short of astounding. I fucking love her for it, but it blows my mind more often than not.

"Just do your fucking job and get her out of danger," I demand.

"Dude, when the fuck have I not done my job?"

"I dunno, but I've never had this much on the line before. I need her safe, man. It's driving me crazy, and nothing has even happened."

"Just chill. We've got this. All you need to do is figure out a way to make her forgive you. Give her the puppy dog eyes. They work on almost every other member of the female population."

"Great, thanks for the advice."

I hang up before he can offer any other words of wisdom and drop my phone onto the cushion beside me.

Evie still refuses to look at me let alone talk to me when she does come back inside. My eyes follow her as she takes herself to the kitchen for snacks before disappearing back upstairs.

I refrain from following like a desperate puppy dog for a while, but eventually, my need to be close to her gets the better of me, and I find myself once again trying to study outside her bedroom door.

It's really not a good place to be. But I put myself in this position, so I deserve to suffer.

Curled up on the floor like a pussy, I barely get any sleep, and when the sun comes up the next morning, I couldn't be any less prepared for my exam.

The alarm on my phone cuts through the silence of the house, making my heart lurch in my chest.

I cut it off as fast as I can, but I've no doubt the obnoxious noise has woken her, and probably alerted her to the fact I'm out here.

As much as she probably wants me to slip out and leave her alone, with my school uniform inside that bedroom, I figure it's the perfect excuse to demand entry.

In all honesty, I could drive home and grab another set. But I don't want to. I want to see her before I leave. See if she got any sleep or if she spent almost the whole night reliving the past few days, thinking about how differently all of this might have played out if I didn't allow her to jump to conclusions.

Getting to my feet, I wrap my fingers around the handle, debating whether to knock and ensure she's awake or just invite myself in.

Deciding on the latter, I push the handle, but it barely moves.

My heart sinks. She locked me out.

Leaning forward, my brow rests against the wood.

"Evie," I call softly. "I need to get to school, and my uniform is in the dressing room."

Silence greets me, and the image of me having to leave wearing only my boxers fills my mind.

"Evie, please. I need to—" Soft footsteps move closer, and hope blooms inside me.

Something moves, releasing the handle, and I push it down and slowly open it, peeking inside.

Evie is already walking back to the bed and slipping under the covers, hiding her body from me.

"Vixen, I—"

"Don't, Alex. Not before your exam. Just get yourself ready and we'll talk later," she says, her voice rough.

She keeps her eyes downcast, refusing to look at me, and my stomach knots. I wonder what it is exactly she's trying to hide from me.

Has she spent most of the night awake like I have? Crying, maybe?

"Okay," I agree reluctantly, stalking across the room to find my uniform.

She's sitting in the middle of the bed with her knees tucked up to her chest when I walk back a few minutes later with my trousers and shirt on, my tie hanging around my neck.

"Evie," I say softly, lowering my arse to the edge of the bed.

She tenses, but she doesn't look up.

"Please, baby. I need to see you before I go. I'm so fucking sorry. I hate this."

Her lips part as if she's going to respond, but she

changes her mind at the last minute and swallows the words.

Reaching out, I cup her jaw, gently grazing her soft cheek with my thumb.

With a little encouragement, she finally lifts her eyes. They focus on my chest for a few seconds before she lifts to meet my gaze.

My breath catches at the pain I see reflected back at me.

Her eyes are bloodshot, surrounded by dark shadows that can only come from a sleepless night.

"Fuck, baby. Fuck. I'm so fucking sorry."

Without thinking, I pull her into my arms and hold her tight.

Her scent fills my nose, and fuck if it doesn't cause a lump the size of a fucking basketball to crawl up my throat.

Closing my eyes, I press my lips to the top of her head.

"I meant it, Evie. I love you. I love you so fucking much, and no matter what, I'm going to get you out of this. You, Blake, and Zay will have the life you always dreamed of. I fucking promise you that."

She sucks in a shaky breath, but she doesn't respond.

Why would she? She's hardly going to return the sentiment, is she?

Knowing that if I don't release her now, I'll never do so, I force myself to relax my arms and push to my feet.

"Good luck with your exam," she says quietly.

Walking backward toward the door, I keep my eyes on her.

"Evie, I know I don't deserve it but..." I pause, expecting her to tell me where to go before I've even made my request. "Can you promise me that you won't leave while I'm gone?"

Slowly, she nods.

"I know what I said last night, but I promise I won't willingly give myself up. I wouldn't do that to my family."

I nod, believing her.

"We'll fix this. I fucking swear to you, you'll be back with them, living your life again before you know it." She holds my stare, desperate to believe me but also not trusting me. It cuts, but I get it. "I'll message you when I'm heading back. If you have a problem, call Theo again, yeah? He doesn't have an exam this morning."

"I will. Go before you're late," she says, shooing me out of the room.

I leave the cabin with a heavy heart and a nod to our soldier who's stationed out the front to protect us.

I try to think of my exam and what the questions are likely to be, but my brain refuses to focus for longer than a few seconds before it bounces back to Evie, wondering if she's out of bed yet and what she's doing.

The sun might be out, but everything is wet from a storm overnight and there are dark grey clouds hanging heavily in the sky, just waiting to soak us once more. Hopefully, that means she'll stay inside. Especially now she knows the truth.

30

EVIE

I'm sitting on the top step of the stairs when the front door slamming rips through the air, making the building around me shake with the force.

I didn't sleep.

And when I did, it was full of fitful dreams about the man who just walked out.

Had I been too harsh, locking myself in the room and cutting him off?

I sure didn't think so at the time.

But this morning when he slipped into the room, my resolve started to crumble.

He looked wrecked. And it was because of me.

Okay, yeah. It was his actions that got us here, but it didn't stop me from feeling bad.

And... did he really spend the whole night sitting outside the bedroom door? The pile of textbooks and an empty bottle of water I passed on the way here sure pointed toward that.

With a sigh, I push to my feet and return to the bathroom to clean up.

Unlike the other day, I'm determined not to freak out at being left alone today.

I'm better than that now. Stronger.

And Alex's exam is only two hours, and then he'll be heading back. To talk.

My stomach knots tightly.

I made that promise to him. I set that plan in motion, and although it felt like a good idea at the time, now, I can't help doubting myself.

I've no idea what I want to say to him.

I'm still so angry that he lied to me. But now I know the truth, I can see how and why he allowed it to happen.

I was so convinced when he found me hiding in the dressing room that he was here for me because he'd handed over a hefty amount of cash for the privilege. I can understand why, in my relief, he wouldn't want to burst my bubble.

Thoughts continue to spin around my mind as I get dressed and head to the kitchen to find some breakfast.

As I find a box of cereal and pour myself a bowl, I can't help missing Alex and his freshly baked croissants.

No, screw the croissants. I just miss him.

The cereal tastes like straw. I'm sure in reality it doesn't, but that numbness from yesterday still floods my body.

After a few mouthfuls, I shove the bowl away and lean forward, resting my brow on my forearms.

My shoulders, my back, my neck... everything is tight. I roll my neck as an idea hits me.

Hopefully, it's exactly what I need.

Abandoning my attempt at breakfast, I grab a glass of water and then the tablet that's been forgotten on the end of the sofa.

Stepping up to the sliding, floor-to-ceiling doors, I question my decision. But in the end, I decide to trust the men who are meant to be protecting me here and pull the door open.

Despite the heavy clouds that line the sky, the sun is currently shining, and I use that as my inspiration as I pull one of the mats from the loungers and lay it out on the decking.

Searching for the YouTube channel I want, I place the tablet on the coffee table and take up my starting position with my hands resting at my sides, focusing on my breathing as the instructor starts the hour-long class.

Smoothly, I move into a forward fold, stretching out my back and breathing in deeply.

The birds sing in the trees around me as I transition to all fours before starting a series of cat-cow poses, emptying my mind and focusing on my breathing and the movements of my body.

I continue with my eyes closed, listening to the soft voice from the tablet and the sounds of nature around me.

I startle when there's a loud bang from the front of the house, but I think little of it as I move to sphinx. It'll just be the security team doing something.

Rolling my neck, I get back on track, pushing into downward dog and then extended puppy.

But the noises continue, interrupting my peace.

The warmth of the sun disappears, slipping behind a dark cloud.

It should be an omen for what's about to happen, but I'm too focused, too in the moment to really think about my surroundings.

A large raindrop slashes against my spine, right between

my shoulder blades as I move again before the heavens open.

Jumping to my feet, I grab the tablet off the side and turn to the house.

But just as I'm about to shut myself inside to continue, the front door swings open, revealing a man dressed head to toe in black, a balaclava over his face leaving only two eyeholes.

My stomach drops into my feet. Without even having to think about it, I know he's not one of Alex's men.

He's not here to protect me. He's here to collect me.

Anger over this whole fucked-up situation burns through me as the tablet crashes to the deck. As fast as I possibly can, I bolt toward the stairs that lead to the woodland beyond. The torrential downpour soaks through me almost instantly, but it doesn't stop me.

I look up as I fly down the steps, immediately wishing I hadn't, because more black-clad figures move out of the shadows until the house is surrounded.

It's not until I hit the ground that I realise I'm shoeless.

But it doesn't matter.

I'm stronger than a few sticks. I haven't lived the life I have to just cower down to these men.

If they want me, they're going to have to catch me.

Spotting a gap between them, I run for it, using the pain from every footstep to push me forward.

Darkness engulfs me as I dive into the trees. The sound of heavy raindrops hitting the leaves above me and the whoosh of my blood past my ears is the only thing I can hear as I continue forward.

I've no idea where I am, if I'm going to stumble into something or someone who can help me, or if this is one of those woodlands that seems to be never-ending, and I'll either be caught or end up dying where no one will ever find me.

Refusing to focus on either of those options, I force my legs to keep pumping.

Sticks, stones, and thorns cut my feet to shreds. The need to cry out with each step is almost overwhelming, but I know I can't. Any signal of where I am other than the snapping of twigs underfoot is more than I want to give away.

I've no idea how many men they've sent to get me, but I saw enough step out of the shadows to know I'm seriously outnumbered.

If I were a betting woman, I wouldn't be putting money on me coming out on top here.

With that depressing thought filling my head, I slow my pace a little in the hope of taking stock of where I am and making a plan.

Other than the rain and my heavy breathing, everything is silent.

As I look back, the house has vanished behind the thick tree cover and I realise I'm alone.

"Oh my God," I gasp, pressing my hand over my racing heart.

For just a few seconds, I allow myself to think I might have done it. I might have outrun the devil and given myself a second chance.

But then, a loud noise comes from my right, and a scream rips from my lips as my heart skips a beat.

Wings flapping a second later clues me into what it was, but it's too late.

"Run all day if you like, sweetheart. We'll find you eventually," a deep, rumbling voice calls.

I've no idea which direction that voice came from. It

seemed to surround me from all angles, making my blood run cold.

You promised Alex you wouldn't leave, a little voice says in my head. But fuck that. The best promise I can make him now is that I'll do anything I can not to be dragged away by them and taken fuck knows where.

I start running once more, hoping like hell I made the right decision on which way to go.

More aware than ever now, I swear I see things moving in my peripheral vision. It occurs to me that they could have been watching me this whole time.

I thought I was beating them, getting away, but really, I'm just part of a sick and twisted game.

Bile rushes up my throat at the thought of them enjoying this cat-and-mouse chase, but I don't have time to do anything about it.

"Evie," an ominous voice calls. "We've got all day. And the longer this takes, the sweeter the reward will be. For us."

A whimper spills from my lips, but I don't stop.

I cut through trees and bushes, branches scratching up my arms and legs as I go. Blood trickles over my sweat- and rain-soaked skin, but I push it all aside. I only have one focus, and that's getting the hell out of here.

I just don't know if it's going to be possible.

"Come out, come out, wherever you are," a taunting voice sings.

"No, no, no, no," I whisper, diving practically head-first into a bush. Thistles slice through my skin and the fabric of my tank gets caught on the branches, but I keep pushing, keep moving. It is the only way to get out of this. The only way to keep control.

Laughter fills the air around me, turning my blood to ice.

It's the reminder I need. This isn't over.
Just keep running, Evie. Keep fucking running.
I squeeze my eyes closed for a beat and think of Alex.
He'd want me to keep running. So I will.
Anything for him.

31
___

ALEX

"Well, aren't you a sight for sore eyes," I say as I walk out of my final exam to find none other than my twin brother waiting for me. His eyes are ringed by dark shadows, and I'm pretty sure, even from this distance, that he's got blood splattered up his neck and forearms. Hazard of the job, I guess. Not sure he should be standing in the middle of Knight's Ridge College looking like a bloodthirsty fucking psycho, though.

"What the fuck are you doing here? I thought you bailed on this place weeks ago?"

He shrugs. "Just returning some shit."

My brows lift.

"Like what?"

"Doesn't matter," he mutters, turning toward the exit and into the rain.

"Tell me you've got good news," I beg as I step beside him.

"Yes and no."

"Just fucking tell me. I don't have the patience for the cryptic bullshit."

"Well, aren't you in a wonderful mood? I'm assuming Evie hasn't forgiven you for being a selfish prick."

"Whatever gave you that idea?" I mutter, more than ready to leave him behind and get back to her. She promised we'd talk once my exam was done, and I'm more than fucking ready.

"I've got some more leads," he says, finally filling me in.

"Is that it?"

"It's better than nothing," he argues.

I refrain from commenting, because right now, I'm not sure if I agree or not.

Unless he tells me that the man who owns my girl is dead, I don't consider it good news.

"We're getting closer," he assures me.

"Yes. But are they?" I ask, voicing my biggest fear.

While we're finding leads and torturing intel out of them, what if they're doing the same? Our location will only be safe for so long before someone figures it out.

I trust our guys to protect us. But we all know that if someone really wants to get to us, it isn't always enough.

"Everything is good, man. You just need to go and grovel at your girl's feet. Maybe while you're down there, prove to her just how pleasurable you are to have around and—"

"Seriously?" I hiss.

"What? I have it on good authority that you're good at that shit."

"From whom?" I ask, regretting the question instantly.

He looks over, his eyes flashing with amusement.

"She told you," I surmise.

"It's locked in the vault, man. Haven't even told Calli."

"You serious?"

"I love her something fierce, you know that, man. But

twin code, Bro." He winks. Actually fucking winks. "I've got your back. Ant though... didn't see that shit coming. So is he—"

"I don't know, D. We haven't really talked about it."

"I assume Evie knows about—"

"She knows everything," I interrupt.

"Ah, no wonder she's pissed then," he mutters knowingly.

"Can you just shut up?" I snap.

He steps in front of me, stopping my attempt to escape to my car to head back to the cabin.

"I might not have had the pleasure of meeting her yet," he says, holding my eyes, "but Calli has, and I trust her judgement. She says that girl is it for you. The Yin to your Yang. The Robin to your Batman," he says with a smirk, making me roll my eyes hard.

"We'll see," I mutter. "She won't be my anything if I don't get back and figure out a way to make her forgive me."

I shove him aside and continue forward.

"I already told you how to do it," he calls after me. "We weren't fucked up from birth for no reason. Use your skills."

"She's not a fucking target," I bark back.

"No, she's your girl. Which means she gets all of you, not just the scraps you're willing to give to a target."

"Fucking hell," I mutter, scrubbing a hand down my face.

"You know I'm right," he taunts.

I glance back over my shoulder at his smirk. "There's no need to look so fucking smug about it, prick."

He chuckles as I pull my keys from my pocket and unlock my car.

"If I don't get called in tonight, maybe we'll head out so I can meet this magical unicorn."

"No. You fucking won't. I've got plans, and they don't involve you."

"Touchy, touchy. You can only keep her hidden from me for so long. What are you worried about? That she'll realise she's settled for the wrong twin?"

I flip him off as I fall into the driver's seat.

"No fucking chance. Laters, man. Got some grovelling to do."

"Good luck," he says before I slam the door and back out of the car park.

I swing by Betties, the bakery Brianna introduced us all to, and pick up one of everything she has on offer. I figure if my skills alone aren't enough to convince her to talk to me, then some freshly baked cakes and pastries should do it.

With my goodies strapped into the passenger seat—yes, they are that good—I head back to the cabin, keeping alert in case I'm being followed.

Confident I'm alone, I take the turn down the long gravel track that will lead me to our little slice of heaven.

Everything is calm and peaceful as I pull to a stop, and I take a minute to soak it in.

I love the city. I always have. But being out here makes me realise just how noisy and hectic it is. Even when we're up in our flats, high above the rest of the city, the buzz of energy is still there. Here, everything slows down.

No one comes to greet me from the blacked-out security truck parked out the front, and I take that as a good thing, before unstrapping my delights and making my way to the front door.

Pressing my hand to the scanner, the light turns green and the locks disengage.

Swinging the door open, I walk inside with a smile on my face, immediately looking around for her.

I've only been gone a few hours, but after yesterday and a night spent alone in the hallway, I'm more than ready to make up and spend some quality time together.

"Honey, I'm home," I shout.

Nothing but silence greets me.

Frowning, I put the box on the kitchen counter and take off in search.

"Vixen?" I call again.

Movement in the corner of the room catches my eye.

"Baby, you scared me for a min—"

My words are abruptly cut off when I discover the person closing in on me isn't Evie but a masked man with a crowbar in his hand.

Oh fuck.

I quickly look around and find he's not alone.

Four of them move closer and before I get to make a decision about what to do next, something collides with the back of my head, sending pain radiating down my neck all the way to my fucking toes. My vision flashes, dark spots cutting my view before they start growing.

"Where is she? What have you done with her?" I slur as my body begins to shut down.

I'm shoved from behind and my legs crumble, sending me crashing to the floor on my knees as someone grabs my arms, binding them together behind my back.

"Tell me where she is. If you've hurt her, I'll fucking kill you all," I warn, but my lack of movement does little to back up my threat.

I'm drowning, my mind swimming and my body useless.

I promised I'd always protect her. That I'd keep her safe.

But I failed.

I failed her, and there's every chance I'll never get to apologise.

"Evie," I scream, desperation oozing through my veins.

"Scream all you like, sunshine. She won't hear you where she is now."

"No, please. Let her go. Do whatever you want to me. But let her go, please."

"Look at you, so pathetic when you beg. Did she know her guard dog is really a puppy in disguise?"

"Please," I whimper before something collides with my head again, stealing the last of my thoughts, my fears, my self-hatred.

You promised her, and you failed...

Want to know what happens next? Find out in Sinful Kingdom!
PRE-ORDER SINFUL KINGDOM NOW

Chapter One

Letty

I sit on my bed, staring down at the fabric in my hands.

This wasn't how it was supposed to happen.

This wasn't part of my plan.

I let out a sigh, squeezing my eyes tight, willing the tears away.

I've cried enough. I thought I'd have run out by now.

A commotion on the other side of the door has me looking up in a panic, but just like yesterday, no one comes knocking.

I think I proved that I don't want to hang with my new roommates the first time someone knocked and asked if I wanted to go for breakfast with them.

I don't.

I don't even want to be here.

I just want to hide.

And that thought makes it all a million times worse.

I'm not a hider. I'm a fighter. I'm a fucking Hunter.

But this is what I've been reduced to.

This pathetic, weak mess.

And all because of *him*.

He shouldn't have this power over me. But even now, he does.

The dorm falls silent once again, and I pray that they've all headed off for their first class of the semester so I can slip out unnoticed.

I know it's ridiculous. I know I should just go out there with my head held high and dig up the confidence I know I do possess.

But I can't.

I figure that I'll just get through today—my first day—and everything will be alright.

I can somewhat pick up where I left off, almost as if the last eighteen months never happened.

Wishful thinking.

I glance down at the hoodie in my hands once more.

Mom bought them for Zayn, my younger brother, and me.

The navy fabric is soft between my fingers, but the text staring back at me doesn't feel right.

Maddison Kings University.

A knot twists my stomach and I swear my whole body sags with my new reality.

I was at my dream school. I beat the odds and I got into Columbia. And everything was good. No, everything was fucking fantastic.

Until it wasn't.

Now here I am. Sitting in a dorm at what was always my backup plan school having to start over.

Throwing the hoodie onto my bed, I angrily push to my feet.

I'm fed up with myself.

I should be better than this, stronger than this.

But I'm just... I'm broken.

And as much as I want to see the positives in this situation. I'm struggling.

Shoving my feet into my Vans, I swing my purse over my shoulder and scoop up the couple of books on my desk for the two classes I have today.

My heart drops when I step out into the communal kitchen and find a slim blonde-haired girl hunched over a mug and a textbook.

The scent of coffee fills my nose and my mouth waters.

My shoes squeak against the floor and she immediately looks up.

"Sorry, I didn't mean to disrupt you."

"Are you kidding?" she says excitedly, her southern accent making a smile twitch at my lips.

Her smile lights up her pretty face and for some reason, something settles inside me.

I knew hiding was wrong. It's just been my coping method for... quite a while.

"We wondered when our new roommate was going to show her face. The guys have been having bets on you being an alien or something."

A laugh falls from my lips. "No, no alien. Just..." I sigh, not really knowing what to say.

"You transferred in, right? From Columbia?"

"Ugh... yeah. How'd you know—"

"Girl, I know everything." She winks at me, but it

doesn't make me feel any better. "West and Brax are on the team, they spent the summer with your brother."

A rush of air passes my lips in relief. Although I'm not overly thrilled that my brother has been gossiping about me.

"So, what classes do you have today?" she asks when I stand there gaping at her.

"Umm... American lit and psychology."

"I've got psych later too. Professor Collins?"

"Uh..." I drag my schedule from my purse and stare down at it. "Y-yes."

"Awesome. We can sit together."

"S-sure," I stutter, sounding unsure, but the smile I give her is totally genuine. "I'm Letty, by the way." Although I'm pretty sure she already knows that.

"Ella."

"Okay, I'll... uh... see you later."

"Sure. Have a great morning."

She smiles at me and I wonder why I was so scared to come out and meet my new roommates.

I'd wanted Mom to organize an apartment for me so that I could be alone, but—probably wisely—she refused. She knew that I'd use it to hide in and the point of me restarting college is to try to put everything behind me and start fresh.

After swiping an apple from the bowl in the middle of the table, I hug my books tighter to my chest and head out, ready to embark on my new life.

The morning sun burns my eyes and the scent of freshly cut grass fills my nose as I step out of our building. The summer heat hits my skin, and it makes everything feel that little bit better.

So what if I'm starting over. I managed to transfer the

credits I earned from Columbia, and MKU is a good school. I'll still get a good degree and be able to make something of my life.

Things could be worse.

It could be this time last year...

I shake the thought from my head and force my feet to keep moving.

I pass students meeting up with their friends for the start of the new semester as they excitedly tell them all about their summers and the incredible things they did, or they compare schedules.

My lungs grow tight as I drag in the air I need. I think of the friends I left behind in Columbia. We didn't have all that much time together, but we'd bonded before my life imploded on me.

Glancing around, I find myself searching for familiar faces. I know there are plenty of people here who know me. A couple of my closest friends came here after high school.

Mom tried to convince me to reach out over the summer, but my anxiety kept me from doing so. I don't want anyone to look at me like I'm a failure. That I got into one of the best schools in the country, fucked it up and ended up crawling back to Rosewood. I'm not sure what's worse, them assuming I couldn't cope or the truth.

Focusing on where I'm going, I put my head down and ignore the excited chatter around me as I head for the coffee shop, desperately in need of my daily fix before I even consider walking into a lecture.

I find the Westerfield Building where my first class of the day is and thank the girl who holds the heavy door open for me before following her toward the elevator.

"Holy fucking shit," a voice booms as I turn the corner, following the signs to the room on my schedule.

Before I know what's happening, my coffee is falling from my hand and my feet are leaving the floor.

"What the—" The second I get a look at the guy standing behind the one who has me in his arms, I know exactly who I've just walked into.

Forgetting about the coffee that's now a puddle on the floor, I release my books and wrap my arms around my old friend.

His familiar woodsy scent flows through me, and suddenly, I feel like me again. Like the past two years haven't existed.

"What the hell are you doing here?" Luca asks, a huge smile on his face when he pulls back and studies me.

His brows draw together when he runs his eyes down my body, and I know why. I've been working on it over the summer, but I know I'm still way skinnier than I ever have been in my life.

"I transferred," I admit, forcing the words out past the lump in my throat.

His smile widens more before he pulls me into his body again.

"It's so good to see you."

I relax into his hold, squeezing him tight, absorbing his strength. And that's one thing that Luca Dunn has in spades. He's a rock, always has been and I didn't realize how much I needed that right now.

Mom was right. I should have reached out.

"You too," I whisper honestly, trying to keep the tears at bay that are threatening just from seeing him—them.

"Hey, it's good to see you," Leon says, slightly more subdued than his twin brother as he hands me my discarded books.

"Thank you."

I look between the two of them, noticing all the things that have changed since I last saw them in person. I keep up with them on Instagram and TikTok, sure, but nothing is quite like standing before the two of them.

Both of them are bigger than I ever remember, showing just how hard their coach is working them now they're both first string for the Panthers. And if it's possible, they're both hotter than they were in high school, which is really saying something because they'd turn even the most confident of girls into quivering wrecks with one look back then. I can only imagine the kind of rep they have around here.

The sound of a door opening behind us and the shuffling of feet cuts off our little reunion.

"You in Professor Whitman's American lit class?" Luca asks, his eyes dropping from mine to the book in my hands.

"Yeah. Are you?"

"We are. Walk you to class?" A smirk appears on his lips that I remember all too well. A flutter of the butterflies he used to give me threaten to take flight as he watches me intently.

Luca was one of my best friends in high school, and I spent almost all our time together with the biggest crush on him. It seems that maybe the teenage girl inside me still thinks that he could be it for me.

"I'd love you to."

"Come on then, Princess," Leon says and my entire body jolts at hearing that pet name for me. He's never called me that before and I really hope he's not about to start now.

Clearly not noticing my reaction, he once again takes my books from me and threads his arm through mine as the pair of them lead me into the lecture hall.

I glance at both of them, a smile pulling at my lips and hope building inside me.

Maybe this was where I was meant to be this whole time.

Maybe Columbia and I were never meant to be.

More than a few heads turn our way as we climb the stairs to find some free seats. Mostly it's the females in the huge space and I can't help but inwardly laugh at their reaction.

I get it.

The Dunn twins are two of the Kings around here and I'm currently sandwiched between them. It's a place that nearly every female in this college, hell, this state, would kill to be in.

"Dude, shift the fuck over," Luca barks at another guy when he pulls to a stop a few rows from the back.

The guy who's got dark hair and even darker eyes immediately picks up his bag, books, and pen and moves over a space.

"This is Colt," Luca explains, nodding to the guy who's studying me with interest.

"Hey," I squeak, feeling a little intimidated.

"Hey." His low, deep voice licks over me. "Ow, what the fuck, man?" he barks, rubbing at the back of his head where Luca just slapped him.

"Letty's off-limits. Get your fucking eyes off her."

"Dude, I was just saying hi."

"Yeah, and we all know what that usually leads to," Leon growls behind me.

The three of us take our seats and just about manage to pull our books out before our professor begins explaining the syllabus for the semester.

"Sorry about the coffee," Luca whispers after a few minutes. "Here." He places a bottle of water on my desk. "I know it's not exactly a replacement, but it's the best I can do."

The reminder of the mess I left out in the hallway hits me.

"I should go and—"

"Chill," he says, placing his hand on my thigh. His touch instantly relaxes me as much as it sends a shock through my body. "I'll get you a replacement after class. Might even treat you to a cupcake."

I smile up at him, swooning at the fact he remembers my favorite treat.

Why did I ever think coming here was a bad idea?

Chapter Two
Letty

My hand aches by the time Professor Whitman finishes talking. It feels like a lifetime ago that I spent this long taking notes.

"You okay?" Luca asks me with a laugh as I stretch out my fingers.

"Yeah, it's been a while."

"I'm sure these boys can assist you with that, beautiful," bursts from Colt's lips, earning him another slap to the head.

"Ignore him. He's been hit in the head with a ball one too many times," Leon says from beside me but I'm too enthralled with the way Luca is looking at me right now to reply.

Our friendship wasn't a conventional one back in high school. He was the star quarterback, and I wasn't a cheerleader or ever really that sporty. But we were paired up as lab partners during my first week at Rosewood High and we kinda never separated.

I watched as he took the team to new heights, as he met with college scouts, I even went to a few places with him so he didn't have to go alone.

He was the one who allowed me to cry on his shoulder as I struggled to come to terms with the loss of another who left a huge hole in my heart and he never, not once, overstepped the mark while I clung to him and soaked up his support.

I was also there while he hooked up with every member of the cheer squad along with any other girl who looked at him just so. Each one stung a little more than the last as my poor teenage heart was getting battered left, right, and center.

With each day, week, month that passed, I craved him more but he never, not once, looked at me that way.

I was even his prom date, yet he ended up spending the night with someone else.

It hurt, of course it did. But it wasn't his fault and I refuse to hold it against him.

Maybe I should have told him. Been honest with him about my feelings and what I wanted. But I was so terrified I'd lose my best friend that I never confessed, and I took that secret all the way to Columbia with me.

As I stare at him now, those familiar butterflies still set flight in my belly, but they're not as strong as I remember. I'm not sure if that's because my feelings for him have lessened over time, or if I'm just so numb and broken right now that I don't feel anything but pain.

It really could go either way.

I smile at him, so grateful to have run into him this morning.

He always knew when I needed him and even without knowing of my presence here, there he was like some guardian fucking angel.

If guardian angels had sexy dark bed hair, mesmerizing green eyes and a body built for sin then yeah, that's what he is.

I laugh to myself, yeah, maybe that irritating crush has gone nowhere.

"What have you got next?" Leon asks, dragging my attention away from his twin.

Leon has always been the quieter, broodier one of the duo. He's as devastatingly handsome and as popular with the female population but he doesn't wear his heart on his sleeve like Luca. Leon takes a little time to warm to people, to let them in. It was hard work getting there, but I soon realized that once he dropped his walls a little for me, it was hella worth it.

He's more serious, more contemplative, he's deeper. I always suspected that there was a reason they were so different. I know twins don't have to be the same and like the same things, but there was always something niggling at me that there was a very good reason that Leon closed himself down. From listening to their mom talk over the years, they were so identical in their mannerisms, likes, and dislikes when they were growing up, that it seems hard to believe they became so different.

"Psychology but not for an hour. I'm—"

"I'm taking her for coffee," Luca butts in. A flicker of anger passes through Leon's eyes but it's gone so fast that I begin to wonder if I imagined it.

"I could use another coffee before econ," Leon chips in.

"Great. Let's go," Luca forces out through clenched teeth.

He wanted me alone. Interesting.

The reason I never told him about my mega crush is the fact he friend-zoned me in our first few weeks of friendship by telling me how refreshing it was to have a girl wanting to be his friend and not using it as a ploy to get more.

We were only sophomores at the time but even then, Luca was up to all sorts and the girls around us were all more than willing to bend to his needs.

From that moment on, I couldn't tell him how I really felt. It was bad enough I even felt it when he thought our friendship was just that.

I smile at both of them, hoping to shatter the sudden tension between the twins.

"Be careful with these two," Colt announces from behind us as we make our way out of the lecture hall with all the others. "The stories I've heard."

"Colt," Luca warns, turning to face him and walking backward for a few steps.

"Don't worry," I shoot over my shoulder. "I know how to handle the Dunn twins." I wink at him as he howls with laughter.

"You two are in so much trouble," he muses as he turns left out of the room and we go right.

Leon takes my books from me once more and Luca threads his fingers through mine. I still for a beat. While the move isn't unusual, Luca has always been very affectionate. It only takes a second for his warmth to race up my arm and to settle the last bit of unease that's still knotting my stomach.

"Two Americanos and a skinny vanilla latte with an extra shot. Three cupcakes with the sprinkles on top."

I swoon at the fact Luca remembers my order. "How'd you—"

He turns to me, his wide smile and the sparkle in his eyes making my words trail off. The familiarity of his face, the feeling of comfort and safety he brings me causes a lump to form in my throat.

"I didn't forget anything about my best girl." He throws his arm around my shoulder and pulls me close.

Burying my nose in his hard chest, I breathe him in. His woodsy scent mixes with his laundry detergent and it settles me in a way I didn't know I needed.

Leon's stare burns into my back as I snuggle with his brother and I force myself to pull away so he doesn't feel like the third wheel.

"Dunn," the server calls, and Leon rushes ahead to grab our order while Luca leads me to a booth at the back of the coffee shop.

As we walk past each table, I become more and more aware of the attention on the twins. I know their reps, they've had their football god status since before I moved to Rosewood and met them in high school, but I had forgotten just how hero-worshiped they were, and this right now is off the charts.

Girls openly stare, their eyes shamelessly dropping down the guys' bodies as they mentally strip them naked. Guys jealousy shines through their expressions, especially those who are here with their girlfriends who are now paying them zero attention. Then there are the girls whose attention is firmly on me. I can almost read their thoughts— hell, I heard enough of them back in high school.

What do they see in her?

She's not even that pretty.

They're too good for her.

The only difference here from high school is that no one knows I'm just trailer park trash seeing as I moved from the hellhole that is Harrow Creek before meeting the boys.

Tipping my chin up, I straighten my spine and plaster on as much confidence as I can find.

They can all think what they like about me, they can come up with whatever bitchy comments they want. It's no skin off my back.

"Good to see you've lost your appeal," I mutter, dropping into the bench opposite both of them and wrapping my hands around my warm mug when Leon passes it over.

"We walk around practically unnoticed," Luca deadpans.

"You thought high school was bad," Leon mutters, he was always the one who hated the attention whereas Luca used it to his advantage to get whatever he wanted. "It was nothing."

"So I see. So, how's things? Catch me up on everything," I say, needing to dive into their celebrity status lifestyles rather than thinking about my train wreck of a life.

"Really?" Luca asks, raising a brow and causing my stomach to drop into my feet. "I think the bigger question is how come you're here and why we had no idea about it?"

Releasing my mug, I wrap my arms around myself and drop my eyes to the table.

"T-things just didn't work out at Columbia," I mutter, really not wanting to talk about it.

"The last time we talked, you said it was everything you expected it to be and more. What happened?"

Kane fucking Legend happened.

I shake that thought from my head like I do every time he pops up.

He's had his time ruining my life. It's over.

"I just..." I sigh. "I lost my way a bit, ended up dropping out and finally had to fess up and come clean to Mom."

Leon laughs sadly. "I bet that went down well."

The Dunn twins are well aware of what it's like to live with a pushy parent. One of the things that bonded the three of us over the years.

"Like a lead balloon. Even worse because I dropped out months before I finally showed my face."

"Why hide?" Leon's brows draw together as Luca stares at me with concern darkening his eyes.

"I had some health issues. It's nothing."

"Shit, are you okay?"

Fucking hell, Letty. Stop making this worse for yourself.

"Yeah, yeah. Everything is good. Honestly. I'm here and I'm ready to start over and make the best of it."

They both smile at me, and I reach for my coffee once more, bringing the mug to my lips and taking a sip.

"Enough about me, tell me all about the lives of two of the hottest Kings of Maddison."

"Okay... how'd you do that?" Ella whispers after both Luca and Leon walk me to my psych class after our coffee break.

"Do what?" I ask, following her into the room and finding ourselves seats about halfway back.

"It's your first day and the Dunn twins just walked you to class. You got a diamond-encrusted vag or something?"

I snort a laugh as a few others pause on their way to their seats at her words.

"Shush," I chastise.

"Girl, if it's true, you know all these guys need to know about it."

I pull out my books and a couple of pens as Professor Collins sets up at the front before turning to her.

"No, I don't have diamonds anywhere but my necklace. I've been friends with them for years."

"Girl, I knew there was a reason we should be friends." She winks at me. "I've been trying to get West and Brax to hook me up but they're useless."

"You want to be friends so I can set you up with one of the Dunns?"

"Or both." She shrugs, her face deadly serious before she leans in. "I've heard that they tag team sometimes. Can you imagine? Both of their undivided attention." She fans herself as she obviously pictures herself in the middle of a Dunn sandwich. "Oh and, I think you're pretty cool too."

"Of course you do." I laugh.

It's weird, I might have only met her very briefly this morning but that was enough.

"We're all going out for dinner tonight to welcome you to the dorm. The others are dying to meet you." She smiles at me, proving that there's no bitterness behind her words.

"I'm sorry for ignoring you all."

"Girl, don't sweat it. We got ya back, don't worry."

"Thank you," I mouth as the professor demands everyone's attention to begin the class.

The time flies as I scribble my notes down as fast as I can, my hand aching all over again and before I know it, he's finished explaining our first assignment and bringing his class to a close.

"Jesus, this semester is going to be hard," Ella muses as we both pack up.

"At least we've got each other."

"I like the way you think. You done for the day?"

"Yep, I'm gonna head to the store, grab some supplies then get started on this assignment, I think."

"I've got a couple of hours. You want company?"

After dumping our stuff in our rooms, Ella takes me to her favorite store, and I stock up on everything I'm going to need before we head back so she can go to class.

I make myself some lunch before being brave and setting up my laptop at the kitchen table to get started on my assignments. My time for hiding is over, it's time to get back to life and once again become a fully immersed college student.

"Holy shit, she is alive. I thought Zayn was lying about his beautiful older sister," a deep rumbling voice says, dragging me from my research a few hours later.

I spin and look at the two guys who have joined me.

"Zayn would never have called me beautiful," I say as a greeting.

"That's true. I think his actual words were: messy, pain in the ass, and my personal favorite, I'm glad I don't have to live with her again," he says, mimicking my brother's voice.

"Now that is more like it. Hey, I'm Letty. Sorry about—"

"You're all good. We're just glad you emerged. I'm West, this ugly motherfucker is Braxton—"

"Brax, please," he begs. "Only my mother calls me by my full name and you are way too hot to be her."

My cheeks heat as he runs his eyes over my curves.

"T-thanks, I think."

"Ignore him. He hasn't gotten laid for weeeeks."

"Okay, do we really need to go there right now?"

"Always, bro. Our girl here needs to know you get pissy when you don't get the pussy."

I laugh at their easy banter, closing down my laptop and

resting forward on my elbows as they move toward the fridge.

"Ella says we're going out," Brax says, pulling out two bottles of water and throwing one to West.

"Apparently so."

"She'll be here in a bit. Violet and Micah too. They were all in the same class."

"So," West says, sliding into the chair next to me. "What do we need to know that your brother hasn't already told us about you?"

My heart races at all the things that not even my brother would share about my life before I drag my thoughts away from my past.

"Uhhh..."

"How about the Dunns love her," Ella announces as she appears in the doorway flanked by two others. Violet and Micah, I assume.

"Um... how didn't we know this?" Brax asks.

"Because you're not cool enough to spend any time with them, asshole," Violet barks, walking around Ella. "Ignore these assholes, they think they're something special because they're on the team but what they don't tell you is that they have no chance of making first string or talking to the likes of the Dunns."

"Vi, girl. That stings," West says, holding his hand over his heart.

"Yeah, get over it. Truth hurts." She smiles up at him as he pulls her into his chest and kisses the top of her head.

"Whatever, Titch."

"Right, well. Are we ready to go? I need tacos like... yesterday."

"Yes. Let's go."

"You've never had tacos like these, Letty. You are in for a world of pleasure," Brax says excitedly.

"More than she would be if she were in your bed, that's for sure," West deadpans.

"Lies and we all know it."

"Whatever." Violet pushes him toward the door.

"Hey, I'm Micah," the third guy says when I catch up to him.

"Hey, Letty."

"You need a sensible conversation, I'm your boy."

"Good to know."

Micah and I trail behind the others and with each step I take, my smile gets wider.

Things really are going to be okay.

DOWNLOAD NOW TO KEEP READING

ABOUT THE AUTHOR

Tracy Lorraine is a *USA Today* and *Wall Street Journal* bestselling new adult and contemporary romance author. Tracy has recently turned thirty and lives in a cute Cotswold village in England with her husband, baby girl and lovable but slightly crazy dog. Having always been a bookaholic with her head stuck in her Kindle, Tracy decided to try her hand at a story idea she dreamt up and hasn't looked back since.

Be the first to find out about new releases and offers. Sign up to my newsletter here.

If you want to know what I'm up to and see teasers and snippets of what I'm working on, then you need to be in my Facebook group. Join Tracy's Angels here.

Keep up to date with Tracy's books at
www.tracylorraine.com

Falling Series

Forbidden Series

Rebel Ink Series

Wicked Knight #1 (Stella & Seb)

Wicked Princess #2 (Stella & Seb)

Wicked Empire #3 (Stella & Seb)

Deviant Knight #4 (Emmie & Theo)

Deviant Princess #5 (Emmie & Theo

Deviant Reign #6 (Emmie & Theo)

One Reckless Knight (Jodie & Toby)

Reckless Knight #7 (Jodie & Toby)

Reckless Princess #8 (Jodie & Toby)

Reckless Dynasty #9 (Jodie & Toby)

Dark Halloween Knight (Calli & Batman)

Dark Knight #10 (Calli & Batman)

Dark Princess #11 (Calli & Batman)

Dark Legacy #12 (Calli & Batman)

Corrupt Valentine Knight (Nico & Siren)

Corrupt Knight #13 (Nico & Siren)

Corrupt Princess #14 (Nico & Siren)

Corrupt Union #15 (Nico & Siren)

Sinful Wild Knight (Alex & Vixen)

Sinful Stolen Knight: Prequel (Alex & Vixen)

Sinful Knight #16 (Alex & Vixen)

Sinful Princess #17 (Alex & Vixen)

Sinful Kingdom #18 (Alex & Vixen)

www.ingramcontent.com/pod-product-compliance
Lightning Source LLC
Chambersburg PA
CBHW050754190726
48285CB00005B/1662